By Your Side

Honeybrook Hollow

Nora Everly

Chapter 1
Paige

Closing time meant two things: the jukebox skipping an old eighties Bon Jovi track and me swearing at my margarita machine, as if it had personally betrayed me.

"Stupid," I muttered as I plugged the cord back in. "You have one freaking job."

The neon sign above the door buzzed softly, casting purple light across the worn floorboards and high-top tables. Twilight Tavern glowed like a magical lavender mirage—magical if you squinted, because it was mostly held together by twinkle lights, duct tape, and spite, kind of like me.

The jukebox warbled, and the margarita machine finally hummed to life like it knew I was seconds from slapping a FOR SALE sign on its face or just straight up tossing it into the dumpster. I started its cleaning cycle and sighed, looking out over the empty bar. Chairs were flipped onto the tables, the floors were mopped, the tip jars had been counted, and the money dispersed. I'd been shutting the bar down by myself and letting everyone go home at closing time the last few months to save money for repairs and improvements. Then once I had this place sparkling from top to bottom, I would throw the biggest grand reopening party Honeybrook Hollow had ever seen.

Most people got a house or a car when they got divorced. I got the Twilight Tavern, formerly known as Bubba's Bar—my ex handed this ramshackle, neon-lit bar over with a signed divorce decree and a smirk that said, "Good luck, hope you know what you're doing." The bar wasn't just an asset on the settlement papers. It was the only thing I'd fought to keep, the one place that felt like mine after years of living in his shadow.

Every battered countertop, leaky tap, and flickering light was proof I'd survived something. Even on nights when the register was low but the overhead felt sky-high, I would walk from room to room, thinking that this place was my pride and joy—the stubborn dream I refused to let anyone else define.

Technically, I was a stay-at-home mom before my divorce. Over the years, Eli made a point of reminding me how little money I earned. During our marriage, he opened this bar, a sandwich shop, and a laundromat, but this place was always my favorite. Somehow, the fact that I managed our books, handled payroll, and placed orders didn't matter to him. I also paid the taxes and took care of our licensing. But most of all, I was a fool. It was so damn stupid to trust him—on paper, it looked like he'd done all the work. Fortunately, I found a mean ass divorce attorney who saw the truth and made sure I got what I deserved. No, what I had *earned.*

So I took this bar and changed it from Bubba's Bar, named after Eli's dad, and into The Twilight Tavern, named for the mountain mist and the way the sky turned purple before the sun set behind the trees.

From the window at the end of Sycamore Street, just a bit out of town, I could see the empty parking lot stretching out under the glow of the old-fashioned black iron lamp poles. Beyond the lot, the land sloped away to the edge of Honeybrook Hollow, where a thick mist curled around the base of the mountain. The peaks loomed above, shrouded in lavender twilight and wreathed in fog, with only the faint outline visible against the deepening night. The silence outside was broken only by the wind sweeping through the lot, carrying with it the promise of another cold, quiet evening at the edge of the world.

It was the kind of blustery fall night in Honeybrook Hollow, Oregon, that made you crave a hot cup of coffee and some peace and quiet curled up in a comfy chair with a good book. But I was okay with this kind of quiet I had found in my bar—where the lights buzzed, the air smelled like lemons and beer, and the weight of everything I'd ever regretted hung in the air like smoke to blow away in the mist outside.

I grabbed my bag and turned toward the rear storage room to check the door and turn out the lights. I was late getting out of here, but it didn't matter. I still had to get up early, as usual. My high school junior daughter, Lark, had an honors chemistry test coming up that she was worried about, and I had promised to help her study for it. And my eighth-grader, Briar, needed a ride to her dance class bright and early. I made a mental note to send Noah a text when I woke up. My oldest was living in Portland now for culinary school, and he actually liked getting updates. Even if it was just, "Your sister stole my eyeliner again."

I passed through the swinging door into the back room, flinching when the outside door creaked. Then the freezer let out a low groan, and my heart skipped a beat as I whirled first toward the freezer, then to the door, then back to the freezer again, hoping it would shut up so I could hear better. The freezer let out a low groan, and I spun toward it like I was about to face down a ghost.

"Shh," I hissed at it because that was normal—scolding appliances instead of people.

A voice—rough, amused, and far too familiar—floated out of the shadows.

"Do you talk to everything in here, or just the lucky freezer?"

I froze. Literally froze, like the freezer had won.

"Depends," I shot back without turning around. "Do you sneak into bars often, or am I just that irresistible?"

Hunter's chuckle rolled through the room, low and warm. "I'll let you decide which answer makes me look better."

My pulse jumped, though I tried to smooth it over with sarcasm. "Either way, you're still trespassing."

He strolled in like he owned the place, boots steady on the floor. "Then it's a good thing you don't press charges for charming repeat offenders."

I finally turned toward him, arching a brow. "Charming? That's a bold word choice."

A grin tugged at the corner of his mouth. "Well, you haven't kicked me out yet."

I narrowed my eyes, reaching toward the corner. "That's only because my bat is over there."

Hunter leaned one shoulder against the wall, arms crossed like he had all night. "Pretty sure you'd miss on purpose."

"Don't test me, Cassidy."

"Wouldn't dream of it, Darlington."

I tucked a loose strand of hair behind one ear, trying to

pretend my pulse wasn't thumping from the fright he had given me.

Note to self: remember to make sure that freaking door was always locked. I didn't need this kind of jump scare in my life. Though I could have sworn I'd already locked it and had already double-checked it. I'd chalk this mistake up to my perpetual exhaustion.

It wasn't like I was expecting anyone at this hour, least of all him. The silence had been comforting, a thin shield I'd wrapped around myself after another long shift. Now, with Hunter's sudden appearance, the room felt smaller, every shadow sharper and more intrusive. Still, despite the jolt, I found myself oddly relieved not to be alone—though I'd never admit that out loud, not to him, not tonight.

The Cassidy family had practically raised me and my younger sister, Piper. We spent almost every day at their place after school when our mother was busy working nights. Hunter was my age and had been in and out of my life like a dependable weather pattern ever since.

He was tall and broad-shouldered, the kind of presence that seemed to occupy a room even when he was simply leaning against a doorway. His brown hair was perpetually tousled, as if he'd just run a hand through it out of absent-minded frustration, and his eyes—pale blue, almost silvery in the dim light—missed nothing. He wore jeans, a gray hoodie that clung to his arms, and a look that said he knew exactly how much trouble he could get into, and he wasn't even sorry about it.

"It's almost two in the morning. You scared the crap out of me."

"I'm sorry. I wasn't trying to sneak up on you. I couldn't sleep, and you texted earlier that the light was flickering again," he said, nodding toward the door leading into the bar.

My hand went to my hip as I answered. "I also said I didn't want to deal with it tonight."

"Well, lucky for you, I'm not dealing. I'm fixing. Let's go." He gave an easy shrug, the kind that said he'd made up his mind and there was no use arguing.

Hunter had always operated on his own sense of logic, quietly reliable, stubborn in the way of people who knew your worst days and never let you forget you had backup.

I tried to muster a glare, but it melted under the light from his lopsided smile. It was impossible to stay annoyed with him. "Fine. I appreciate it. I don't mean to be such a grouch."

"Grouch? You? Nah. But I can come back tomorrow if you'd rather go home and crash. I don't want to mess with your sleep."

"Don't worry about it. I no longer have a set sleep schedule. All I have left now is chaos and insomnia with a dash of caffeine and stress to keep me going."

"That's relatable." He gestured to himself. "I mean, here I am in the middle of the night, right?"

With a grin, he led me back into the bar, his gaze sweeping the room, scanning like he was doing a safety check. He always did that. Hunter was the kind of man who couldn't help taking care of people, even if it meant showing up to boss my flickering light back into submission or whatever else was falling apart in this place. We moved through the familiar space of the bar, the wood floors creaking under our steps, the shadows playing tricks in the corners until the overhead light flickered again with a sharp buzz.

He paused, hand grabbing onto the pull cord. "You

know, I'm pretty sure this thing has it out for you," he said, half-grinning, half-serious.

"Maybe it's just jealous that the margarita machine gets more of my attention," I shot back, feeling the tension ease between us, replaced by the easy, offbeat rhythm that always seemed to settle in when he was around.

"The girls with Eli for the weekend?" he asked.

Eli, my cheating ex-husband, was now engaged to my high school nemesis. Do not get me started on that. Twenty years of marriage had gone up in smoke when my son caught them in the act a couple of years back. He'd told me immediately, but even our emergency therapy session couldn't erase the sight from his mind. Noah would be scarred for life, and my grudge against my ex and his mistress would last for the rest of eternity.

"No, they're home. Sleeping. Or fake sleeping. Teenagers are like raccoons; adorable, but you never truly know what they're up to. My grandpa is with them. They've been binge-watching *Friends* together when I'm at work. Technically, they're old enough to be alone, but I don't like the thought of them being by themselves this late at night."

"Those girls are something else." My kids knew Hunter and his family well. He had reached honorary uncle status. He'd been over to my place countless times with his flavors of the month for dinner. The phrase 'serial monogamist' fit him to a T. But, come to think of it, he'd been single ever since I'd filed for divorce. Weird.

He grabbed a stool and dragged it across the floor with a soft scrape to set it beneath the troublesome light.

"You know, on second thought, it is late. You really don't have to do this tonight. Plus, I can't keep taking your help without paying you. I feel bad. Let's go."

With a sidelong smirk, he climbed up and got to it.

"Seriously?" I crossed my arms. "You're going to ignore my boundaries *and* climb my furniture?"

He glanced down with a grin. "Boundaries are for people who don't remember your prom dress or sat next to you in kindergarten. And I'll never take your money."

I groaned. "Hunter. Oh my god."

"That thing was purple satin. You looked like a fancy cupcake. Kind of like that Hello Kitty dress in our kindergarten class photo. Sparkly."

I shook my head, a smile tugging at the corner of my mouth despite my determination to remain annoyed. "Whatever. I don't remember anything about kindergarten, and you didn't even go to prom."

"Because I was helping my dad fix his Mustang. And because Eli was your date."

"He was also the prom king." I pursed my lips in disgust.

"And you were the queen," he shot back. "He was such an ass. You deserved better."

Over the years, Eli had tolerated my friendship with Hunter. Probably because Hunter was rarely without a girlfriend, and we'd all known each other since kindergarten. Sometimes I wondered how I ended up married to Eli, but then I'd come home from therapy and remember that all my problems began when my dad cheated on my mom and left us. Needless to say, I had issues.

"Yeah, then you took me home and went back to kick his ass. We were always fighting about something. God, I should have never married him," I muttered. Eli was the biggest mistake I'd ever made. But I couldn't bring myself to regret it too much since the three loves of my life were the result of our marriage. My children made the entire fiasco worth it. Noah, Lark, and Briar were my heart.

Hunter sent me a look filled with sympathy, and I looked away. Then he tightened a random bolt with a tool I didn't even see him pull out of his pocket. "So is it weird if I say happy early birthday?" he said out of nowhere.

"Huh?" I narrowed my eyes. "What are you up to?"

"Nothing. Just pointing out that you're single. I'm single. And we had a deal. Remember?"

"Oh my god." The memory slammed into my head like a thunderbolt.

"We were going to get married at forty if we were both unattached," he said casually, stepping down off the stool and wiping his hands on his jeans. "And I turn forty tomorrow."

"It was a joke," I sputtered.

"Sounded more like a pact to me," he shot back, along with a grin.

"Well, I used to think tequila counted as hydration, and I married a jackass. We were dumb teenagers back then."

He shrugged. "You still drink tequila."

I threw my arms out to the sides. "Exactly my point. I never learn, Hunter."

He laughed, and I loved hearing it, like a warm patch of sun breaking through the clouds.

"You've still got it, you know." He was more serious now. "That prom queen thing."

"Thanks. Maybe I do, but I don't want it anymore. It caused me nothing but trouble."

His voice dropped. "Have dinner with me, Paige." We met eyes. His were earnest. And I knew mine were completely confused. He quickly looked away. "I mean for our birthday. No big deal."

The room went quiet—just the soft buzz of the appliances and the distant sounds of the fall night outside the windows.

Was he asking me out? Like on a date?

My sisters would love it if I went out with him. Since my divorce, they'd been hinting that I should go out with him. But I immediately rejected the thought. He had to be kidding. Or it was just a birthday thing like he'd said.

But was it?

"You've lost your mind. And we don't even have the same birthday—"

"Maybe I have lost my mind." He cut me off and stepped closer, but not close enough to touch. "But it's just dinner. Nothing more. Think about it. It could be fun."

"Okay..." I whispered. "I'll think about it." I blinked away whatever emotion was threatening to claw up my throat. "I need to lock up and get home to the girls."

"I'll walk you out." As I reached my car, fumbling in my bag for the keys, Hunter stepped forward and gently took them from my hand before I could protest. "Let me help you," he said quietly, unlocking the door and holding it open. I felt a sudden heat rush to my cheeks, flustered not just by the gesture but by how easy he made it all seem. I mumbled a thank you, trying to disguise my awkwardness as I slid into the driver's seat, aware of his watchful eyes and the way my heart fluttered unexpectedly.

He didn't say more. Just waited for me to start the car, waving goodbye as I took off.

I drove through the quiet streets in a haze, turning his words over and over in my mind. Honeybrook Hollow at night was a patchwork of sleepy porches, with their lights glowing golden in the dark, and tidy lawns scattered with fallen leaves that whispered across the pavement in the breeze.

Sycamore Street—the main drag through town—was mostly dark, except for the neon sign flickering pink in the window of Something Sweet, my sister's bakery, and the corner store's open sign buzzing faintly. I passed the library, its stone lions watching over the square, and the town hall with its clock stuck forever at eight-fifteen. It was the kind of small town where nothing really changed, but tonight, everything felt tilted, off kilter.

I barely noticed the turns as I headed home, headlights sweeping past familiar mailboxes and picket fences. The stillness wrapped around me like a scarf, tight around my neck. Somehow, it made my thoughts louder, as my head throbbed, echoing questions I didn't have answers for.

Something was off with Hunter tonight. Asking me to dinner was not part of our usual script. I brushed it off. He probably felt sorry for me because of the divorce.

As I pulled into my driveway, the porch light cast a gentle glow across the cracked path, illuminating the jumble of rain boots left on the porch by the girls earlier. The house was quiet from the outside, the kind of silence that suggested tired children were asleep just inside. Sitting in the car for a moment, I took a deep breath. My confusion hadn't faded, but as I looked at the warm glow spilling from behind the curtains, a little sense of calm settled in.

My grandpa opened the door as I walked up the steps and wished me goodnight as he headed for his car. Whatever awaited me tomorrow, at least I was home for the night.

Chapter 2
Hunter

I should have left when she told me she didn't want to deal with the light. I should have gone home like a normal person, fed my cat, and watched some crap on TV. But instead, I stood in the middle of her bar like I'd stepped into the future I was supposed to have.

She looked tired. Beautiful, but tired. She always looked like that lately, like she was holding her whole life up with one hand and flipping the bird with the other. That was always my favorite thing about her. The attitude that wouldn't quit. Paige could make me laugh like no one else.

Back at home, my cat greeted me by jumping onto the counter and knocking over a cup, meowing at me as if I'd been gone for years, rather than just an hour or so.

"What have you been up to, Ozzy, you little menace?" I scratched behind his ears, smiling when he leaned in and started purring.

My townhouse looked cozy and homey, but in a way where everything was in its place, and nothing quite felt like it was lived in. The walls were a soft slate blue, and the floors were worn wood that creaked with each step. My favorite leather armchair sat beside the fireplace I never used, with a stack of books I kept meaning to read piled on the end table. In the kitchen, under-cabinet lights glowed against the tiled back-splash, creating an illusion of warmth. I filled the space with soft rugs, framed photos of my family, and mugs I'd collected over the years. It looked like a home. But most nights, it felt like a waiting room for something that had never arrived.

I dumped food into Ozzy's bowl, made a cup of tea, and then checked my phone.

The Cassidy sibling group chat had gone hard today. There were six of us. My baby sister, Charlotte, had shared too many old man birthday memes to count. Deacon had posted gym selfies, Tucker had shared pictures of his kids sleeping under the table at his ex-wife's house, Spencer shared pics of his new place—he'd just moved in with his girlfriend, and Brody had started a list for my birthday barbecue—looked like steaks were on the menu. I stared at it for a long time. I should be looking forward to my birthday, but I wasn't.

Tomorrow, I'd be forty.

I hadn't told anyone about the pact. Paige remembered, of course. She remembered everything.

We were seventeen when she said it. I was driving her home from prom after she'd had a fight with Eli and ditched him in a rage. On her way out, she stole a tray of cupcakes from the hotel ballroom. We pulled over and parked at the makeout spot along the Sweetbriar River. She climbed into the bed of my truck, hair still curled, tiara crooked. We looked at the stars and made the pact, toasting with cupcakes to seal the deal.

She'd said it offhand, like a joke.

But somehow, it had felt more like a promise. Even so, I shoved it to the back of my mind and kept it there for years.

I headed out to my back steps, Ozzy curled up beside me as I sat down and thought about what I should have said tonight. I had fought the urge to tell her she was beautiful. That I admired how she'd raised three kids, spent her time building her business, all the while holding herself together through a divorce that would have flattened most people.

Instead, I'd joked about the pact and asked her to dinner.

Because that's what I did. Hid the truth behind a smirk. Fixed what I could and left the rest. That's probably why I'm still single.

I leaned back against the railing, looked up at the stars, and let the cool night sink into my skin as I checked my texts. My father had sent me photos of the restoration job he was working on, a '67 Camaro he'd found in pieces and was determined to bring back to life. I texted back that we'd get started on it soon. He was an insomniac like me, so I wasn't worried about waking him up.

My family owned Cassidy's Automotive. It had been a fixture in the area since my grandfather had opened it up decades ago. My brothers and I worked with our father on rebuilds and repairs for cars, trucks, motorcycles—basically, if it had an engine and wheels, we could fix it. We all had our specialties. My favorite work is rebuilds; I liked taking broken things and making them into something better.

I set the phone down, smiling when Ozzy climbed into my lap like a little brown furnace and purred, headbutting my arm. He was a cranky rescue with half a tail and a judgmental stare. I'd found him wandering along the trail behind my townhouse when I was out for a jog. He had no chip, no owner, no one but me. So I kept him.

I thought about Paige again, how she had looked at me tonight after I'd asked her to dinner. She'd been annoyed with me, I could tell. She was also flustered and curious, like she couldn't decide whether I was a problem or a solution.

She had called me safe once. I overheard her tell her sister, Piper, that I was the only man in her life besides her grandpa and her son who hadn't given her a reason to cry or yell or run screaming like a banshee into the night.

She didn't know I'd heard her. Or that I had memorized her words and kept them close to my heart. I walked back inside, closed the sliding door, and stood in my kitchen like a man trying to decide if he was having a midlife crisis or developing feelings for his best friend. Ozzy ran off down the hall, expecting me to go to bed.

I flicked off the kitchen light, and the room sank into a gentle silence. Ozzy meowed his protest from the hall, but even he seemed to respect the stillness that settled in when I allowed myself to think too much. The truth was, I didn't know what I wanted anymore. Not really.

I used to imagine my life was mapped out—organized, predictable, safe—but somewhere between learning to repair broken things and loving people who didn't always stay, I lost the script. Maybe that's why the idea of Paige, with her sharp tongue and stubborn hope, felt like both a threat and an irresistible temptation.

I wandered to the window, absently tracing the pane of glass, listening to the distant sound of the wind outside. The urge to call her, to hear her voice and ask if she was awake too, tugged at me. But I didn't. I knew better than to turn this restless loneliness I was drowning in into a confession or whatever it was that I was feeling.

Instead, I rinsed out my mug, turned off the faucet, and

tried to focus on something else—cars, work, my family, Ozzy.

There was a time when I thought I would marry someone soft. Someone gentle who wanted a white picket fence and Sunday dinners. Someone who would bake cookies and hum while we folded the laundry together, someone who reminded me of my mom and the way my family had been before she died. I'd dated a few, well, more than a few women like that over the years. But none of them had ever made me feel like Paige did when she cursed out her appliances.

She'd been on my mind more and more since her divorce. It was confusing. No, it was maddening. No, she needed help, and her asshole husband was out of the picture, so I stepped up. She was my friend. The best friend I'd ever had, and I was not about to screw it up by confusing my care for her with feelings that were most likely based on the fact that I hadn't had a date in over a year.

I ran a hand down my face and poured the rest of my tea in the sink. The cup clinked gently, the sound echoing in the quiet like a reminder of how alone I had become. This house wasn't empty; I had Ozzy, but it sure as hell was lonely.

Shit.

I shook my head to clear it. I needed sleep. That's all this was, so I scooped Ozzy up and went to bed.

I woke up to my phone blowing up with texts—more than I usually got on my birthdays. Apparently, turning forty was a huge deal. The messages came in bursts—old friends from high school, acquaintances from town, even some of my regular customers from Cassidy's Automotive. I thumbed through them, bleary-eyed, not sure whether to laugh or groan at the exclamation-pointed well wishes and blurry memes.

The calendar was relentless: another year older, and I was still circling the same questions like a moth at a porch light. Still alone, still lonely, and still unsure what to do about it.

Outside, early-morning light pressed pale and insistent at the window. I should get up and get moving, but the thought of facing the day—my fucking birthday, of all days —felt heavier than usual. I wanted to stay wrapped up in the borrowed warmth of sleep, but Ozzy was sitting in the middle of my chest, glaring at me, ready for breakfast and attention. The house was quiet, but the world outside was already awake—neighbor's car doors slamming, birds skittering across the roof, but all I wanted to do was go back to sleep.

My phone buzzed again, this time with a message from Paige.

Paige: Happy birthday, you old fart. Don't get out of bed. I'll be there in ten minutes to drop off your birthday coffee.

Me: Thanks. How do you know I'm still in bed?

Paige: We share common enemies: insomnia and mornings. I made an educated guess.

Gently, I shifted Ozzy to my side and rolled over. "Ten more minutes," I mumbled as he headbutted my chin.

Chapter 3
Paige

Today was supposed to be quiet. A soft reset after the chaos I'd experienced yesterday. I'd earned a peaceful day, damn it—the kind of day where nothing broke, no one cried, and the biggest emergency would be running out of lime wedges before happy hour.

Naturally, that's not how my day started off.

First up: Briar. My thirteen-year-old champion of passive resistance. I stood in her doorway like a worn-out general surveying the battlefield—hands on hips, voice already tired.

"You're going to be late. We have to get Lark to your father's house, you to dance class, and I have to be at the bar for the beer delivery."

She didn't even look at me. "I'm too tired to care."

"You need to care, or we're all going to be late, and then it's total anarchy. Is that what you want? Chaos? Mutiny in the ranks?"

"Ten minutes," she muttered, already burrowed deeper under the covers like a disgruntled groundhog. Briar's room was a cute mess: mismatched throw pillows, tangled fairy lights, and a sprawl of books and half-folded laundry that made it look less like a disaster and more like a teenage girl's version of cozy.

I nudged aside a stray sock with my toe and tried again. "Briar, please. We have to get going. You have dance class and you can't be late. Then, after, your dad will pick you up."

Unintelligible grumbling came from beneath her pillow. I took a deep breath. Counted to five. Walked away before I said something I couldn't unsay. Like how sometimes I wanted ten more freaking minutes, too.

In the hallway, Lark drifted past like a hoodie-clad ghost. Earbuds in, expression unreadable, eyes only halfway open.

"Don't forget your chemistry notes," I reminded her, trying to keep my voice light. "Your dad said he'd work with you today, then I'll work with you in the morning tomorrow if we can manage to get up a bit earlier. The beer delivery changed. I'm sorry for the rush, sweetheart."

She didn't say anything, just gave me a sleepy smile and wrapped me in a quick, warm hug before heading into the kitchen.

And just like that, the morning had begun. Not with peace. Not with quiet. But with the usual chaos wrapped in teenage moods and giant hoodies.

By the time I wrangled Briar out the door—with a smoothie, mismatched leg warmers, and a half-hearted apology for her tone—we were officially behind schedule. Again.

I dropped Briar at dance and Lark at Eli's place and waved goodbye like I hadn't just barely survived the morning. I rested my head on the steering wheel. I finally had a moment to breathe.

Then I remembered Hunter's birthday. I sent him a text, then headed to Coffee Cabin to procure his usual birthday latte before I had to meet the beer man at Twilight Tavern. And by the way, I did all of this *without* thinking about our stupid pact.

Hunter Cassidy didn't like birthdays. He claimed he didn't want anyone making a big deal out of them, which was a lie, because he *definitely* wanted someone to make a big deal. Just not in a balloons-and-cake kind of way. More like a "coffee delivered with a smirk that said I'm thinking about you" kind of way. Quiet, just like him.

So that's what I was doing—driving across town bright and early to pick up a latte and a cinnamon crumble muffin from Coffee Cabin, one of the many businesses my grandparents had opened in town; they were the entrepreneurs of Honeybrook Hollow, and my youngest sister, Eliza, ran the place for them.

I gripped the steering wheel a little tighter, a thousand anxious thoughts buzzing through my head about the damn pact. I kept telling myself it didn't matter, that Hunter was just Hunter—my safe place, my constant for so many years.

I was used to quiet mornings and predictable routines, but now my nerves were fluttering, and it confused me.

No, I wasn't the weirdo; he was. This was all his fault. He's the one who started it by bringing up that damn pact. And okay, fine. I couldn't get it out of my mind, damn it. Lying to myself was one of my most insidious coping mechanisms, at least that's what my therapist always said. I had thought it was bingeing on Doritos whenever I was PMSing, but whatever.

Back to the task at hand. And the inevitable freakout to follow.

"It's just coffee between friends," I muttered to myself

as I pulled into the Coffee Cabin drive-thru line. "*Child-hood* friends. Like, I've seen him pick his nose. This is thoughtful, not flirty. Thoughtful friends exist. It's fine. It's his birthday coffee for eff's sake, and we've known each other forever. It would be weird *not* to bring him coffee."

"Hello there." Eliza's voice crackled through the speaker. She sounded suspiciously amused, and I scowled.

"Hey, Eliza."

"Paige Darlington. To what do we owe the pleasure of your company at this ungodly hour?"

"Large vanilla latte, two extra shots, cinnamon muffin. Plus my usual, please. And hold the commentary." Ever since my divorce became final, my sisters, friends, acquaintances, customers—basically everyone I knew had been sharing their opinions about Hunter and me, suggesting we should become an item. I was over it. Living in a small town was so freaking fun.

"Ohhhh," she drawled. "Birthday delivery, huh? Are you bringing that man your feelings in a cup? And adding a muffin this year. Interesting."

"Yeah, okay," I sighed and pinched the bridge of my nose. "I will tip you zero dollars and block your number."

"Um, rude," she cheerfully chirped. "Pull forward, please."

By the time I got our coffee and muffins secured in a tray, my nerves had ratcheted up from "mild butterflies" to "full internal earthquake." What was I doing? Why was I sweating? I hadn't worn makeup. I was in leggings. This was aggressively platonic attire. Except I'd definitely picked the hoodie that made my boobs look nice. So there was that.

The drive across town was brief but oddly cinematic in its quiet tension. My grip on the steering wheel was a little too tight. Every red light felt like a cosmic test of resolve, every pedestrian a potential audience to my anxious errand. The car was filled with the warm, reassuring fragrance of coffee, but my pulse skipped with each familiar landmark. It was both a comfort and a torment, as if the whole town was in on my secret.

But what secret?

How could I be keeping a secret when I didn't even know my own damn mind? I let out a small scream of frustration, then bit my lip.

By the time his townhouse came into view, my heart was performing a frantic drum solo somewhere behind my ribs.

I parked in his driveway and stared at the front door for a solid minute before getting out. The tray shook slightly in my hands. Great. I was going to spill coffee on his crotch and seduce him by accident.

Seduce? What the hell? I needed an emergency shut-off switch for my out-of-control brain. Ever since he'd suggested going to dinner together, I'd been off balance.

I knocked.

He opened the door in gray sweatpants, and he was freaking shirtless, abs galore—who knew he had freaking abs like that? Not me, damn it—I counted, there were six of them. Gah! His glasses were askew, hair sticking up on one side like he'd fought off a bear in his sleep. Plus, he was cuddling an adorable brown cat against his chest.

And somehow, the sight of him—half-asleep and rumpled—made that out of control thing in my head short-circuit.

"Abs," I said stupidly. "Glasses. Cat."

He grinned at me. "Good morning to you, too."

"You wear glasses now?" I tried again, sounding more like a caveman discovering fire rather than a grown woman finding out that her best friend could wear the shit out of a pair of slutty little glasses.

"I've worn glasses since I turned thirty-seven. You've just never caught me before the contacts go in. And this is Ozzy. I found him on the trail when I was jogging. I guess I haven't told you about him yet either."

"Well, you look very... distinguished," I said, realizing too late that was the sort of thing someone's old ass *aunt* might say. But, I mean, I was almost forty, so I guess it was appropriate.

He arched a brow, amused. "Distinguished?"

"Like a hot librarian," I blurted. "And the freaking cat? Cute!" I didn't say anything about his abs. I mean, I was a lady, damn it.

There was a pause—the kind where two people simultaneously question all their life choices.

"I brought your birthday coffee," I added quickly, holding up the tray like it could shield me from my own words.

His mouth twitched. "Thank God. I was worried you came over to insult my sleepwear in addition to gawking at my glasses."

"I would never," I said, stepping inside before I lost my nerve.

His house smelled like cedar and something woodsy— like cologne and clean laundry and safety, if safety had a scent. It was familiar, but that safe feeling I always used to have here was now coupled with a surge of something else. Something new. I set the tray down on the counter and refused to look directly at him. I'd been here a million times before. My kids had been here. My stupid ex-husband had even been here. What the hell was wrong with me?

He followed, scratching at his hair. "So. The usual

coffee, thank you. Muffins too? This is nice. Just like old times, except you added my favorite muffin. Thanks."

"Right, old times. Sure. Except you never looked like a sleepy romance novel lumberjack when you used to answer the door, and I usually had one or more kids with me."

His head jerked up. I stared at the muffins like they were the most fascinating objects on earth.

"Paige," his voice was a low growl, and I felt it from the top of my head to the tips of my curling toes. *What the hell was going on?*

I pretended not to hear the way my name sounded, all gritty with sleep and full of warmth. Instead, I focused on fussing with the lids on the coffee cups. My hands trembled, so I lined them up like soldiers, buying myself a moment. "I said nothing. Forget it. You didn't hear a thing."

"You said *lumberjack.*"

I slammed my eyes shut as if that could make me disappear. "It was meant clinically."

"Clinically? Uh-huh. Okay."

We stared at each other across the kitchen island like teenagers playing chicken with our hormones.

I shoved the muffin toward him. "Happy birthday. Don't get all weird about it."

He smiled—slow and dangerous. "I think I like it when you get weird about it. This is kind of nice. And did I mention that I've always liked that sweatshirt?"

"I'm leaving." Heat pooled beneath my collar, prickling my neck. He reached for the muffin with a reverence that made it seem like I'd offered him something rare, some talisman instead of half-stale carbs from Coffee Cabin. He broke it in half, the gesture careful, deliberate, and I wondered if he was stalling, too.

"No, you're not leaving," he finally said. "You're gonna stay and have coffee with me. It's our birthday tradition."

He was right. I wasn't going anywhere. I couldn't. I didn't want to leave.

He took a sip of the latte, made a satisfied sound that landed somewhere uncomfortably close to a groan. I watched his throat move as he swallowed, and I knew I turned bright red. I had to look away before I started analyzing it like a scene from *Bridgerton*.

"You doing anything today?" I asked, trying to steer us back toward safer shores.

"Cassidy birthday barbecue. You know the drill. Too much meat, unsolicited opinions, a game of lawn darts that will absolutely end in someone getting stabbed."

"Sounds wholesome as usual."

"You should come. You're basically family."

The word *basically* hit like a dart in its own right, and *family*, for some reason, was downright painful.

"Right," I said. "Practically like a cousin or something."

He didn't say anything for a second, just traced the rim of his cup with one finger, his attention suddenly fixed on the swirls of foam as if they held an answer. I picked at the sleeve of my coffee cup, wishing I could peel myself out of this skin, out of this moment, and float into something less complicated.

"That's not what I meant," he finally said.

For a breath, it was as if everything in the room contracted—coffee scent, late-morning sunlight, the sweet ache of almost. Then the moment passed, as moments do, and he looked away.

"I know," I said, my voice a little too soft.

He stepped closer. Not close enough to touch. But close enough that I felt his warmth.

I looked up at him. "This is getting weird, isn't it?"

"A little," he admitted, still smiling.

"Okay. Good talk."

He handed me the other muffin. "Let's just eat and pretend this isn't a slow spiral into whatever the hell this is."

"Perfect."

We stood in his kitchen, both pretending the air wasn't buzzing between us, chewing awkwardly, sipping our coffee, and *not* making eye contact, because that's what emotionally constipated best friends did when they were maybe-sort-of starting to catch feelings for each other.

Or not, what did I know about this kind of situation?

Chapter 4
Hunter

"I have to go," she said, reaching for her things like they might protect her from whatever had just passed between us.

I nodded. Too quickly. "Yeah. Totally. Makes sense. You probably have a busy day."

She grabbed her purse, slinging it over her shoulder, clearly ready to leave. But she hesitated, her fingers tightening around her keys. Without really thinking, she stepped back toward me and wrapped her arms around my waist in a quick, tight hug. I hugged her back, feeling the tension and comfort mixed together, neither of us quite knowing what to do with our hands. Then she pulled away, going for a friendly kiss on my cheek—only I turned at the exact moment, and her lips grazed the corner of my mouth instead. We both froze, eyes wide, too startled to say anything. The air felt charged and awkward, the kind of moment that would replay in my head for days.

She lurched out of my arms so fast she nearly collided with the kitchen counter, cheeks flushed and eyes darting anywhere but mine. We both cleared our throats at the same time—hers high and embarrassed, mine low and gruff —which only made things more ridiculous. The awkwardness hung between us, but a tiny, reluctant smile tugged at her lips, and I couldn't help but laugh softly.

She shuffled toward the door, keys clutched in one hand like a shield. Her steps were hesitant, almost deliberately slow, the silence stretching out until it snapped.

Before she reached the handle, I tried to lighten the mood and said, "Don't trip over all this awkward tension on the way out."

She shot me a crooked grin, rolling her eyes. "Only if you promise not to schedule an emergency therapy appointment after I leave." The tension cracked just enough for us both to let out nervous, awkward laughs, the sound lingering in the charged air as she finally turned the knob.

She paused at the door. Looked back at me. Then didn't say anything at all.

And that was somehow worse than a goodbye.

The door clicked shut behind her, and I stood there in my stupid gray sweatpants and smeared glasses, holding the second half of a muffin I hadn't asked for but now never wanted to throw away. The kitchen still smelled like vanilla and cinnamon, and her shampoo—whatever she used that made her smell like lemon cookies, lavender, and defiance.

Ozzy padded into view, tail twitching, and gave me a look like *Well, that could've gone better.*

"Shut up," I muttered, crumbling part of the muffin into his bowl.

He sniffed it, unimpressed.

I leaned back against the counter and ran a hand down my face. My heart was doing something it hadn't done since high school—slamming around in my chest like it had no respect for my boundaries. What the hell was happening to me?

I liked Paige. I even loved her. That wasn't new. She was my best friend.

But whatever *that* was? Whatever it was that had just happened between us was new. And terrifying. And oddly kind of amazing.

She'd called me a hot librarian and a lumberjack.

I was going to be thinking about this all day.

It was just coffee. Just a muffin. Just our usual offbeat banter, but this time it had veered one millimeter too close to flirty and made both of us retreat like we'd stepped on an emotional landmine.

But she hadn't exactly retreated, and neither had I. We'd stood there, biting into our muffins like we were afraid our feelings might escape if we didn't keep our mouths full.

She hadn't run. Not right away. She'd lingered. And then we'd almost kissed. What would have happened if we had?

God, I was in trouble.

I took a sip of the latte she brought me, the one with the extra shots, because she knew I hated sweet drinks unless they had enough caffeine to cause heart palpitations. It tasted perfect. And somehow worse than anything I'd ever had.

Because now I wanted more.

More than coffee. More than a shared history and inside jokes and late-night repair calls. I wanted mornings like this, minus the awkward exits. Maybe I wanted to wake up next to her instead of watching her walk out the door with muffin crumbs on her sweatshirt and a joke stuck in her throat. Or maybe not. I'd just turned forty. Perhaps it really was a midlife crisis and nothing more.

Ozzy jumped on the counter and pawed at the empty muffin wrapper.

I picked it up and held it just out of reach. "Nope. It's evidence now. Something happened here, Ozzy, and I need to figure it out."

He meowed in protest. I sighed, grabbed my phone, and opened our text thread like a glutton for punishment. There was her last message from last night, a sarcastic 'happy birthday,' followed by a winking emoji that she would absolutely deny using.

No new texts. And no clue to help me figure this out.

I tossed the stupid wrapper in the trash and went to get ready for the barbecue. I lingered in the shower, took my time getting dressed, all the while thinking about Paige and the confusing swirl of feelings flooding my mind.

I arrived late, which in Cassidy terms meant "just in time to get heckled." The Cassidy property spread out like a patchwork of memories around an old, rambling farmhouse. It felt homey and cozy, shaded by a wide scattering of mature trees. The massive sycamore tree in one corner was my favorite; growing up, I'd climbed to its top more times than I could count. That's where we built tree forts as kids and camped out under the stars. The grass was patchy from years of games and roughhousing, and the flower beds along the edges had clearly been trampled by children or animals —or both.

The backyard was already full—what used to be just my father and siblings had expanded to include my niece and nephew, my baby sister's husband, Cade, Spencer's girlfriend, Lucy, and Larry the Llama, Lucy's odd pet, who was also the star of her best-selling children's book series.

Larry was wearing a red bandana and was currently being fed carrots by Tucker's kids, while Lucy narrated his backstory as if it were an epic fantasy tale. She waved a half-eaten cupcake for emphasis as she explained that Larry had recently made peace with his rival, a goat named Deborah. Spencer stood behind her, grinning like he'd already decided he was never letting her go.

Brody was playing DJ, toggling between outlaw country and 80s power ballads like his life depended on the playlist. Deacon was overseeing the drink cooler with all the seriousness of a man guarding nuclear codes, and Cade—Charlotte's husband-slash-police-chief in Sweetbriar, the next town over—was running crowd control and passing out jalapeño poppers while wearing aviators and an apron that said *Grill Sergeant*, like this was just another Sweetbriar crime scene. And then there was my father, manning the grill with Tucker and smiling like the happiest man in the world to be surrounded by his family.

I met eyes with Spencer, who was holding a beer and wearing a grin that said, "*I know things.*" He clocked me, turned to Charlotte, and said something I couldn't hear—but she turned toward me like a heat-seeking missile the second she did.

"You're late," she said, handing off a stack of paper plates to Cade like a general distributing orders.

"I'm thirty minutes behind. That's not late. That's fashionably overwhelmed."

"You smell like cinnamon," she said pointedly as she brushed my shirt with a knowing grin.

My mouth opened in surprise. "That's extremely specific."

"Paige brought you muffins, don't bother denying it. We already know."

I sighed. "Are you psychic now?"

She wasn't psychic. I knew this bit of information had

come from Eliza. She told Lucy. Lucy told Spencer—big mouth Spencer—who couldn't keep a secret if you paid him to or even if you taped his mouth shut. Yeah, we'd been doing birthday coffee every year, but this year had included muffins and weirdness, and it was hard to hide the weird vibes from people who knew you well.

She turned to my brothers with a satisfied smile. "That's a yes. It *was* more than birthday coffee. Confirmed." She held her fist out for a bump.

Spencer strolled over, can of Coke in hand, grinning as he bumped it. "Was it *birthday muffins* or *I-want-to-kiss-you muffins?*"

"I hate all of you," I muttered.

Tucker popped his head up from behind the grill. "So you *did* kiss her. Really?"

"I said no such thing."

Brody leaned over the cooler. "You didn't *not* say it, either."

I glanced toward the llama—*the llama*—as if Larry could save me from the trainwreck that was my family's emotional meddling. Larry stared back, unimpressed.

"Can't a man show up to his birthday party without being emotionally dissected by his siblings and a barn animal?"

Tucker waved his spatula in the air while my father chuckled. "Not in this family."

"Let him be," Dad called out.

"Thank you!" I huffed. "Let me be. You heard him."

Brody cracked open a beer. "Forget that. We want details. For bonding purposes."

Deacon held up his own beer like he was about to propose a toast. "Should we start designing wedding invitations? Because I have a font picked out."

"Stop it," I said, slamming my eyes shut in frustration. "There's no wedding. There's no relationship. It was *just coffee*. Birthday coffee, like every other year. Jesus Christ."

"And muffins," Charlotte added helpfully. "This time, there were *muffins. And* she's divorced, *and* you are between women. *Muffins*, Hunter. Cinnamon crumble. Your favorite."

I turned toward Larry, desperate for a distraction. He made eye contact, then farted loudly and trotted away with the kids, as if his work here was done.

"Great," I muttered. "Even the llama's judging me."

Charlotte handed me a cupcake from the picnic table—vanilla with too many sprinkles, just the way I liked it. "Eat this. Try not to overthink your entire life while you chew. Just go with the flow."

I took the cupcake and escaped to a lawn chair beneath the sycamore tree like a man retreating from war. I unwrapped the paper slowly, trying not to look like someone scanning the driveway for signs of the woman he may or may not have feelings for.

She wasn't coming. I already knew it. Didn't stop me from wishing she would.

Charlotte flopped into the chair beside me, dragging a cooler over with her foot.

"So, Paige. You. You and Paige. Both single for the first time in, well, ever. Right?"

"Yeah." I closed my eyes. "Can I just enjoy my cupcake and slowly die of emotional repression?"

"Nope. Not when you've got that look on your face."

"What look?"

"The 'I want to kiss her but also, I might pass out' look."

I sighed. "When she brought me coffee this morning. It

was weird," I confessed. "Don't say anything to them." I swung my hand toward the yard.

"Weird bad or weird *hot*?" she whispered, before twisting her fingers over her lips like she was locking them.

"Yes."

Charlotte leaned back. "You've waited like over two decades. What's your next move? Sending her a strongly worded greeting card? Or owning your feelings and using your words like a brave little toaster?"

"I haven't exactly been waiting. It's not like I was celibate or something." I licked frosting off my thumb. "I don't want to push her. But mostly I don't know how I feel. This could all be a result of a midlife crisis, you know," I added under my breath.

"Hunter." She turned to me, serious now. "You are the least pushy man on the planet. You once apologized to a raccoon for walking too close to its trash can."

My lips tipped up at the corner. "In my defense, it had a knife," I joked.

"You deserve something that's yours," she said. "And I think we both know she's been yours since you were kids. You belong together. I want this to happen for you."

In the distance, Larry honked like an angry goose, and the kids shrieked with laughter.

It was chaos. Beautiful, full-hearted chaos.

And the only thing missing was Paige and her kids. They should be here, too.

I looked down at the crumpled cupcake wrapper in my hand and sighed. "I don't want to mess it up. She's the best friend I've ever had. Plus, what if I don't have romantic feelings for her? What if she doesn't for me either? What if this is all just because we're both single at the same time? Like you just said, that's never happened before." I decided not to tell her about the pact. I'd never hear the end of it.

"You are having feelings. It's obvious and it's real. You've been repressing them forever because she was married." She nudged my shoulder. "And you won't mess anything up. What is meant to be always finds a way. I believe that. I mean, hello? I experienced it firsthand with Cade."

The backyard glowed with late-afternoon sun, golden light spilling over the weathered picnic table and dented cooler. It was messy and loud and home. And for the first time in a long time, it didn't feel like enough.

I didn't answer her. I couldn't. Because if I said what I suspected I really felt, it would all be out there. No take-backs. No more hiding behind tools, flickering lightbulbs, and muffins. No more hiding behind our friendship. Which, aside from my family, was the most essential thing in my life.

My phone buzzed in my pocket.

I pulled it out; my thumb was still stained with frosting, and I saw her name.

Paige: Sorry, I bailed on the barbecue. Blame it on work. Really, it was more of a social-overwhelm-slash-what-am-I-even-doing situation. Anyway. Hope the steak was good. And that no one let Larry into the house.

I stared at it, rereading that middle line until it burned.

Typed back.

. . .

Me: Steaks are on the grill now. I wish you were here.

Paige: Happy birthday.

Me: Thanks

Three dots blinked.
 Stopped.
 Started again.
 Then vanished.
 And just like that, I was a teenager again, waiting on a maybe that was never going to happen.

Chapter 5
Paige

Family dinners were sometimes like minefields, and this one was no exception. It was only a few days after Hunter's birthday, and I still couldn't get him out of my mind. Not just because of what he said—though that would've been enough. The pact. The way he'd looked at me when he mentioned it, like he wasn't entirely joking. But mostly, it was that kiss. Or...whatever it was. A misfire. A half-second mistake. My aim had been for his cheek, but then he turned at the last moment, and suddenly my lips were on the corner of his mouth. It wasn't a real kiss. It shouldn't have meant anything. So why was I still thinking about it?

My family was also obsessed with the subject. If I had a dollar for every time someone asked me when I was going to start dating again. I could finally afford a vacation somewhere tropical and warm. They were driving me crazy.

It was almost a sport now, the way they couldn't help sneaking glances at me whenever the conversation lulled. I'd learned to recognize the way their eyes would flick from their plates to my face, then dart away again—hopeful, nosy, brimming with anticipation, as if at any moment I might announce something dramatic about me and Hunter. Every time I picked up my phone or let my gaze wander toward the driveway, a ripple of silent speculation swept through the yard. It was only a matter of time before one of them broke and said something.

The first offender: My grandmother.

She sat down next to me at the picnic table, holding a plate loaded with baked beans, a burger, and some kind of kale salad that I had no intention of acknowledging because it had raisins in it. *Raisins*. Ew.

"Well, honey," she said, patting my hand like I was a spinster in a Regency novel, "you're not getting any younger."

"Thanks, Grandma," I muttered. "What a comforting thing to say at a family barbecue."

We were at the Honeybrook Inn for our monthly Darlington weenie roast. Two of my sisters were here with their significant others, two came alone, like me, and my girls were here too. All I wanted was to stuff my face with hot dogs and relax, but that seemed unlikely with the specter of their matchmaking tendencies hovering over my head like a fricking storm cloud.

The heart of our family was the inn. The Honeybrook Inn, referred to by locals simply as The Honeybrook, which my grandparents had owned for as long as anyone could remember. My grandpa had inherited it from his grandmother, who'd inherited it from her grandfather, and so on, stretching back to some sepia-toned photograph of a dusty Main Street and a hopeful wooden sign. The inn itself was a patchwork of old timber and newer paint, with creaking floors that told stories with every step and flower boxes that overflowed from every window in the summer.

Tourists adored it—something about the promise of small-town peace and the proximity to some of the best ski resorts in Oregon. People returned year after year, scribbling their gratitude in the battered guestbook, promising to come back for the autumn harvest festival or just a piece of the homemade cherry pie. It wasn't fancy, but it was ours, and the way it held together through every family storm was almost miraculous.

My grandparents' house was tucked right at the back of the property, beyond the clusters of lilacs and the rickety swing set, private but close enough that you could always catch a whiff of whatever was simmering on my grandmother's stove. From their kitchen window, you could see straight across the sprawling lawn to the inn's front porch. Their house was flanked by a small red barn and a ramshackle chicken coop. Just beyond that was Grandma's rescue animal enclosure, complete with goats, a miniature donkey, and a goose who had beef with the UPS guy.

Near the porch was the outdoor kitchen my grandfather built from old barn wood and stone, with a giant grill, prep counter, and long wooden table that had seen more birthday candles and root beer floats than I could count. I loved it here. It was peaceful. It was home.

My family was chaotic, messy, and occasionally scandalous—but it worked. Mostly thanks to my grandparents, who refused to let the sins of their oldest son be passed down to the next generation. Grandpa always said he wouldn't live in a world where his five granddaughters didn't know each other. So, through "gentle" persuasion and a lot of stubbornness, he made sure we became a family.

I was the oldest granddaughter. Piper was next—we shared the same mother. Lucy and Cara were the same age, born to different mothers. My father was married to Lucy's mom while cheating on her with Cara's mom. Eliza came after. Dad left Lucy's mom for hers, and they were still married and living in Portland. Probably pretending none of this ever happened.

Everyone in Honeybrook Hollow knew my dad was a serial cheater, but this was the kind of town that wouldn't say it out loud unless you were new and asked the wrong question. However, people loved my grandparents and us girls, so the scandal faded into lore and eventually became a story about resilience—or at least, a testament to stubborn family bonding.

Piper was curled up on a blanket, feeding her new boyfriend, Ren, strawberries like he was royalty. But I wasn't about to tease her. Ren was my divorce attorney; he was as tough as nails and brilliant. He was steady, loyal, kind, and precisely what Piper needed in her life. When I realized he was single, I set him up with her so fast I nearly gave myself whiplash. It was in the top five of my life accomplishments as far as I was concerned. With my three kids and sticking it to Eli being the top four.

Lucy was off somewhere with her boyfriend, Spencer—Hunter's youngest brother—probably making out behind a tree. And Cara and Eliza were by the firepit, roasting hot dogs and arguing about whether cappuccinos were acceptable at weddings or if only champagne and sparkling cider were appropriate. "Discussing" (arguing about) dumb stuff was their favorite hobby.

Two-thirds of my kids were around, too. Noah was in Portland at culinary school, probably cooking dinner for his girlfriend. Briar was in a lawn chair, scrolling with her usual vaguely offended face. Lark was under a tree nearby with a book, but she kept glancing at her sister instead of reading. The girls were acting odd. Which immediately put me on high alert.

Briar was tough, mouthy, and fiercely independent. She was also dramatic and stubborn, and I loved that about her. Lark was quiet and studious, but even more stubborn. And when the two of them were pretending not to be having a conversation, something was definitely up.

I cracked open a Diet Coke and took a long swig, watching them with narrowed eyes.

Grandma leaned in like she was about to deliver state secrets. "I saw Hunter in town the other day. He's still as handsome as ever."

"Oh my god." I choked on the soda. It went up my nose and everything. "Are you serious right now?"

She handed me a napkin, entirely unbothered. "I'm just saying. You two used to be thick as thieves."

"We still are," I said, dabbing at my face. "He's just—"

"A man who shows up when you need help. Fixes things. Looks at you like you're more than just tired bones and stubborn pride."

I stabbed a baked bean and gave her my best *please stop matchmaking* glare. "You're very nosy. Are you aware of that?"

"I'm old," she said, totally unrepentant. "It's the only hobby I have left."

"We're not talking about this." I resisted the urge to tell her Hunter had asked me to dinner. She would shit a brick and then double her efforts.

"You're both finally single at the same time." She pushed with a wink. "Wasn't it his birthday the other day? I heard you brought him muffins. Next year, bake them yourself. I'll give you my grandmother's recipe. I mean, you could do worse than a handsome man like Hunter."

I could do worse. And I had. Exhibit A: my ex-husband.

"You heard, did you? From Eliza? The damn muffin."

"Of course. She keeps the family abreast of all the pertinent news in town."

"That's it," I declared. "Coffee Cabin has lost my business. It's official."

"Okay, sure, you can't resist our mochas, and everyone knows it. All I'm trying to say is it's time to get out there again, honey."

"Nope. Not worth it. I'm choosing to die alone," I said. "The plan is to adopt a few cats. One kid is already out of the house. The other two are teenagers. Piper and I have a date next week to go caftan shopping. My future is set."

"We'll see," she tutted. "You just need more time."

"Yeah. Like, *all* of it. All the time for the rest of my life. Men are not worth the trouble."

"You know that's not true. Look around this yard. Good men are everywhere."

I rolled my eyes and shoved a forkful of beans into my mouth with extra flair.

"I'll let it go," Grandma said sweetly. "For now."

I watched Briar and Lark again, narrowing my gaze. Briar was now whispering to her sister behind a strategically placed napkin. Lark looked miserable and totally guilty.

I got up and made my way over, planting myself between their chairs like a one-woman truth commission.

"What's going on?"

"Nothing," Briar said, her eyes fixed on her phone.

"Yeah," Lark echoed too quickly. "We're totally fine."

"That was the least convincing 'totally fine' I've ever

heard," I said, crossing my arms. "Spill it. Don't make me tickle it out of you. You know I'll do it."

They exchanged a look.

I waited. Wiggling my fingers for emphasis.

Finally, Lark sighed and nudged her sister. "Tell her."

Briar hesitated, then muttered, "Danielle told me to quit dance."

I gaped at her. "I'm sorry—what? You mean your father's fiancée and my high school nemesis is telling *my daughter* what to do? The hell you say?"

"She said Dad's having a hard time financially, and that dance is too expensive, and maybe I should think about stopping so there's more money for... everything else."

My jaw clenched. "Did your father say that? Did he agree? What did he say? Tell me everything before I lose my ever-loving mind."

"No," Briar said. "He just stood there. He didn't say anything. It was almost like she was telling me that for him."

Of course, he didn't say a word—the weak-ass loser. I ground my teeth together so hard my head pounded. I would never say anything bad about him to the kids. Or at least I would try my hardest not to. "And by *'everything else,'*" I finally asked, "do you mean Danielle's kids?"

Briar shrugged, but her face had gone tight. "Probably. And a new couch for the living room. Um, he said he was going to come talk to you soon."

I took a breath. Then another. I was trying to be reasonable. But my baby girl had just been told to give up the one thing that made her feel strong and joyful after going through a very hard time because her dad couldn't be bothered to advocate for her.

"Oh, I'm going to kill him," I said. Damn it. I slapped a hand over my mouth.

"Mom," Lark, my little peacemaker, put her hand on my arm.

"No." I took her hand. "It's okay." I tried to dial back my anger. "Not like *murder*, murder. Not like *prison* murder. Just a little bit of murder. With threats, I mean words—bad ones. And maybe some salad tongs." *Well, that was an utter failure.*

Briar cracked a small smile. Lark did too, but quietly.

"Dance is not optional," I said. "You hear me? I don't care what Danielle says. That's *your* thing, Briar. And you get to have your thing. The court and a freaking judge said you get to have your thing." My voice rose along with my temper. "So you're keeping it no matter what I have to do."

She nodded, blinking quickly. "Okay. Thanks."

I took her hand too and looked between both girls. "Next time, just tell me, okay? Don't sit over here like you're in a spy thriller. The Darlington girls do not keep secrets." Except for me, who was keeping a huge one about Hunter, but whatever.

Lark snorted. "We weren't very good at it."

"No, you were terrible," I said. "Remind me never to cast you as spies."

I stood up and brushed the grass from my jeans.

"Also," I added, already plotting a truly impressive rage-text to Eli, "remind me never to let Danielle speak to any of my children ever again." I decided I could badmouth her, maybe just a little.

I was muttering murder scenarios under my breath when we made our way back to the firepit. I'd nearly decided that rusty salad tongs were my weapon of choice when Briar slipped her hand into mine.

"You okay?" I asked.

She shrugged. "Mad. But also kind of hungry."

"Fury burns calories," I said solemnly. "Let's feed it."

We rejoined the crowd around the fire just as Grandpa appeared with his usual paper plate stacked dangerously high—burger, hot dog, beans, potato chips, and an extra helping of whatever dessert someone dared to leave unattended.

"You girls hungry?" he asked, giving us all a once-over with his Grandpa Radar™—fully capable of detecting emotional instability, heartbreak, or hidden contraband.

Briar nodded.

"Then get you a plate, sweetie," he said. "I didn't raise this family to skip dinner over drama."

"Technically, you didn't raise me," Briar said. "And how do you know there was drama?"

He pointed at her with his fork. "I'm still claiming you. And I have eyes, don't I? I know what drama looks like when I see it."

Piper appeared as if out of nowhere, strawberry in one hand, probably sensing family tension like the bloodhound she was. "Okay, why does Paige have her *do not engage* face on?"

"It's my regular face," I protested weakly.

"No, it's the one where you're mentally drafting an email that starts with 'per my last message' and ends with jail time. What's going on? Let me help."

I sighed and waved a hand. "Danielle told Briar to quit dance class to save money. Apparently, they need a new couch."

The ripple was instant. Cara dropped her drink. Lucy gasped so dramatically you'd think someone spoiled the ending to a true crime documentary. Eliza whispered, "That witch," which in Eliza-speak was basically a declaration of war.

"Maybe we should kick her ass a little bit," Lucy grumbled.

"I'll get a shovel and pick a spot behind the barn," Cara offered. "You know, if it gets out of hand."

"I'll provide the alibis," Spencer added.

"Guys," I said, rubbing my forehead. "We're not going to kill her or beat her up or even talk to her."

"Speak for yourself," Ren muttered. "I am on this. No charge. This was settled."

Grandpa just stood there, nodding slowly, like he was running calculations in his head. Finally, he jabbed his fork toward Briar. "You want to keep dancing?"

Her eyes widened. Hope shining through. "Yes."

"Done. I'll pay for it. Forget about Danielle and whatever she wants. Forget about Eli, too. Problem solved—no conflict, no arguments. We'll keep our little Briar-girl out of the middle."

"Grandpa—" I started, instantly launching into my default protest. "That's not necessary. I've got it."

He gave me a look that could stop time. "You've been doing everything yourself for too damn long, Paige. Let me do this one thing. I won't even tell your mother about it."

I groaned. "Now it sounds shady."

"Good," he said. "Keeps things exciting."

"But I can—"

"Paige." He stepped closer, his voice gentle now. "Let her dance. Let me help. You've taken care of everybody else. It's okay to let someone take care of you for once."

I looked around the firepit—at my sisters, my girls, the way Piper had slid an arm around Briar's shoulders, and how Lark had quietly handed her a marshmallow and a Hershey Bar. These people were mine. Messy, loud, and way too involved, but all *mine*.

"Okay," I said, voice soft.

"Okay?" Grandpa repeated, eyes narrowing like he didn't quite believe it. "Really?"

I nodded. "Okay."

"Well, alright, done deal. Dance with me, honey." Grandma clapped her hands together in satisfaction, then she grabbed Briar and spun her in a circle before pulling her into a big hug.

I heaved out a relieved sigh. Briar would be okay; Grandma's hugs could work magic. And Grandpa had been helping us solve all our problems since we were born.

Grandpa smiled, satisfied, and said to Briar. "Great." He held out a hand. "Now let's go eat some questionable kale salad whatchamacallit and pretend your great grandma doesn't add raisins to everything."

Briar grinned and followed him toward the buffet table to fill a plate.

I sank back onto the picnic bench, exhausted but a little lighter. Piper handed me a strawberry and leaned her head on my shoulder.

"We're not going to let either one of them mess with the girls," she said quietly. "Or Noah."

"I know."

She paused. "But if you need us to come up with some interesting revenge, we *do* have access to a barn and an entire chicken costume from last Halloween. And Larry is usually down for anything."

I snorted. "Don't tempt me."

Piper drifted off back to Ren to make s'mores, and I was left alone with my half-finished Diet Coke, the scent of firewood, and the sound of Briar laughing with my grandpa.

I should've felt better.

And I did. Mostly.

But under the relief was something else. A kind of tired that lived in my bones. The kind that came from fighting battles no one else saw—again and again—while trying to keep everything running and everyone smiling.

My phone buzzed in my back pocket.

I pulled it out and saw Hunter's name.

Hunter: Just checking in. You okay?

Just two words.

But they cracked something open in me.

Not "how was the barbecue" or "what happened." Not pushy or prying.

Just *okay*.

Like he could feel that tonight had cost me something.

I stared at the screen for a moment, thumb hovering.

Then I typed back.

Me: Yeah. Kids are fed. Grandpa's mad. Family's rallying. So… the usual. Thanks for asking.

Three dots flickered, then stilled.

Then finally—

Hunter: Anytime you want to talk. You
know where to find me.

I stared at the message long enough that the screen dimmed.
    Then I hit save on the moment.
    Tucked it away somewhere soft.
    And went to be with my girls.

Chapter 6
Hunter

Weekly dinners at the Twilight Tavern were a ritual for me and my brothers. Comfort food, cold beer, and the exact same argument every week over who owed for the wings. But none of that was why I showed up tonight. This time, I was here for her.

I knew the signs with Paige. When she started deflecting, joking too much, brushing things off— it usually meant she was hurting. Quietly. She wouldn't come to me. So I went to her.

The bar smelled like fryer oil, lemon cleaner, and old pine from the dark wooden floorboards. Every table had a little battery-powered candle Paige had hot-glued into little mason jars. The jukebox still only played '80s music because she hadn't been able to justify the cost of updating the selections. And yet, it was still the best place in town because she had made it that way.

The place buzzed with energy, a warm pulse that seemed to shimmer just beneath the laughter. Twinkling strings of lights traced the beams overhead, casting a soft glow over everything. The mismatched wooden tables, covered in ring marks from hundreds of glasses dripping with condensation from ice-cold beers, edges worn smooth by years of elbows, knowing glances, and secrets whispered between sips, everywhere, there was the hum of voices, the clatter of glasses, and the spark of a place everyone loved.

Tonight, it was packed. Local crowd, mostly. Paige's regulars. Plus, a few tourists who'd wandered down from The Honeybrook. The kitchen was slammed. Two of the servers wove through the crowd with trays full of sliders and nachos, laughing and keeping pace with the rhythm of the bar.

Paige was behind the counter, pouring drinks and tossing sass like it was currency. The words *It's five o'clock somewhere* stretched across the chest of her snug long-sleeved T-shirt, and her hair was up in a high ponytail. There was a smudge of something on her cheek that only made her look more gorgeous. I couldn't get her out of my head, but I was currently refusing to think about why. She had gone from my best friend, Paige, to the most beautiful blonde bombshell I'd ever seen. Objectively speaking, I'd always recognized she was pretty; it was evident to anyone with eyes. But now she was *hot*. Big brown eyes, tall, curvy body...

Damn it. Stop.

I slid into the seat at my usual table with my brothers and scanned the room. The light flickered above us, and I scowled. It needed to be replaced, not repeatedly tinkered with. I wish she'd just let me buy her a new one.

Paige moved behind the bar, ponytail bouncing, sleeves shoved to her elbows, eyes sharper than any knife in the kitchen. Every so often, she'd send a nod or a word toward her crew—quick, efficient, never lingering. I liked watching her like this, running her kingdom, making the chaos look choreographed.

She hadn't seen me yet, and I hadn't gone to the bar to say hi since she was busy. Or maybe she had—because the second the waitress dropped off our beers, a couple of my former classmates made a beeline for our table, and she shot them a glare.

"Hunter Cassidy," the blonde one—Ashley?—drawled, leaning a little too far into my space. "Haven't seen you in ages. How's life treating you?"

I smiled politely, leaning back enough to put an inch of space between us. "Busy. Working a lot."

"That shop still keeping you tied down?" she asked, fingers brushing my arm. "Bet you don't get much time for fun. You were always there back in school, right? Working for your dad?"

Deacon smirked behind his pint, enjoying the show way too much.

I answered with a noncommittal "something like that" and reached for a wing. She laughed and touched my shoulder this time.

Out of habit, my eyes drifted toward the bar—and found Paige watching. Or rather, *glowering*.

She was sliding a beer down the counter to a regular, but her eyes flicked back to me in between motions. Her mouth was set in a tight, annoyed line, and she quickly turned to refill a pitcher, like I hadn't caught her looking.

"Not tonight, yeah?" I said gently. "Brother night."

"Gotcha," she said, excusing herself with a grin. "Maybe another time?"

I nodded. "Sure. See you around."

Brody leaned in, low enough that only I could hear.

"You seeing this? Pretty sure your bartender's about to follow her and break her hand off for touching you."

"She's not *my* bartender," I said, but the corner of my mouth betrayed me as it twitched up in a satisfied grin.

Deacon chuckled. "Not yet."

I ignored them both and caught Paige's gaze again, just for a second, before she looked down, busying herself with wiping down the bar that, from my vantage point, looked already clean.

Yeah. She'd noticed, and she didn't like it. Clearly, she was jealous—and *I loved it.* But at the same time, I wanted to reassure her that she was all I was thinking about, that I only had eyes for her. But I couldn't do that yet. I didn't want to risk scaring her off or putting pressure on whatever was happening between us.

There was something else going on, though. Underneath the sound of laughter and clinking glasses, there was tension brewing—a charge that made the hair on my arms stand up. Paige was moving a little too fast, her smile a little too thin. When she caught my gaze again, she held it for a second longer than usual, just long enough that my chest tightened.

It was more than her potential jealousy. She was stressed out; something was going on that I didn't know about—yet.

That was when I noticed her sisters at the bar. Piper raised her glass to me in a silent toast, Lucy gave a tiny wave, then blew a kiss to Spencer, and Eliza pretended not to notice me at all, probably feeling guilty for spreading the muffin gossip. Cara, who usually kept to herself, was talking to Jasper, the new bartender, and the way she tucked her hair behind her ear made me wonder if something was going on between the two of them.

The air felt heavy with anticipation, as if everyone was waiting for something to tip the balance.

"She's about to snap," Spencer said from beside me, sipping his beer. "It's gonna be epic and most likely horrifying. Lucy is worried, but she won't say why. It's personal business. Probably about her shithead ex."

"She'll be fine," I said, but I didn't take my eyes off her. No matter what happened, I would make sure she came out of it as unscathed as possible. I would throw myself in front of a train for her if it would spare her any pain.

"She's got the same look my ex used to get before she cussed out the vacuum cleaner," Tucker observed. "Stressed the hell out."

He had a point. She was on edge tonight.

At the bar, her sisters were pretending it was "Sister Night." But anyone could see they were watching her like hawks. Protective. Waiting. Ready to pounce if needed.

Paige waved to one of the servers at the tap and hollered, "Table six needs another round and a reminder that flirting doesn't get them a discount."

She snorted. "Already handled it."

Then the door opened, Eli walked in, and Paige froze in her tracks.

He had that same too-clean, too-confident vibe he always did. Button-down crisp, hair freshly trimmed, and wearing a smile like he'd practiced it on the way over.

Eli swaggered to the bar like he owned the place—like he still had any right to be near her. I felt a hot spike of disgust before I even heard him speak. "Paige," he said. "Hey. Got a minute?"

Her indifference hit him harder than any insult. "No". Not a "maybe later," not a "go away"—just a flat, cold no.

I saw her hands clench tight around that bar rag, like

she was trying not to shatter right there in front of everyone. I wanted to reach out and tear Eli's smug grin off his face.

The room held its breath. Piper's sharp look at Paige was almost like a warning. Or maybe a shield. I wasn't sure what Eli thought. Maybe he still thought he had some claim to her. God, how wrong he was.

Paige's voice barely broke the silence: "What do you want, Eli?"

I felt my jaw tighten. That name on her lips was bitter and broken. Eli shifted uncomfortably, looking at the floor like the arrogance was slipping away. Good. He deserved to feel small.

"Can we talk? Just for a second."

Her jaw clenched harder. She was steel, but I could see the wear beneath the surface, the way she was holding herself together just enough not to fall apart.

"Make it fast," she said, voice brittle as cracked glass.

Eli hesitated. And that hesitation was all Piper needed to stand. The atmosphere thickened, and I knew every sister there was ready to defend Paige, while I was ready to end him. Fury radiated through me like a god damn furnace. I ground my teeth together, trying to cool off. I knew she could handle herself, and I had to let her do it.

Paige didn't flinch, but I could see the storm in her eyes, that wild flash of fear and fury barely contained. Piper shifted closer, shoulders squared, letting Eli know—without words—that his time was running out. The whole bar felt it, the way loyalty can turn sharp and dangerous in an instant.

Eli opened his mouth to say something, but Paige didn't give him the chance. She tossed her towel on the bar and turned sharply.

"Not here."

Every step she took toward the kitchen was deliberate. I

could feel the tension rippling off her, daring him to follow, daring him to try.

He lingered a moment, maybe weighing his chances, but then hurried after her. I wanted to yell at him to stay away, that he didn't deserve her, never had, never would.

As they disappeared through the kitchen door, the room exhaled, and Piper gave the nod. Sisters rising, ready for whatever storm Eli thought he could bring.

I stayed rooted to the spot, fury simmering under my skin. Because he'd broken her heart once, and if he thought he could do it again without consequence, he was dead wrong.

"It'll only take a second." Eli tossed over his shoulder. But they didn't care what he had to say; they followed anyway.

"Dude is definitely not scared enough." Deacon shook his head. "I never liked that prick."

Spencer stood. "Back door?"

"Back door," I confirmed, already moving to be there for her. I'd stand by her side while she faced him, but I wished she would let me just pick her up and carry her away from his bullshit. I wanted to fix this, to make everything okay, but I knew it would only piss her off if I interfered.

Spencer's eyes met mine, searching for agreement—maybe for permission, maybe for backup. The air was thick with the promise of confrontation, everyone acutely aware that lines were being drawn, stakes raised.

We slipped through the kitchen and out the back just as Paige's voice rose through the gravel-scented alley.

"You want to *sell* my house?!" she shrieked. "*Your children's home?*"

Inside, the entire tavern hushed; she was that loud. Even the jukebox seemed to lower itself into a pause.

"It's not just your house. We should split it." Eli said. "My new lawyer said it should have been considered marital property—"

"Oh, you do not want to start with legalese and technicalities. You left, Eli. You moved out. You moved *on*. You don't get to come back and claim pieces of the life I rebuilt."

"I need the money. I'm not trying to hurt you."

"I do not care enough about you to let you hurt me. But threatening to take away your kids' home? What kind of father does that? You are pathetic."

"I'm just saying—it could help us both, financially, I mean. You could pay off the bar, take a break. Or maybe even sell the bar. Think about it. We could sell and split it, and then we could both be set."

"Are you crazy? I'm not selling anything. You think I *want* a break? This is my place. *Mine*. I don't need a fucking break."

"You're running yourself ragged. It's not sustainable, Paige."

"And whose fault is that?" She was on fire. Furious. "You're choosing Danielle's comfort over your daughter's dreams. You're trying to cut Briar's dance class so you can buy new furniture for your fiancée's living room! They told me everything."

"I'm doing my best—"

"Your best sucks!"

Behind me, I heard Eliza suck in a breath. Lucy folded her arms. Piper stayed quiet, her jaw set like stone.

"He's gone too far," Cara whispered, voice tight.

"I'm texting Ren," Piper muttered.

Eli took a half step forward, hands held out placatingly, like he thought being reasonable would work now. "You don't have to make this harder than it is."

"Oh, you have *got* to be kidding me," Paige snapped. "You don't get to pull the 'I'm the reasonable one' card. Not when you're standing in *my* parking lot, outside *my* bar, telling me to give up the home we raised our children in. That house is mine, and it's going to stay mine. *Forever*, you stupid prick."

He opened his mouth. Closed it.

Then he noticed all of us standing there.

Her sisters. My brothers. The bar staff. Me.

And for once in his life, Eli did the right thing.

He turned and walked off. Stalked across the parking lot, got into his car, and left.

Paige exhaled like she'd been holding her breath since he arrived. Her shoulders slumped for half a second, just enough to feel the cost of staying upright. Then she looked up and saw us.

"Did you seriously all follow me outside?" Her eyes were bright with something sharp and defiant, and for a heartbeat, no one moved. Then the tension snapped—just a little, just enough for breath to return—and the crowd shifted closer, a ripple of solidarity.

I hung back behind the others, the urge rising in me to swoop in and hold Paige, to take her home and make sure she was okay. Every instinct screamed at me to shield her, to make things easier. But I knew her too well—her pride wouldn't let her leave before she'd finished her job. She needed to stand her ground and prove she could handle this, and I respected that. Still, I watched from the edge, wishing I could do more, wishing she'd let me carry some of the weight for her.

Jasper stepped forward, holding out a glass of water. Paige took it, her fingers steady but pale, and drank it. "Thanks," she muttered.

Piper was the first to break the silence, her voice low but sure. "We wanted to make sure you didn't kill him," she said gently.

"You looked like you might," Eliza added.

"No one would have blamed you," Lucy said.

"I have alibis," Spencer offered with a grin, breaking the tension.

She let out a short laugh. "I don't even know what to say to that."

I stayed quiet, watching her. "You okay?" I finally asked.

She gave me a look. "Do you even need to ask?"

"I'll always ask."

"I know. You're always here when I need you." Her expression softened, barely. "Thanks for not jumping in."

"You didn't need me to. You had it covered."

That pulled a breathy laugh out of her. Not quite amused, but close enough. "He's just so—*ugh*."

"I know."

"Do you think there's a planet somewhere where men like that turn into frogs instead of middle-aged, deadbeat, cheating assholes?"

"I can only hope. But hey," I added. "I'll send him to another planet whenever you want. Just say the word and I'll handle him."

She sighed, nodding her thanks to me, then looked at her sisters. "Sorry, guys."

Piper just waved her off. "Please. We were one dramatic moment away from storming in like the Sisterhood of the Traveling Murder Charges."

"Maybe tomorrow I can get through the night without needing a rage fest and a court-appointed mediator," Paige muttered.

"This will be over soon," Piper said, as they all turned

back toward the door. "By the way, I called Ren; he's on it. That asshole will not be taking the house. Get that worry right out of your mind."

"Thanks." She looped her arm through Piper's. "Talking to Ren is probably better than committing murder."

The cool night air followed us in as the kitchen door swung open and we filtered back into the warm, noisy light of the tavern. The jukebox, as if sensing the all-clear, picked up in the middle of "Hit Me With Your Best Shot". Glasses clinked. Chairs scraped. Conversations slowly returned to normal.

By the time I sat down again with my brothers, Paige was back behind the bar like nothing had happened, the servers were making their rotations, and Jasper was pouring drinks.

"Is she going to be okay?" Tucker asked. "That was bad."

"She will be." I shrugged, trying to downplay my worry for her, running a thumb along the condensation of my glass. "She always is." But the words felt less certain than I wanted, less reassuring than I'd intended. Around us, the tavern buzzed as everyone went back to their evening.

I watched her from across the room as she tucked a strand of hair behind her ear and smiled at someone at the bar. It wasn't a big smile. Not her real one. But it was enough to make me stay put—for now.

She caught me looking and gave the tiniest shake of her head, like she knew exactly what I was doing and was too tired to argue about it. And then she moved on to the next customer and returned to work.

I stayed where I was, beer in hand, letting Spencer and

Deacon argue over ranch versus blue cheese on wings while I kept an eye on her.

When closing time rolled around, the tavern's energy had faded to a gentle murmur. The regulars trickled out with nods and waves, the last glasses were stacked, and the bar lights flickered low. I said goodbye to my brothers, then started stacking chairs on tables while Paige finished tallying the register—her movements were precise and practiced, eyes focused anywhere but on me.

She clicked the lock on the door and gave me a tight smile. "You don't have to help. I got this," she said, voice quiet but clear. The way she straightened her shoulders made it obvious: she wanted space, not comfort.

"You know I do," I insisted.

"Okay. Thank you..." she whispered.

I watched her for a moment, wanting to bridge the distance but knowing better than to push. There was a rawness in her eyes, a tension in her posture that told me tonight wasn't the night for easy reassurances or clumsy gestures. Instead, I just nodded, stacking the last chair and letting the quiet settle between us like a fragile truce. We moved through the familiar motions of closing up—her wiping down the bar, me checking the back door—each of us careful to keep our words light and our distance respectable, as if any sudden move might shatter what little calm we'd managed to reclaim.

Once finished, we headed to the door in silence. "Are you okay to drive? Tonight was a lot."

Paige hesitated before answering, her fingers tightening around her car keys. She took a slow breath, and for a moment I thought she might actually tell me how she felt. But all she said was, "Yeah. I just need a minute before I get going." I nodded, respecting her need for space, even as concern tugged at me. The air between us was thick with everything left unsaid, but I chose to trust she'd reach out if she needed me, at least for tonight.

"Just making sure," I replied, stepping outside into the cool night beside her. The street was empty, darkness pressing in with only the distant hum of traffic. Paige crossed her arms, gaze fixed ahead. I wanted to offer something that might lighten the weight she carried, but she shook her head—barely, just enough for me to know the conversation was over before it started.

"I'm fine," she said, keys clenched in her hand. "Really, I'll be okay, I promise. I don't feel like talking about it. I'll see you tomorrow."

She didn't linger. A quick wave, a determined stride toward her car, and she was gone, leaving me standing under the streetlamp with nothing but the echo of her footsteps fading into the night.

I stood outside for a long moment, listening to the quiet city and letting the chill settle into my skin. It was the kind of night that made every sound carry—a distant dog barking, the hum of a stoplight changing, the crinkle of leaves skittering across the sidewalk. I thought about texting Paige, just a simple "made it home?" or "let me know if you need anything." But I knew better than to crowd her, so I slipped my phone back into my pocket and let the silence stretch. In the end, I just took a deep breath and headed toward my car, the faint glow of the tavern sign behind me a reminder that sometimes, the hardest part is knowing when to let someone walk away on their own.

I drove home beneath a sky brittle with stars, and the silence back at my place echoed the unsaid words between us. Tomorrow, maybe, things would feel less fragile.

Chapter 7
Paige

If there was anything sacred in my life, it was my day off. No alarm. No bar. No customers were asking if we served food, even though they were holding a menu in their hands. Just me in my leggings, mug of tea in hand, ignoring the sink full of dishes while pretending my house didn't smell vaguely like a teenager's gym bag and the stale onion rings from last night's dinner.

It had been a little over two weeks since the confrontation with Eli, and I hadn't yet heard from him; radio silence. Ren said things were okay—for now, anyway—though I knew better than to take "okay" at face value when it came to Eli. He was plotting something, I knew it.

Hunter hadn't mentioned us going to dinner again, but he texted me every morning, just quick notes to check in. I saw him on his brother nights at the bar, and we chit-chatted like we used to. It felt like my life had slipped back to almost normal - but part of me didn't like that. Going back to how things were *before* wasn't as comforting as I thought it would be.

Noah was home for the weekend, lounging on the

couch, cocooned in an oversized hoodie, his bare feet sticking out from the edge of the old quilt he refused to let me throw away. He'd outgrown it years ago and now used it more like a weighted comfort blanket than actual warmth. He was on a break from culinary school, where he was learning how to make fancy sauces and sending me texts about knives I couldn't afford to buy for him—not yet, anyway.

The girls were out, Lark was spending the night with a friend, and Briar was with Eli; it was his turn. She said she'd be okay and promised to call me or Grandpa if she wanted to be picked up at any point. Grandpa had become the de facto middleman between me and Eli. He dropped them off and picked them up whenever it was Eli's turn to spend time with them. Briar and Lark had reassured me multiple times that they would tell me everything. No more attempts to protect me from the truth.

I sat on the couch with my tea, feet propped on the ottoman, as the late evening sun slanted in through the blinds enough to warm the edge of the rug. The living room was small and overstuffed—two faded armchairs, a too-squishy couch, and a crooked bookshelf filled with everything from classic novels to cookbooks to romance novels that seemed more like wishful thinking than reality.

The girls' shoes were in a pile by the front door. An empty mug and a hair tie sat on the windowsill. A full laundry basket waited to be folded on the floor. I needed to clean up, but I wasn't going to waste this rare one-on-one time with my son by mentioning the dirty dishes or the fact that I had approximately seven hundred loads of laundry to do.

He was here. That was enough. Especially since I knew something was wrong. He hadn't told me yet, but he would.

Then he sniffed, voice thick and rough. "She dumped me over text."

My heart squeezed in a way I hadn't expected. So that was it. He was hurting, and not just a little, but from a broken heart. My baby's first real taste of heartbreak, and it was crushing to realize I couldn't take this pain on for him.

"She didn't even call?" I asked softly, my mind racing. How long had he been carrying this alone?

He shook his head, voice barely above a hoarse whisper. "Nope. Didn't even have the decency."

I swallowed the lump in my throat. "She's clearly blind," I said, trying to keep my voice steady. "And stupid, too, because you're amazing. Honestly, she needs therapy and a serious reality check." He snorted, but the sound was watery, and a tear slid down the side of his nose. I handed him a tissue without comment, giving him the dignity of not drawing attention to it. For a minute, we just sat like that, the clock ticking softly in the kitchen, the house holding its breath.

"You have to say that," he muttered. "You're my mom."

"No, I don't. I could say nothing and just judge her in silence like a normal person."

That got a weak smile out of him. He leaned against me on the couch, and I let him, resting my head lightly on his as I pulled him into my side. It had been a long time since I'd been able to hold him like this, and I wasn't going to be the one to end it. I had almost forgotten how this felt, to hold my kids this way. Like when they were my little babies and I had the power to solve all their problems with hugs and kisses.

"I feel like I'm dying," he whispered. "My heart actually hurts."

I kissed the top of his head, my heart breaking right

along with his. "I'm so sorry, sweetheart. I know this means nothing right now, but you're going to be okay, I promise."

He nodded against me, and I squeezed him tighter.

A long time ago, like a decade or more, I had felt this way about Eli. How sad was it that I had felt nothing but relief when we divorced? Nothing but resignation and the slight thrill of finally being free of him. We'd married young, and almost immediately, I'd regretted it. But before I could do anything about it, Noah was on the way.

"Want me to make you a grilled cheese? I'll cut them into triangles like when you were little." I asked, knowing he'd refuse, but I needed to offer it anyway.

He shook his head, wiped his face, and managed a shaky exhale. "Maybe later. Can I sit here with you for a while?"

"Always," I said. I squeezed his hand, feeling the familiar ache of wanting to fix everything and knowing I couldn't. So I just stayed, letting the silence hang, the sunset darkening the room a little more with every passing second.

My phone buzzed on the side table.

I ignored it.

It buzzed again.

I finally leaned over to check.

Hunter: Just checking in. You okay?

A small rush of warmth and reassurance washed over me. He always seemed to know when I needed a lifeline. It was as unnerving as it was soothing.

Then it rang.

I was ready to see Hunter's name—but it wasn't.

It was Ren calling.

I answered. "Please tell me this is about anything other than Eli."

"Can't," he said, clipped and direct. "His attorney formally requested a meeting to discuss selling the house and reducing child support."

I closed my eyes. "Of course they did."

"I already responded," he said, his tone sharpening. "I have a motion prepared challenging both. They're going to have to fight for it. And trust me, they will lose."

I stared at him in surprise. "Wait—you didn't even call me first?"

"Paige, you hired me to protect you and your kids, not sit around and wait for Eli to do the decent thing. This is me doing that. And like I said before, no charge for family. I'm with Piper now, that makes you family."

I paused, caught somewhere between startled and grateful.

He continued. "He's claiming reduced income. I have my doubts about that based on the bank records we pulled during the divorce. I'm digging deeper and will have an answer for you soon. On a more personal note: I'd love to toss that motherfucker through a window."

"He's such a—" I glanced over at Noah and stopped myself. "Never mind."

"You can say it. I called him worse during the divorce, remember?"

"Yeah. I owe you a lot." I let out a slow breath. "Thanks, Ren."

"You don't owe me a thing. You're doing everything you can to keep things stable. He's the one trying to knock the whole thing over. We're not letting him."

That one hit me square in the chest. "I appreciate you."

"Seriously," he added. "Let me be ruthless. It's my favorite part of the job. I love it."

I rubbed my eyes. "I'm just tired of feeling like the punching bag."

"You're not," he said firmly. "You're the one still standing."

We hung up, and I set the phone back on the table. I leaned back into the couch and let my head fall against the cushion.

Noah was still staring at the ceiling.

"You ever wish you could just hit pause for like, a week?" I asked.

He snorted. "Try a year."

I reached out and rubbed his shoulder.

"Are you okay?" Noah asked. "I mean, with me gone. And Dad's gone too. And that I'm not working with you at the bar anymore and—"

"Shh," I cut him off. "I'm fine. Don't worry about me. You just concentrate on becoming the best chef in the world, okay? I'm good, I promise."

"Why don't I believe that?" He looked hurt.

I hesitated, rubbing circles into the fabric of his sleeve as I contemplated how much to tell him. He was an adult. He was a man now, and lying about things he already knew were happening was not right.

"I don't know, Noah. Some days it feels like things are unraveling faster than I can tie them back up." The room was quiet except for our breathing. I looked at the muted television, absently watching colors flicker across the screen.

Noah's voice was softer now. "I get it. I felt that way when I caught him with her."

"I hate that you saw that." I swallowed the knot in my

throat. "Sometimes I wish I knew how to make it easier for everyone. For you. For Lark. For Briar, you're hurting so much because of this."

Noah leaned against me. "Maybe we're all just getting by for now. But that's enough, isn't it? We have each other, and he's going to lose all of us if he doesn't quit acting like an asshole. Not just you."

I managed a smile, feeling a fragile sense of comfort settle between us. For a moment, the world outside faded, and it was just us, quietly holding on. When I first left Eli, I'd made a promise to myself never to say anything against him, but to always be there if the kids needed to unload. I didn't answer Noah, as I tried my best to keep it.

"Do you promise to call me if you need me?" He broke the silence. "I'm not a kid anymore, even though I was acting like a baby tonight."

"You were not acting like a baby. Everyone hurts like that sometimes; you have to get it out. And I promise I'll call you. As long as you do the same." I brushed away the stray thought of how quickly life kept shifting beneath our feet. Noah smiled, and for a second, I thought it was possible to believe we would be okay.

But then my phone buzzed on the table, a sharp note slicing into our moment. I glanced at the screen, saw Eli's name, and felt the old, familiar jolt of dread. Noah watched my face change and knew before I did that whatever peace we'd found had slipped away.

I picked up, bracing myself for whatever storm waited on the other end.

My stomach sank as I answered. "What?"

"Is Briar home?"

I straightened. "What do you mean by '*is Briar home*'? She's supposed to be with you."

"She was in her room. Or I thought she was. But I went to call her for ice cream, and—she's gone. She's not answering her phone. I thought maybe she came back to your place."

I stood, my heart already thudding. "No. She didn't. She's not here, and she hasn't messaged me."

"Text Grandpa," I told Noah. "Ask if he has Briar."

"What's happening?" he asked as he fumbled for his phone on the coffee table to do what I said.

"Lark's not answering either," Eli added, voice rising.

"Grandpa doesn't have her," Noah informed me.

"I'll call her phone," I said to Eli. "Hang up and start calling Lark again. No, don't call Lark, call the police."

"I already called the police. I did it before I called you." Eli clicked off, and I turned to Noah, who was already standing.

"Briar's missing," I said. "Can you call Lark?"

He started dialing.

My phone buzzed again. It was Hunter. I answered this time.

"Paige," Hunter said immediately, his voice deep and steady. "Is everything okay? You usually answer right away—"

His calm tone washed over me, quieting the frantic edge in my chest just enough to let me breathe.

"No. Nothing is okay. Briar is not at Eli's. He thought she might've come home, but she's not here either. She's not answering her phone. I don't know where she is."

He didn't hesitate. "I'm calling Cade and my brothers. We'll head out now. Don't panic—we'll find her."

"Thank you," I said, my voice shaking. "Eli has called the police already. Maybe Cade already knows what's going on."

Noah's voice cut in. "Lark's fine. She's still at Maddie's like she's supposed to be. She heard there's a party. Someone's parents are out of town. She thinks Briar might've gone, and she's texting you the address."

I grabbed my keys and shoved on my sneakers.

"Can you pick up Lark and bring her home?" I asked Noah.

"On it," he said, already heading out.

As the door shut behind him, I stood there in my quiet living room, staring at the phone in my hand and hoping to God that we were just dealing with a harmless teenage screw-up. And not something worse. I copied the address straight into a group text—Hunter, Cade, and Eli. Then I texted, called, and left a voicemail for Briar to call me immediately.

> Me: She might be at a party just outside of Willowmist Falls. I'm heading that way.

Noah grabbed his keys and took off to pick up Lark. I barely had time to grab my jacket before I was out the door, too, with my phone clutched in my hand like it might give me one more piece of certainty if I squeezed it hard enough.

Willowmist Falls wasn't far, but the roads out that way were narrow and winding, all dark trees and spotty cell service. My headlights barely cut through the black.

Every minute that passed without hearing from Briar made my pulse throb louder. It echoed in my ears, pounding cold dread through my veins. I'd almost made it to the edge of the woods near the address of the party when my phone buzzed.

Hunter: Found her. She's safe. I've got her
in the truck.

I had to pull over.

Hands on the steering wheel, forehead against it, I burst into tears, loud sobs shaking my shoulders as I almost crumbled apart.

I gathered myself together and texted back.

Me: Where are you?

His reply came fast.

Hunter: Heading toward your place now.
She's quiet but okay. I'll see you soon.

For a moment, the woods pressed in on all sides—silent and ancient, as though they held their breath too. I rolled down the window, letting the cool night air sting my cheeks, grounding me. The tension in my chest softened, just a notch, replaced by a jumbled relief that made my hands tremble as I started the engine again.

Mist curled over the asphalt as I turned around, headlights carving pale tunnels through the trees. I kept glancing at my phone, half expecting another message would come through, half-dreading it.

What had she been thinking? And why hadn't I known something was wrong? Why hadn't I sensed that she needed me?

The road home blurred beneath me, each landmark I passed loosening the knot in my stomach.

By the time my porch light winked into view, I was in a state. I killed the engine and stepped out, running toward my porch, heart hammering in my throat, bracing for whatever was coming.

Chapter 8
Hunter

The roads out near Willowmist Falls were just as bad as I remembered, narrow and potholed, dark as hell even with my brights on. I'd already looped past a couple of bonfire parties and what was obviously still the popular makeout spot when I saw her.

She was walking on the shoulder, arms crossed, head down, ponytail swinging behind her with every hurried step. Her sweatshirt sleeves were pulled over her hands, and even from behind, I could see the tension in her shoulders.

But that wasn't what made my heart hammer.

It was the truck behind her.

Old. Rusted. Rolling slow. Too slow.

I rolled my window down and leaned out. "Briar!"

She froze, turned, and the second she saw me, she bolted. The truck behind her spun around, gunned it, and took off, tires skidding as it sped away into the dark behind me.

Briar didn't stop until she hit the passenger door.

I threw it open. She climbed in, gasping, pale as hell.

"Are you okay?" I asked, checking the mirrors, trying to get the license plate, but the truck was gone.

She nodded too fast, blinking hard, arms wrapped around herself. "I didn't know what to do. They weren't doing anything. Just driving slow. I really didn't want to go into the woods, and—"

"Okay," I said, trying to keep my voice even. "You're safe now. Everyone's out looking for you. Your mom is terrified."

That cracked her. Her face crumpled, and she covered it with both hands. I found my phone in the console and sent a text to Paige, then Cade, to let them know I'd found her.

I didn't say anything. I reached behind the seat and pulled out the clean jacket I kept back there. I passed it over to her, along with the crumpled pack of travel tissues in the cupholder. She yanked the jacket on and buried her face in the sleeves.

"I didn't mean to scare anybody," she mumbled. "I just —I didn't want to be at my dad's house anymore. And I didn't want to make Mom feel worse. Everything's already hard."

"I get it," I said quietly, pulling back onto the road to take her home.

She sniffed, hard. "Danielle acts like me and Lark are a problem. She makes it feel like every time I breathe, I'm taking something from her kids."

My hands tightened on the wheel.

"She says things like, 'We all have to make sacrifices now,' and then looks right at me. Like I'm supposed to feel guilty for existing. I don't know what her problem is. Grandpa is paying for dance now. She hates me. I know it. And when he's there, my dad doesn't say a word."

I let her talk. Let it all tumble out in angry, breathless pieces while I fought back the urge to find her father and cave his face in with my fist for allowing this to happen.

"She treats Lark and me like we're extra. It's as if we're the ones who don't fit into their perfect little family. And Dad just lets her. Lark says to ignore her, but I can't. She said we have to go to his place, or Mom could get in trouble with the judge because of the custody stuff."

Listening to her, something fierce burned in my chest—I wanted to protect her, to go to war for her if I had to, the same way I would for her mother. I've known her since she was a baby, and it made me sick to think Eli could stand by and let this happen, let her feel unwanted in his own house. How could he?

I didn't say what I was thinking. That Danielle had no business parenting anyone. That Eli had no business letting her even try. And I wished she had said something to Paige, because there was no way this would have happened if she had known how bad it was. And that if it were up to me, she'd never go back there again.

"I didn't know what to do. I thought about calling Mom, but I didn't want to make her deal with more crap." She wiped her nose. "But it just—it all sucked, so I snuck out. Everyone at school was talking about this party—I screwed up. I'm horrible."

"Maybe you screwed up. But you're not horrible," I said. "You're a kid who got stuck in a really bad situation and didn't know what to do."

She was quiet, sniffling into her tissue. Then, so soft I almost didn't hear it, "Is Mom gonna be mad? I promised I would call her if I got upset. I didn't call her. That makes me a liar. I broke my promise."

I shook my head. "She won't be mad. She'll be relieved when she sees you. That's all."

We turned onto her street.

The porch light was on. The front door was open, just the screen pulled shut, and Paige stood there in leggings and an oversized sweatshirt, arms crossed over her chest, pacing just inside the frame.

The second she saw my headlights, she stepped outside.

I pulled into the driveway and put the truck in park.

"She's right here," I called out. "She's okay."

Briar looked up. Her whole face crumpled again.

"I'll walk you in," I added.

We got out. Paige met us halfway.

"Briar," she breathed, voice shaking.

"Mom," she cried, and launched herself into Paige's arms.

Paige wrapped around her like a shield, one hand in her hair, the other around her back.

"I'm so sorry," Briar said between sobs. "I didn't want to make things worse."

"You didn't," Paige whispered. "You didn't. I promise. It's okay. Shh. I'm just glad you're okay. You're home now, you're safe. I've got you."

I stayed back, hands in my pockets, heart still pounding from the what-ifs. But watching the way Paige held her kid like she was piecing her back together was the only thing that really mattered.

Eventually, she looked over Briar's shoulder at me. Her eyes were glassy, but alert. "Thank you," she mouthed. Then she pulled out of Paige's arms and ran to me, throwing her arms around my waist in a giant hug. "You saved me, Hunter, and you listened."

Embarrassed, she darted away back to the house and ran inside with Paige following closely behind.

I pulled out my phone and called Cade.

"Hey," he answered. "How is she?"

"She's safe. I found her walking along the highway. But there was a truck. Old. Red and white, but rusted. I'd say it was a Ford F-100, 1959, if I had to guess. It followed her slowly as she walked. Took off when I pulled up."

Cade's voice dropped. "You get a plate?"

"No. Too dark. But it felt wrong. It seemed like whoever was in it was up to no good. Could have just been a kid messing around, but it couldn't hurt to check it out. I can't shake it, man. It gave me a bad feeling."

"I'll make a few calls. Check in with patrol. We'll see if anything like that's been reported. And I'll send a car out there to look around."

"Thanks."

We hung up just as Noah's headlights swung into the driveway behind me.

He stopped haphazardly and barely had it in park before he and Lark were climbing out. Paige must've already texted them.

Lark didn't even pause—she sprinted to the front door and disappeared inside.

Noah spotted me and exhaled. "You're the one who found her?"

I nodded. "She's okay. Scared. Shaken up. But okay."

"God." He dragged a hand through his hair. "Okay. Thank you. Okay."

He looked like he'd aged five years in an hour. I clapped a hand on his shoulder and gave it a firm squeeze.

"You did good," I said. "Getting the info. Picking up Lark."

He nodded, still dazed. "Thanks."

I turned to go, to give them space, but then the screen door opened as another car pulled into the driveway. Paige stood there, arms crossed, her mouth a firm line as Eli burst out, running toward the porch.

"Is she okay?" he asked, looking around Paige into the house like he had a right to be inside with them, as if this entire situation wasn't his fault.

"She's safe," Paige said flatly. "And staying here tonight."

"I was worried—"

"You weren't watching her," she bit out. "I know she's not a baby, but she's still only thirteen. How long did you leave her alone? What the hell, Eli?"

That shut him up. She didn't raise her voice. Every word was edged with glass.

"I—" he attempted to answer before Paige cut him off.

"She didn't feel welcome in your house, Eli. That's a problem."

"I didn't know she was gone," he muttered weakly.

"And that's an even bigger problem."

No one said anything for a long, stretching beat. Then Briar's voice floated through the screen door. "Is he gone?"

Eli flinched. But that was all Paige needed. "You should go," she told him. "We'll talk tomorrow."

He hesitated, like he might protest. But then he saw Noah standing beside me, glaring at him, and Lark hovering just inside the doorway. The fire in Paige's eyes.

And me. Just waiting for the chance to take a swing at him.

He turned and walked back to his car without another word.

When the taillights disappeared, Paige exhaled.

I didn't move.

She looked at me, like she wasn't sure what to say next. "Will you stay for a minute? Please?"

That hit me harder than it should've. "Yeah," I said softly. "I'm not going anywhere."

Inside, the house had the stillness of something sacred, like everyone was holding their breath. The lights were dim. Briar and Lark had disappeared down the hall, and Noah had collapsed into the corner of the couch with his phone and a glass of water.

"I'm going to tuck them in," Paige said quietly, brushing her hair back with one hand. "Like when they were little. I need to. I have to make this okay somehow."

I nodded.

"I'm going to bed too," Noah said as he stood.

"I'll tuck you in too," she told him with a trembling smile. "No arguments."

"Okay, Mom," he whispered before giving her a quick hug.

They disappeared down the hall, and for a few minutes, it was just me and the tick of the old wall clock.

I wandered into the kitchen, opened a few cabinets until I found mugs, tea bags, and the scratched-up electric kettle she always kept on the counter. It rattled a little when it boiled.

By the time she came back out, her shoulders had fallen, and her eyes were glossy but dry.

She looked at the mugs. "Thank you, Hunter."

"Of course. Let me take care of you. Please. Tell me what you need, and I'll do it."

"I have no idea what I need. I can't believe this happened. I think I'm in shock." She sank onto the couch, curling her legs up beneath her and wrapping her arms around her stomach like she was trying to hold herself together from the outside in.

"I'm here. I won't leave you alone, I promise." I brought her a mug and sat down beside her. Not too close. Just close enough in case she needed a hug or something.

She took the tea with both hands and held it without drinking. "They're okay," she said softly. "They're all going to be okay."

"They're safe. They're home. With you where they belong."

She looked at the tea, then slowly turned her head toward me.

"I almost lost her tonight."

"You didn't."

"I could have." Her voice cracked. "She was out there and scared, and I wasn't there and—" Her mouth trembled, and she pressed the mug to her lips like it could stop the horrible thoughts I knew were rushing through her mind.

I wanted to tell her about the rusted truck I'd spotted following Briar earlier, warn her just in case, but even thinking about it made my chest tighten. This wasn't the moment—she was barely holding it together, and the last thing she needed was another worry piled onto everything else. No, I'd keep it to myself for now, stay vigilant, and do whatever I had to so Paige and her kids stayed safe. If it came down to it, I'd put myself between them and anything that tried to get close, no questions asked. She didn't have to know all the details; she just had to know I'd do anything for them.

I set my mug on the coffee table and reached for her, opening my arms and hoping she'd come to me. I had no idea what to say to her; this was all I could think to do.

She didn't hesitate; she set her mug next to mine and let

me pull her into my side. Her forehead rested against my shoulder. Her breath hitched once. Then again. And finally, she let it out.

I didn't say anything. I just held her, heart pounding in rhythm with hers, and thought that if this were all she ever let me give her, I'd still give it gladly. I'd give her anything.

She didn't move for a long time. Just breathed against me, silent and heavy and warm as she cried. I didn't push her to talk. Didn't say any of the thousand things in my head.

Eventually, she murmured, "I used to be really good at this."

I glanced down, resisting the urge to kiss the top of her head. "At what?" I murmured.

"Being strong. Holding it all together." She gave a biting, bitter laugh. "Now I'm out here crying into your shoulder like we're starring in some kind of Lifetime movie."

"You're allowed to fall apart."

She pulled back just enough to look up at me, eyes still shining. "Not really. Not when they're looking at me like I'm the only thing holding their whole world up."

"You are," I said, voice quiet. "But that doesn't mean you have to carry it all alone. I'm here. I've got you. Always Paige. I hope you know that."

Her eyes didn't leave mine.

There was something raw there—wounded, yes—but also tired. So tired.

"I used to think if I just kept doing the right thing, eventually the universe would let up. Like there was some kind of finish line where I'd finally earned a little bit of peace."

I nodded slowly. "I think a lot of people believe that. That goodness is supposed to equal safety."

She gave a hollow laugh. "And then Eli blew up our lives." Her voice dropped. "He told me once I was too much. Too intense. Too everything."

The desire to find him and hurt him as much as he'd hurt his family was strong. "You're not too much. You're perfect. You are everything, Paige, and it's never too much."

"Yeah, well. I believed him."

I wanted to reach for her hand, but I didn't. I kept still. She could come to me if she wanted.

"He made me feel like I had to shrink. Like the only way to be lovable was to need nothing."

"That's not love."

"I don't want my kids to feel that way. I want them to come to me, to need me, to know I'll be there no matter what. Why didn't she come to me?"

"She was scared. She loves you, Paige. She's just a kid. Kids do stupid shit sometimes. Remember all the dumb stuff we used to think?"

"Okay. That makes sense. Yeah, maybe you're right."

For a long moment, the only sound was the tentative sounds of the world outside, the rain barely tapping at the window, the wind whispering through the trees.

I watched her, not daring to speak, deciding to let her fill the silence if she wanted to. My fingers flexed restlessly on my knee, a silent offering for her to hold onto.

She looked down, twisting the edge of her sleeve between her fingers. "Do you ever wonder if there's another version of you somewhere—one who didn't get broken somewhere along the way?"

"Sometimes," I said. "But I like this version of you and me. I'm glad I'm here for you tonight, Paige. I love that you're letting me be."

A tear slipped down her cheek, but she didn't brush it

away. Instead, she let it hang there, shimmering in the soft glow emanating from the end table lamp. "I'm so tired of trying to be small for people who don't even see me anymore."

"Then don't," I murmured, my voice as soft as I could make it. "Let them miss out. Let them regret it."

She let out a sigh, a sound half sorrow, half relief, and finally—finally—she reached for my hand. Her grip was tentative, but it was warm. I squeezed back, grounding her, holding on for both of us.

"Maybe I'm allowed to want more," she said, her voice trembling at the edges but steadier than before. "Maybe I'm allowed to need things too."

"Yeah," I told her, my thumb tracing gentle circles on her skin. "You absolutely are."

"I think I know that now." Her mouth twisted. "Took a divorce, therapy, and half a bottle of tequila with Piper, but I know."

"You don't have to be small with me," I said before I could stop myself.

"I've never fallen apart like this. If Eli were here with me right now, I'd be shoving everything down. The fear, the worry, the horror of those minutes when I didn't know where my baby girl was."

"I've got you, Paige," I promised her. "It's okay to let go. Get it all out."

She stilled. Her gaze held mine, and I saw it there—just for a heartbeat—that flicker of knowing as she recognized the fact that I'd always seen her and liked her for exactly who she was.

"I'm scared," she whispered. "Not just of Eli and his stupid plans. Of everything. Of what happens next. Of wanting something again."

My throat tightened. "You don't have to figure it all out tonight."

She let out a shaky breath and leaned back into me again, this time resting her hand over my heart like it was the only solid thing in the room.

"You always feel like home," she said softly. "With you, I can breathe. You're safe, Hunter. You didn't push me or crowd me. You just knew what I needed. You always do."

She looked up at me then, her voice quieter. "Do you have any idea what that means to me?"

My pulse stuttered. "I know you, Paige. I'd never want you to do something you weren't ready for."

She didn't say anything else.

So I sat there and held her until the tea went cold on the table, and the weight of everything she'd carried finally started to melt away.

We didn't speak after that.

There wasn't anything else that needed to be said.

She stayed curled against me, one hand resting lightly over my heart, her breathing growing steadier with every passing minute. The distant creaks of the house settling, and the low tick of the wall clock, counting down the seconds, were the only sounds in the room. I didn't move, tried to be as still as possible. She needed me. She needed peace. But mostly, she needed some damn rest.

After a while, her fingers slipped, and her hand slid down to rest between us. Her weight shifted ever so slightly, heavier now.

I glanced down.

Her eyes were closed. Long lashes brushing the soft skin beneath them. Her mouth parted slightly in sleep, her face finally free of tension.

She'd fallen asleep in my arms. And god help me, I

wasn't about to wake her. Carefully, I adjusted us both, only enough to lean back into the corner of the couch, one arm tucked around her shoulders, the other cradling her legs across mine. She didn't stir, just breathed a little deeper.

She smelled like lemon, spice, and that lavender laundry detergent she always used. But more than anything, this felt right. Holding her like this felt more right than anything I'd ever experienced.

I let my head rest back against the cushion.

The living room faded into a gentle blur. The only light came from the little lamp in the kitchen, casting everything in warm gold. Outside, the breeze shifted the porch chimes, soft and slow as I drifted off to sleep, feeling more at home than I ever had in my life.

Chapter 9
Paige

I woke up warm.

Which was immediately suspicious, because I didn't remember going to bed. And I definitely didn't remember falling asleep with someone wrapped around me like a weighted blanket with stubble.

I opened my eyes slowly.

Couch cushion. Old throw blanket. Dim morning light filtering through the curtains.

Chest rising and falling beneath my cheek, a stubbled chin resting against the top of my head.

And—oh god.

Hunter.

His arm was still around me, his hand resting lightly against my knee, like we'd fallen asleep mid-conversation. Like this wasn't something altogether, wildly inappropriate that would short-circuit my nervous system the second I remembered how real it was.

It felt like I belonged right here.

He was so warm.

So right.

My whole body tensed, just slightly, like maybe if I didn't move, the feelings wouldn't catch up to me.

Which, of course, was when Hunter's voice rumbled low and sleep-heavy beneath me. "You okay?"

"Yeah," I whispered. "I just..."

He cracked one eye open, his gaze amused and still soft with sleep. "Freaking out?"

"Only a little bit," I muttered. "I'll try to keep it together."

I shifted away, and he let me go, stretching out with a low groan and scrubbing a hand through his hair. I sat up, brushing wrinkles from my sweatshirt, my heart thudding loudly in the morning quiet.

Then I heard footsteps.

Noah rounded the corner, rubbing his eyes, wearing pajama pants and a wrinkled t-shirt. He looked half-asleep and mildly annoyed to be vertical.

He took one look at me. One look at Hunter. Then he raised an eyebrow, as if he were the parent and I was the one getting caught past curfew. "Morning," he said, voice dry as dust.

"Don't," I warned before he could make it weird.

"I need more sleep." He raised both hands and walked back to his bedroom, disappearing without another word. "It's too early for this. But, if it matters, and if this is a thing now, I approve."

"Your kids are exactly like you," Hunter said under his breath. "Kinda scary."

"Yeah," I sighed. "I'm going to check on Briar."

I knocked gently on Briar's door before easing it open.

She was curled on her side in bed, hugging a Squishmallow to her chest. Her eyes were open and tired, but clearer than last night.

"Hey," I said softly. "How are you feeling?"

She shrugged. "Tired. But better. I'm sorry for sneaking out."

I sat down on the edge of her bed and brushed her hair back from her face. "You scared the hell out of me."

"I know. I'm so sorry." She hid her face behind the Squishmallow. "I don't know what I was thinking—"

"Hey. I love you. Nothing you could do will ever change that. You freaked out; it happens to the best of us. But promise me that next time you'll come to me. Please. Or Grandpa, or any of your aunts, Lark, Grandma, anyone. Just don't run off alone. I want you to be safe, sweetheart."

"I promise. I will." She peeked out, and I brushed her tears away. "I love you, too, Mom. I'm so sorry—"

"I forgive you. No more apologizing, okay? It's done, and you're safe. You want breakfast? Tea? A loud distraction?"

She shook her head no. "Can you stay with me for a minute? Is it okay if I sleep a little bit more?"

"Yeah. Of course." I slid into bed beside her and pulled her into my arms, wondering why it took a trauma to make my teenagers want to cuddle with me.

"Do you regret marrying Dad?" Her whispered question shocked me, though I should have known it was coming based on how he had been behaving lately. "I kind of hate him right now. I don't know if I'm supposed to say stuff like that out loud—"

I squeezed her tight, then brushed her hair over her shoulder. "You can say anything you want to me. I'm your vault. I'm the safest space in the world for you, Briar. I promise."

"Okay. Are you sorry you had kids with him?" Her voice was tiny, barely audible.

"No." I pulled back to look into her eyes. "Never. Not for one single second. I think women might sometimes marry the wrong man. But we always, *always* get the right kids. You, Lark, and Noah are my whole heart. Please believe that."

"Okay," she whispered, snuggling herself deeper into my arms. "I believe you. I love you, Mom."

"I love you, too, sweetheart. Forever and ever. To the moon."

She didn't say anything else, but after a few seconds, she relaxed and let out a huge, trembling sigh.

And from the other room, I heard the soft creak of the old floorboards, the kettle clicking on, the sound of Hunter moving around my kitchen. And for the first time in what felt like forever, I didn't feel like I had to do it all alone.

After a while, Briar drifted back to sleep, and I eased myself off the bed without waking her.

The house was still quiet, except for the faint sound of the kettle finishing its cycle and a pair of mugs being set on the counter. When I stepped into the kitchen, Hunter was already pouring cups of tea, like he did this every day.

He held out a mug to me. "Thought you might need this."

I took the mug and let the warmth settle in my hands like armor. "This is perfect. Thank you."

He reached out and tucked a stray lock of hair behind my ear. My eyes widened, and I hissed in a breath as he leaned against the counter, his mug cradled loosely in one hand, eyes on me but gentle about it. "You want me to go?"

I looked at him. The flannel sleeves were rolled up, exposing strong forearms I had no business noticing. His hair was sleep-rumpled, his expression tired but steady, like nothing could shake him. And somehow, just standing there in my kitchen, he made me feel more grounded than I had in weeks.

But at the same time, something in me shifted. The way he looked at me—calm, unwavering—sent a ripple through my chest. Like my body knew something my mind wasn't ready to admit. He felt safe, yes... but suddenly, he also felt dangerous in a way I couldn't name. "No," I said, quiet but certain. "Not yet."

He nodded like he already knew I was going to ask him to stay.

We stood there, sipping in silence, when someone knocked on the front door with the exact energy of a hurricane warning.

I cracked it open to find Piper standing on the porch with a paper bag in one hand, Ren at her side, carrying a box of take-out coffee cups like a breakfast-themed rescue squad.

"Don't panic," she said, sweeping past me into the kitchen. "We're not here to smother you. We're here to feed you, assess the situation, and report back to Mom, Grandma, Grandpa, and... I guess everyone. Hunter." She smiled at him with knowing eyes. "I'm glad you're here. Good. Finally."

Ren followed, setting the coffee down on the counter. "For now, I want you to avoid communicating with Eli. Direct him to me."

"Got it. No screaming fits or threats. Check. The kids are okay, for now. They're home, safe, asleep."

Piper opened the bag and began pulling out pastries and foil-wrapped breakfast burritos. "Food helps. Now you don't have to make breakfast. Just eat and try to relax."

Ren gave me a look and jerked his head toward the back yard. I followed him outside, away from curious ears.

"Are you okay?" he asked, keeping his voice low.

"I think so."

"And Briar?"

"She will be."

"Good. Because I'm about to go full scorched earth, I heard from his attorney."

I clutched my hands together. "Oh my god. Is it bad? I mean, aside from what happened with Briar? Could it be worse?"

He leaned one shoulder against the wall, arms crossed. "He wants primary custody. Probably so he can avoid paying child support to you. He's accusing you of working crazy hours. But unfortunately for him, he is currently cohabitating with someone who is absolutely tanking any shot he has at appearing stable."

"Are you kidding me?" My blood turned cold as his words sank in. "This is all about Danielle, it has to be. She is a piece of work. Always has been. He's gone crazy. And hello? The kids are teenagers; they won't stand for this. I mean, doesn't he realize they are fully capable of forming their own opinions? Is he trying to ruin his relationship with them forever? He's already on beyond shaky ground with Noah. I mean, look what happened last night for fuck's sake!" I slapped a hand over my mouth, afraid of getting too loud.

"I don't pretend to know how people like him justify their actions," he answered. "From what you've told me, he's obviously prioritizing her kids at the expense of yours. The court will likely be concerned about the minimal attention and emotional support being given to his own children. If it even gets that far. And Briar walking out and ending up in danger? Not a good look."

I swallowed. "You really think he won't be able to change things? I mean, I thought this was all settled."

Ren's eyes sharpened. "He's not getting the house. He won't get primary anything. And at this point, he'll be lucky if he walks away without supervised visitation. If he pushes this, I will nail him to the wall, Paige. You don't have to worry about a thing."

I closed my eyes, a deep breath filling my lungs for the first time in what felt like days. "Thank you."

"You already did the hard part. You're free of him," he said softly. "Now I just clean up the mess he's trying to make."

I nodded, blinking quickly. "I should get back in there before Piper starts planning my second wedding," I joked to hide that I was about to cry. Or scream. Or have some other kind of uncomfortable emotional outburst. Ren was used to it, though. He'd seen it all when I was going through the divorce.

Ren smirked. "To Hunter?"

I rolled my eyes. "You're as bad as she is."

We stepped back into the kitchen to find Piper leaning against the counter, plating muffins and burritos, like she'd already claimed setting up breakfast as a personal challenge. Hunter stood across from her, holding his coffee and watching her like she was a one-woman sitcom.

"Everything okay?" Piper asked.

"Everything's handled," Ren said simply.

Hunter caught my eye but didn't press. That was one of the things I liked most about him—he waited until you were ready to talk.

Piper handed me a burrito, warm and fragrant in its foil. "Eat before you start overthinking. You've already reached your brain's daily freakout limit. It's early, but I know it."

"Is that a medical opinion?" I asked, peeling it open.

"It's a sister opinion. Arguably more qualified."

Ren clapped his hands together. "Alright, our mission is complete. We've fed, assessed, and emotionally triaged. Time to go."

Piper kissed my cheek on the way out. "Call if you need anything. Or don't. We'll probably show up either way to bring you and the kids dinner later."

Ren and Piper left in a flurry of takeout wrappers and quiet affection, and for a moment, the house was still again. I sank into a kitchen chair with my burrito and let the comfort of everyone being safe under my roof sink in.

Until the sound of a door creaked down the hallway.

Lark shuffled in first, wearing fuzzy socks and an oversized sweatshirt with a glittery bunny on it. She squinted at us like we were an optical illusion.

"You're still here?" she asked Hunter, rubbing her eyes. "I mean that in a nice way. A surprised way. Mornings are not my thing," she mumbled. "Hi."

"Hi." He grinned. "Breakfast is on the table."

She grunted and grabbed a burrito.

Then Briar padded in, clutching a blanket around her shoulders like a cape. She looked a little pale, but steadier on her feet than last night.

She looked at Hunter. "Thanks for finding me last night."

"Anytime, kiddo. I'm glad I was there to help."

She gave a shy nod and leaned into my side when I held out my arm.

Noah followed next, hair sticking up in ten different directions. He grunted a good morning and stared at the muffin box like it was a mirage.

My kitchen had never felt this calm in the morning.

And I couldn't remember the last time I'd sat down and simply relaxed into a morning. And even though Eli was attempting to ruin everything again, I wasn't worried. Ren was more than capable of handling everything. He'd done it before. And this time, I had Hunter on my side.

Hunter sat across from me, took a sip of coffee, and leaned back in his chair just enough to stretch his legs out under the table, bumping mine lightly in the process. I didn't move away, and neither did he.

"Thanks for staying," I said finally, voice low.

Eventually, the quiet began to shift again.

Lark yawned, grabbed a muffin without saying a word, and disappeared back to her room like a sleepy little zombie.

Briar gave me a small, tired smile, then mumbled something about finding her phone charger and vanished just as quickly.

Noah followed, rubbing his face and muttering something about texting one of his friends in town for lunch. He stopped long enough to give me a long hug from behind my chair, then wandered down the hall.

And just like that, it was just Hunter and me, with two half-finished cups of coffee cooling on the table. I watched the sunlight shift across the tile and smiled at him.

"I thought I was going to lose my mind last night," I said softly, tracing my finger along the rim of my mug.

Hunter didn't interrupt.

"I mean—I did lose it a little bit, when I was alone in my car and on the couch with you, I guess. I'm not always good in the moment. But later? That's when it all hits. But it didn't hit this time. I got to talk it out instead of crying into my pillow. Because you were here with me."

"I'm glad I was. Thank you for letting me stay with you. I was worried. Still am, if I'm being honest."

I looked at him, and his gaze was so warm, so open, it made something in me ache a little. "You always seem to show up when I need you," I whispered.

"Not always." He took a slow sip of coffee, watching me over the rim. "Not when you were married. But from now on, I'll never stop trying to be."

I swallowed hard, eyes burning again. "You make everything feel easier."

"That's all I want. You do the same for me and you always have, Paige."

The silence that settled between us then wasn't awkward. It was weighted, but warm—like we were both standing on the edge of something neither of us wanted to rush.

"I'm scared," I admitted.

"I know. So am I."

"But I'm also tired of feeling alone."

"I know that, too, and I feel the same way." He reached across the table and slid his hand over mine. His thumb brushed along the side of my hand, slow and careful, like he didn't want to startle me.

"You've been carrying everything for so long," he said quietly. "I know you're exhausted."

"I don't have a choice."

"You do," he said gently. "You just haven't had help you trusted in a long time. And I don't mean your family, they're amazing. I mean a man. *Your* man."

I didn't say anything. Couldn't. Because if I opened my mouth, I might cry. And I wasn't sure I had any tears left after last night.

"You don't have to explain anything to me, Paige," he added. "I've seen you at your best and your worst. I've known you forever. None of what you're going through scares me."

I looked down at our hands. His skin was rough, calloused from work. Mine were dry from dishes, hand sanitizer, and the constant use that came with being a mom, a bartender, and a woman who did too much. But our hands looked right together.

My breath caught. And maybe it was because the house was at peace again. Maybe it was because my heart was still wide open from last night. Maybe it was just that I was tired of pretending. But I stood up. Walked the few steps around the table. And slid into his lap.

He stiffened for a second, surprised, and then his arms came around me like they were meant to be there. I tucked my face against his neck, breathing him in—cedar and soap and the faintest hint of coffee.

"You sure about this?" he asked, voice low.

"No," I whispered. "But I want to be."

His hand moved up my back, fingers gentle, his touch light. "Then we'll go slow."

I pulled back just enough to look at him.

His eyes searched mine, careful and patient.

Then, finally, he leaned in and kissed my forehead.

And when he pulled back, I didn't move. I just curled into him again, my arms around his shoulders, my face buried in the soft fabric of his shirt. We sat there for a long time, holding each other, while the sun rose a little higher and the rest of the house stayed miraculously still. And for the first time in years, I didn't feel like something was about to fall apart.

"I'm sorry if I've been weird," I said.

"You've been going through a lot lately," he said, voice steady. "I'm sorry I backed off if you didn't want me to."

For a moment, we simply looked at each other, eyes searching, thoughtful and unhurried. There was a vulnerability hanging between us, as if we were both quietly measuring the distance we'd come and the space that was left to close. I saw the flicker of uncertainty mingling with hope in his gaze—the silent questions we were both too careful to voice but still lived behind every blink. I wondered what he saw in mine: hesitation, maybe, but also a willingness that hadn't been there before. It felt like the room was holding its breath, waiting for one of us to decide if this was safe ground or just another edge to fall off of. And as our eyes held, something eased in me—I recognized the steadiness in his, the gentle invitation to trust, to stay a little longer in this fragile, sunlit peace.

"No, I needed the space, so much is going on. I just—" I hesitated. "Sometimes it's easier to pretend I don't feel anything than deal with the possibility that I might."

Hunter nodded slowly as relief suffused his features. "Yeah. I get that. Obviously, because I feel the same way. I'm sorry for being weird, too. That last thing I want to do is push you too far. Or push you at all."

I drew back to look at him, the morning light slanting through the kitchen window and catching in the strands of his hair. I didn't know what this thing between us was exactly, but for the first time in a long time, it didn't feel scary to want something. It felt like maybe I *should* want this.

"Thank you for being here for me," I said softly.

He gave a quiet smile, a little sheepish. "Well, you make it hard not to. Especially since you're always there for me, too."

I let out a breath that might have been a laugh, but maybe also a sigh of relief. "You're dangerous, Cassidy."

He tilted his head, lips tilting up at the corner. "I've been told."

We stayed like this—close, quiet, no pressure.

"This is nice," I said softly.

"Yeah," he murmured. "It is."

"I don't know what I want yet," I whispered. "No, that's not it. I'm not sure I even know how to want anything anymore."

"That's okay. I don't either."

"I just know I don't want to fight whatever is going on with us, and I don't want to hide from it anymore."

His hand found mine, fingers lacing through mine loosely.

"Then we won't," he said, like it was that simple. And maybe it was.

We sat there a while longer, wrapped in quiet, and I let myself just exist in that moment—with him, in my kitchen, in the stillness. No expectations. No labels. Just comfort.

When I finally got up, he followed, gathering the mugs and rinsing them in the sink like he'd done it a hundred times before.

Chapter 10
Hunter

The clatter of a socket wrench echoed off the concrete floor of the shop as I straightened up and stretched my back. I'd left Paige's house and gone straight to work. My shirt was stuck to me in places I didn't want to think about, and there was a smear of grease across my forearm. It was a warm day, and the fan overhead might as well have been stirring soup.

Cassidy's Automotive looked exactly as it had since Dad took over the place from my grandfather when I was a little kid. The walls were lined with tools, pegboards filled with wrenches, and sockets sorted by size. An old fridge hummed in the corner, covered in fading bumper stickers and notes scrawled on taped-up paper. The smell of motor oil and rubber was baked into the concrete, and the front office always had a faint aroma of coffee and air freshener. I loved that it rarely ever changed in here, but I wouldn't mind the addition of an air conditioner.

We were working on the old '67 Camaro he'd acquired, and I was trying to get Paige out of my mind so I could focus on the task at hand and not screw it up.

Dad leaned against the open garage door, sipping coffee like he didn't notice the heat at all. "You're quiet today. Everything okay?"

I shrugged. "Just thinking."

"That wouldn't have anything to do with a certain bartender we both know, would it?"

I shot him a look, and he grinned over the rim of his travel mug.

"You think I don't notice things? The look on your face is intense."

"It's complicated," I muttered as I wiped my hands on a rag, stepped outside into the morning air, and squinted up at the sky.

"Complicated? *Pfft.* You look like you're waiting on a delivery that ain't coming," he observed. He held his mug of coffee and looked every bit the grizzly bear he'd always been —hair in a ponytail, beard like a lumberjack, coveralls pulled down at the top and tied around his waist.

"Just thinking," I repeated. "Trying to figure stuff out is all."

"Don't hurt yourself."

I grinned, grabbed my water bottle, and wandered over to sit on the steps.

"You know, when I turned forty," he said, lowering himself beside me with a groan, "your mother gave me a card that said, 'You're not old, you're vintage.' Then she made me a cake and we spent the rest of the day with you kids."

I chuckled. "I remember. I miss her."

"Paige?" He asked, confused.

"Mom." She died when I was barely a teenager. Cancer. She'd hardly been sick before she was gone. It had been that quick.

"Ahh, I miss her too. Always will."

"You never dated anyone after her."

He fell quiet, gazing out over the patch of sunlit yard as if searching for something hidden in the shadows of the fence. The silence hung heavy between us.

I fiddled with the cap of my water bottle, unsure what to say—unsure if words could even reach the place he had drifted to. Grief doesn't ask for permission; it just arrives, settles in, and makes itself comfortable.

"Why would I?" he finally said, his eyes shifting to mine. "She was the love of my life. The mother of my babies. I'll never find anyone better, and I'll never be happier than I was when she was here."

"Aren't you lonely?"

He let out a low chuckle, though it sounded rough around the edges. "She used to say I could fix anything, but I never figured out how to fix a broken heart." My throat tightened. I wanted to reach over, to say something that might fill the space she'd left behind, but the words wouldn't come. Instead, we both sat there, letting the sun warm our shoulders, each lost in memories that never really faded. He looked away as a sad smile crossed his face. "I'll be with her again. Just a matter of time."

"Dad..."

"I understand you now," his whispered voice was both sad and knowing.

"Understand what?" I shifted, suddenly scared of what he was about to say.

"There's an old saying, you know? Something about how it's better to have loved and lost..."

"Yeah," I whispered. "I know the one."

"I had decades worth of birthdays spent with your mother. Memories that I cherish, some of them I share with you." His sharp eyes met mine and wouldn't let go. "You've spent all of your birthdays with us. I love you, son. Love spending your birthdays with you. But I want more for you. You seeing anyone these days?" he asked me as if he didn't already know the answer.

I shrugged. "You know I'm not."

"Been a while, hasn't it?" He nodded like he understood more than he let on. And maybe he did. There wasn't much I could hide from him, even now, maybe especially now. "Paige still calling you every time her sink makes a funny noise?"

I tried not to smile. "It's usually the deep freezer. Or the neon sign. Or a few of the lights," I paused. "It's not quite run down, but the place needs some work."

"Well, you're handy, aren't you? She still single?" As if he didn't already know that Paige was not dating anyone either. He knew everything, and he always had.

I looked at my water bottle like I could climb into it and avoid where this conversation was headed. "Yeah. She's still single."

"How long are you planning to pretend she's not the reason you're still single, too? You haven't had a date since she filed for divorce from that asshole she married."

I didn't answer.

Dad clapped a hand on my shoulder. "Well, if you're waiting on a sign, son, I think the universe already sent it. It's purple and flickering, and bright flashing neon. Wake up and pay attention." He nodded, thoughtful as he sipped his coffee.

"Uh, I guess, um..." I had no idea what to say, so I stopped talking.

He grinned at me like he had an ace up his sleeve, and I braced myself. "I just found out from her mother that she closes the tavern by herself most nights. You believe that? That little girl I used to babysit after school is standing in that bar alone while everyone else clears out. I don't much like the thought of it."

I sat straight in surprise. "Seriously? Alone?"

He nodded, watching my reaction. "Yup," he answered. "All by herself."

"She was alone a few weeks back when I fixed the light. But I'd just assumed it was a one-off, like everyone had just left. Why didn't I realize? Why didn't she tell me? I don't like it either."

He looked at me sideways. "What are you going to do about it?"

"I guess I could replace the evaporator fan motor on her freezer. I was meaning to get to that. It might take a few nights of work if I stretch it out. Plus, she has no idea what the problem is aside from the noise it sometimes makes."

His eyes crinkled, approval warming his face. "There you go. Subtle, but effective. Sometimes, a wrench and a little common sense go further than a card and a bouquet of flowers. I'm sure the door gaskets could use some work, too. Possibly the thermostat."

"Good thinking. And her margarita machine is a menace."

"Don't know why anyone would want one of those when you could have an ice-cold beer, but that's not for me to say."

I grinned at him without answering.

"She needs a man like you. This is a good thing you're doing," he added the last part under his breath.

"Yeah. I mean, I guess so."

"Well, you know where I'll be if you need help with that margarita machine of hers."

"Might take you up on that."

"Good. Now go on home and shower. Don't show up there tonight all sweaty."

"Yes, sir." I chuckled as I swiped my water bottle and mock saluted him as I headed for my truck.

"Love you."

"Love you too, Dad."

Back at home, the kitchen lights shone overhead like a spotlight while I peeled apples over the sink, trying not to overthink what I was doing—but failing. All I'd been doing lately was overthinking and avoiding taking action. But that was over. I'd already showered, dressed, and formed a plan.

Ozzy launched himself onto the counter, tail twitching with judgment. He promptly knocked over my measured bowl of sugar with one paw; he didn't seem to like it when my attention wasn't solely on him.

"Seriously, man?" I muttered, brushing sugar off the edge into a paper towel. "You've got three scratching posts and a cat tree, and you pick my pie station for your chaos?"

He flopped dramatically across the counter like he was exhausted by my incompetence, then purred like he hadn't just ruined my prep. I slid him gently to a stool with one arm and grabbed the bag of sugar.

The pie dough was already resting in the fridge, waiting to be rolled out. I was using my dad's recipe—flaky, buttery crust with just a touch of cinnamon in it. He used to make it for Mom every Sunday for dessert, even if she never asked. Said it was his love language. It must be genetic.

I sliced the apples thin, tossed them with cinnamon, lemon, sugar, and a fresh swipe of nutmeg over my microplane before layering them into the crust with practiced hands. The smell hit me square in the chest.

Paige loved this pie. When he realized how much, my

dad started saving some for her and Piper to eat every Monday after school, back when he used to babysit them.

I'd caught her once, curled up at the counter with her math book open and a plate of pie crumbs beside her, eyes shining from what my dad referred to as being food drunk.

"Your dad made this?" She'd asked after the first time she tasted it. "My future husband better be able to make me a pie every Sunday, just like it."

I smiled at the memory, pressing the top crust into place.

Maybe I wasn't trying to win her over with pie.

Maybe I was just trying to remind her that I already knew what she needed—that I knew *her*.

I brushed the crust with egg wash, sprinkled it with sugar crystals, and tossed it in the oven. Then I leaned back against the counter, watching the timer tick down like it was a countdown to a new future.

When it finally rang, I set it on the counter to cool, its golden crust crackling as it met the air. I packed it carefully—warm, fragrant, still a little too hot but perfect all the same.

I slid into my truck, pie riding shotgun, and headed to Paige. The road narrowed, streetlights thinning until only the sound of the tires on gravel kept me company. At the very edge of town, almost swallowed by the dark and mist, the Twilight Tavern waited. Its parking lot stretched under a scatter of tired lamp posts and the pulsing violet haze of the neon sign, painting the world in a strange, hopeful hue.

I pulled in and cut the engine. For a minute, I just sat there, pie in hand, letting the silence settle. The parking lot was empty except for Paige's car.

She was still here. Alone, probably tired, too damn stubborn to ask anyone for help. That part hadn't changed. But something in me had.

I'd stopped by this place a hundred times. Shared a laugh, a drink, a story. But this... this wasn't just dropping in anymore. My pulse was too loud in my ears for that.

I stared at the tavern door, feeling the weight of the pie in my hands. I wasn't sure when it had shifted—when *she* had shifted in my mind—but now I couldn't look at her without feeling like the ground under my feet was just slightly off. Like I was leaning toward something I couldn't take back.

And suddenly, I was nervous. Anticipating the way she'd look at me. Speak to me. Whether she'd feel it too, that something was changing.

I blew out a slow breath, ran a hand over my face, and opened the door.

I knocked once on the glass and pushed the door open. Frowning at the fact that it was unlocked. The creak it made was loud enough to make a horror movie proud. I made a mental note to oil the hinges for her.

A split second later, I heard it—a sharp inhale, followed by the low, fierce scrape of something solid on the floor.

Then Paige appeared from behind the bar like a vengeful goddess, gripping a baseball bat with both hands.

"Jesus, Paige! It's me. Hunter. Don't kill me."

Her eyes were wild, breath shallow. "You scared the *hell* out of me, Hunter Cassidy. I was this close to going full Final Girl on your ass. Everyone just left. I was about to lock up and finish closing."

"Pretty sure I just lost ten years off my life," I muttered, heart hammering.

She lowered the bat but didn't let go of it. "You can't just sneak in here after hours like some bar-hopping vampire. I've got baseball bats stashed in every corner for a reason. I also have pepper spray in my apron. I'm almost forty, for fuck's sake—I'm in perimenopause, also known as the coming of rage. I could have killed you. You could be dead right now, then what?" She huffed, chest rising and falling as her wild eyes met mine.

I knew I'd scared her, and I felt terrible. "Yeah, I can tell that you're fully prepared for everything," I said, holding up my free hand and the brown paper bag in the other. "But in my defense—I brought you a pie."

Her grip loosened. Slightly. "Store-bought or bribe-grade?" Her eyes narrowed.

I grinned. "I made it."

She blinked at me, and her hand loosened on the bat. "You *baked* a pie?"

"Of course I did. You think I'm just some guy who fixes cars and broods under the moonlight like a sneaky bar-hopping vampire? I'm a man of many talents, Paige. Baking included."

Slowly, she leaned the bat against the bar. "Okay. I'm listening."

I walked toward her, set the pie down on the counter like it was an offering to a very tired, very pretty deity, and slid onto a stool. "Apple. Homemade crust. Sugar crystals on top. A little bit of cinnamon and fresh nutmeg. Don't act like you're not impressed."

"Your dad's pie? *The* pie?" She crossed her arms and tried to look skeptical, but the twitch of her mouth gave her away. "Did you come here to woo me with baked goods and late-night handyman heroics?"

"Yes," I said. "I'm also here to work on your freezer."

That earned a smile—small but genuine. "So you just

happened to bake a pie and wander over to repair my cursed appliances?"

"Yeah, that, and I heard you were closing the place alone. I don't like that."

Her brows lifted, but she didn't argue.

"And yes," I added, "I might've planned to bribe you with the pie. You're not fond of accepting help, you know. Are you sure that stubborn is not your middle name? Joanne seems too tame for you."

She lifted her chin as an amused grin slid across her face. "You're trouble. Have I mentioned that before?"

"You're the one who keeps texting me about mysterious freezer groaning noises at two in the morning. And the endless curse of your margarita machine."

She smirked, finally walking around the bar and sliding into the stool next to me. "It sounds like it's dying. Or haunted."

"I'll take a look. But only after you have some pie. And then you're going to let me seriously fix them. Not just a patch here or a new wire there. Okay?"

"Hmph." She eyed the pie and dodged my request. "You always show up to places like this? With tools and baked goods? Or is this special treatment?"

"Only for you. And absolutely special treatment." I let her dodge it. Flirting with her was more fun than insisting she let me help her.

She bit her lip, fighting a smile, and losing the battle.

"Fine," she said, reaching for the pie. "But if this crust sucks, I'm firing you."

"You don't even pay me," I teased.

"Then I'll just spread rumors about your subpar pastry skills all over town. Or I'll tell your dad on you."

"I'll take that risk." I'd packed paper plates and forks in the bag.

Before she could cut a slice, I picked up a fork and scooped up a perfect bite, holding it out to her. "Taste test. Official duties," I said, nudging the fork closer. She met my eyes, her mouth twitching, and then wrapped her fingers around mine, guiding the fork to her lips. For a second, neither of us moved. It was just her touch, warm and sure, and the way her gaze didn't waver.

She took the bite. Chewed. Paused. And then let out a low groan that I had absolutely no business hearing while sitting in her mostly empty bar this late at night.

"This is infuriating," she muttered, hand over her mouth while she finished chewing.

"What is?"

"You being *good* at everything. It's annoying."

I grinned. "Just wait till I fix your freezer."

"Oh, stop it. You're going to ruin my whole worldview about men. I've been cultivating it for decades, Hunter. This is serious."

"You're welcome."

She shook her head but took another bite, and I couldn't stop watching her. Her ponytail was a little loose, and her cheeks were flushed and lovely. Her sleeves were shoved up like usual, and her sweatshirt said *Whiskey Helps* across the front in curling script. And maybe whiskey could help. But I was starting to think maybe I could, too.

She looked up and caught me staring.

"What?" she asked, cheeks turning a pretty shade of pink.

"Nothing," I said. "Just thinking this might be the best pie I've ever made."

"Oh my god," she groaned. "Stop flirting with me, or I'm going to throw a bar mat at your head."

"Promise?"

She laughed, and it was the kind of sound that made everything else in the room blur out. Then her expression softened, just a little. "Thanks for showing up. I know you're joking around, but it means something. Having someone around at the end of the night. It won't be for long, just until I save enough to fix this place up the way I want it."

My chest tightened. "You never have to thank me for showing up, Paige. I'll always be here for you."

She blinked. Looked down at her pie. "That's dangerous talk, Cassidy."

"Only if you don't mean it back."

"I'm here for you, too, Hunter. Always."

We sat there for a second too long.

Then she cleared her throat and shoved the pie box toward me. "Go fix my haunted freezer before I start writing your last name in hearts."

"Yes, ma'am." I stood and grabbed the tool bag I kept stashed under the counter at the side of the bar, and as I walked past her, I bent close and murmured just loud enough for her to hear: "You already know how to spell it, and it would look great next to *Paige*. Now we have the pact and the potential of *the* pie every Sunday. Think about it. You. Me. Your birthday. Dinner. It's all back on the table whenever you're ready."

She didn't say anything. But she was definitely still blushing when I walked into the back room.

As I made my way to the back room, my mind kept circling around Paige—her laughter, the warmth in her eyes, the way she said my name. The truth was, being around her always made my heart race a little faster, and tonight was no different. I wanted more than just these quiet moments and inside jokes; I wanted all of her, but the fear of pushing too hard, too soon, lingered at the edges of my thoughts. What if I ruined the comfort we'd finally found just because I couldn't hold back how much I cared?

There was a pull between us I couldn't ignore, but I knew I had to be careful. She deserved patience. Still, it was getting harder to pretend I didn't notice the way her smile stuck with me long after she looked away.

Shaking my head, I forced the thoughts away, determined to focus on the work instead of the ache in my chest. I busied myself with the repair, letting the steady rhythm of my hands and the hum of tools drown out feelings I wasn't ready to face. Fixing the freezer was easier than trying to untangle the mess of emotions Paige stirred up, and for now, I'd rather hide behind the comfort of routine than risk saying too much.

"So, the evaporator fan motor's making a noise. I hear it this time," I called as I crouched down with my flashlight. I frowned, angling the light deeper into the housing. "That's weird."

Her footsteps echoed over the floor behind me as she approached. "What?" she asked, bending to look over my shoulder.

"See right here?" I pointed. "It looks like the wiring has been loosened. Not frayed. It's like someone actually unscrewed part of the clamp here." I glanced up at her. "But it could be nothing. Maybe it rattled loose on its own."

"This place is full of quirks," she said, waving it off. "It's just old."

"You're probably right," I muttered as I fixed it.

Chapter 11
Paige

After he went into the back, I took another bite of the pie and paused mid-chew. The taste hit me like a memory: buttery crust, just the right amount of cinnamon, a whisper of lemon. Not too sweet, not too tart—precisely the way his dad used to make it.

My heart thudded once, low and hard.

I hadn't tasted this pie in years. Not since Mondays after school when his dad used to save two slices for me and Piper to eat. God, I loved his dad. I used to joke that I'd marry the first man who could bake me a pie like this.

And now here he was.

Offering it to me like it wasn't the most intimate thing anyone had done for me in over a decade. I stared down at the crust, suddenly unsure if I wanted to laugh, cry, or crawl under the bar and scream into a towel.

The jukebox hummed in the background, softly looping through its endless playlist of '80s classics. The front of the bar was clean. All I had left to do was my weekly inventory. Everything was still. Quiet.

But inside me, everything was shifting.

He'd baked *the* pie. His dad's pie. *For me.*

He remembered. All of it.

And he didn't bring it up like it was some clever trick or romantic ploy. He just set it down in front of me like it was obvious. Like feeding me comfort, and history was just what you did when your best friend needed a reminder of who they were.

I curled my fingers around the edge of the bar and took a slow breath. I didn't know what this thing between us was yet. Not really. But I knew what that pie meant.

It meant he saw me.

It meant he remembered me—not just who I'd become after the divorce or the version of me that yelled at margarita machines and ran on coffee and stress—but the girl I used to be. The one who ate apple pie in his dad's kitchen and told herself she wasn't falling for her best friend, even back then.

And maybe that girl never really stopped.

Maybe she kept her feelings shoved into the back of her heart because she wouldn't dare risk losing her very best friend, not after losing her dad. Not after losing Eli, then getting him back, then losing him again, then marrying his stupid ass. And especially, not after losing her belief that she could ever hold onto anything worth having.

I wouldn't say it out loud. Not yet. Maybe not ever. But as I stood there in my empty bar, heart doing an offbeat drum solo in my chest and the taste of cinnamon still on my tongue, I let myself whisper it just once inside my head:

He brought me his dad's pie.

That wasn't nothing, it was everything.

Back to reality. I cleaned up my plate, boxed the pie back up, grabbed my laptop, and got to work. I used to dread inventory. Not because it was hard, but because it was always done in silence. Alone. After hours. I'd pace from shelf to shelf, counting liquor bottles and dry goods while trying not to let the empty space feel like a metaphor for my life.

Tonight was different.

Tonight, Hunter was here, sleeves rolled up, kneeling in front of my industrial freezer like some kind of off-duty, blue-collar romance novel cover model. And I was going from the front of the bar to the back, counting bottles of liquor and pretending I wasn't distracted by the way his forearms flexed when he used a socket wrench.

Every so often, he'd mutter something under his breath —something about a stripped screw or a faulty something or other—and I'd make a noncommittal sound to disguise the way I was definitely *not* imagining what it would be like to kiss him while he was covered in grease and nonjudgmental competence.

My head was a battlefield. One half screaming *Nope. Too soon. Absolutely not.* The other whispering, *but what if...*

"I'm adding 'professional freezer whisperer' to my resume," Hunter called out.

"You're gonna need your own section on the town attractions website," I called back. "Right next to the Honeybrook Inn and Larry the Llama from Lucy's books."

"Don't forget local pie hero. Maybe I should enter the Harvest Festival baking competition."

I snorted. "Modest, too."

The door creaked, and I heard him walk into the main bar, wiping his hands on a rag. I didn't turn around immediately. I crouched to count the backup cases of tonic water and told myself to focus. My pen hovered over the order sheet. "Huh," I muttered.

"What?" he asked. "Something wrong?"

"We're missing two bottles of Jameson. Jasper signed for them last week. Or at least that's what my supplier emailed me."

"Does the supplier ever mess up?"

"No. Not so far, anyway. I'll figure it out. Never mind."

When I stood, Hunter was leaning against the bar, his dark sweatshirt sleeves pushed to his elbows, wiping his hands on a rag.

"Maybe they're just misplaced," he suggested.

"Probably." I tried to sound casual, but I never misplaced shipments. Ever. I jotted a note to check with the distributor in the morning and allowed myself to be distracted.

He looked unfairly good. Like, I was just a tired divorced woman trying to rebuild my life, and he was over there looking like a lumberjack, guardian angel, handyman, kind of good.

"All fixed for now," he said, like it was no big deal.

I blinked. "Seriously?"

"Evaporator fan motor was shot. I patched it for now, but I'll order the part and come back when I get it. And I tightened those wires too."

"Thank you."

He brushed my ponytail over my shoulder, his eyes crinkling as he smiled at me. "You're welcome."

My heart stuttered. That was the thing about Hunter. He didn't just *do* the things—he knew what they meant—being here. Helping. Staying.

I leaned against the bar beside him and sighed. "You always make things feel easier. I know I keep saying it, but it's true."

"That's my goal."

"I thought your goal was to bring me baked goods and flirt shamelessly."

He gave me a slow, dangerous smile. "Multi-tasking."

I reached for my laptop and my list and tried to get my voice under control. "Well. You passed the pie test. It is perfection."

"Thank god," he murmured. "I was really hoping to make it through the day without you telling my dad on me."

I glanced at him sidelong. He was watching me again. Not in a creepy way. In a *trying to memorize your face in this moment* kind of way.

"Stop looking at me like that," I muttered.

"Like what?"

"Like you know what I'm thinking. Like you see me."

"I do see you. I've always seen you."

His voice was low. Quiet. And it knocked the air right out of me.

I turned away, under the guise of tallying how many bottles of tequila we had left on the shelf. "Careful," I said, forcing my tone to stay light. "You keep this up and I might accidentally agree to have dinner with you."

He didn't laugh.

When I looked back, he was still watching me. Thoughtful. Steady.

"Paige," he said softly. "I didn't do any of this by accident."

The room went still.

I cleared my throat. "Okay. Time to change the subject before I combust. What's next on your fixer-upper list? I have some money saved up to get started."

He didn't push for more. Just smiled like he knew the exact page I was on and was happy to wait for me to catch up. "I was thinking about checking that margarita machine again," he answered, all casual and cool. "You said it made a noise like a dying banshee?"

"Only during full moons and karaoke nights. But seriously, it only seems to do it when I'm the only one around to hear it, usually after I come back from a day off. Weird."

He chuckled, grabbed his tool bag again, and headed toward the back.

I tried to breathe through the sudden surge of nervous energy.

I was in trouble.

Because if I let myself think too long about how easily he slid into my life—how good it felt to have him here, fixing things, bringing me pie, *seeing* me when I wasn't even sure I wanted to be seen—I was going to start hoping.

And I didn't know if my heart was ready for that.

Hope was a dangerous thing.

Chapter 12
Hunter

A few nights later, the margarita machine finally let me hear what Paige had described. I winced as it groaned like it was possessed, then sputtered out a sad mechanical wheeze. I examined it, flashlight in my mouth, elbow-deep in wires and regret, half tempted to throw it in the dumpster and buy her a new one.

"There!" She shouted as she came running out of the back room. "Hear that? It's haunted, I swear."

"Yup, it's definitely a hard sound to miss."

"Right?" she muttered. "It's sentient, I know it. Watch out before it kills us both. Death by tequila and triple sec."

I got to work, frustrated as there seemed to be nothing actually wrong with it. "Every time I think I've figured you out," I muttered to the machine, "you prove me wrong. Just like the woman who owns you."

Behind me, Paige hummed faintly as she organized something behind the bar. I couldn't tell what—she could've been stacking napkins or alphabetizing tequila—but it sounded like she was in the zone.

If I hadn't been falling for her already, this would have pushed me closer to the edge.

There was something unexpectedly adorable about the way she concentrated, humming her off-key little song as if the rest of the world had slipped away. She always bit her lip when she was deep in thought, her brows scrunched in mock severity, only to soften moments later with a half-smile when she found whatever she was searching for. Even with her hair falling messily around her face and her sleeves pushed up, she managed to make the mundane—stacking boxes, straightening bottles—look cute. She wasn't trying to be, she just was.

Weirdly, tonight reminded me of being with her after school when my dad still watched her and Piper. Once high school started, they started going straight home instead of riding the school bus with me and my brothers back to our place. I had never let myself feel how much I had missed her after that. She started hanging out with Eli, and they began dating. And they got married soon after graduation. We had obviously remained friends, but not quite as close as when we were kids—until now.

It felt like she was mine again.

Mine? I brushed the thought aside and glanced her way, grinning to myself as she worked. Hiding a smile while she hummed her little song and jolted me back to the past—at the kitchen table, doing homework together, fighting back a grin as she hummed.

I tightened the last bolt, adjusted the switch, and listened as the machine whirred back to life. Still not quite right, still running weird—but functional. I stood and wiped my hands on a towel, watching her out of the corner of my eye.

She had one knee propped on a barstool, reaching up to

adjust a box on the highest shelf, hoodie riding up just enough to show a sliver of skin. Nothing overt. Just soft, pale skin that I'd give just about anything to trace with my fingers.

I looked away. Fast.

"I'm done for now. And the freezer seems to be holding steady," I called, trying to sound casual. "I don't hear it anymore, do you?"

"Nope." She grinned at me. "And the margarita monster?"

"She lives," I said, walking toward her. "Every time I work on it, there's a different problem. I think she's just dramatic. Needs attention."

"So, basically, me in machine form."

I laughed. "Exactly. Little high-maintenance, kind of unpredictable, but if you take care of her, she runs like a dream."

She gave me a look over her shoulder. "Flattery won't get you out of inventory next week," she joked. "You're my helper now. It's official."

"I'd do your inventory every night if it meant I got to spend time with you like this." The words came out softer than I meant them to.

Her smile faltered for a second. Not completely—but enough that I saw the flicker of something cross her face. Fear maybe. Attraction hopefully.

I cleared my throat and leaned against the bar, careful to give her space. "Anyway. You're all set for now."

"You don't have to keep fixing things for me. I was only kidding about the inventory. I take too much help from you, Hunter."

"I know I don't have to," I said, echoing what I'd told her earlier. "I want to. And you help me too. Who's the one who brings me chicken noodle soup whenever I'm sick? Who drives all the way to McDonald's for fries and a Coke whenever I get a migraine? Who makes sure I have my favorite sugar cookies and an ugly sweater for your Christmas party every year? And let's not forget about the annual birthday coffee, now featuring cinnamon crumble muffins. You're there for me, too, Paige. Please don't pretend that you're not."

She didn't reply. Just lowered the box she'd been fussing with and ran a hand over her ponytail. The motion lifted her hoodie again for a second, and I forced myself to look at the jukebox instead of her waist.

I was dangerously close to falling apart in the middle of a bar that smelled like the usual lemon cleaner but now also faintly like her shampoo.

"I should head out," I said, even though I didn't want to. "You good here?"

She nodded, surprised. "Yeah. Just finishing up. Thanks for coming."

"Anytime."

I hesitated in the doorway, one hand on the knob.

She didn't look at me, but her voice stopped me. "Hunter?"

I turned.

I fully intended to wait for her in the parking lot. I just couldn't be around her anymore without kissing her.

Then she said, so quietly I barely heard her: "I can't stop thinking about the pie. It was my favorite."

"I know. I remember." I didn't wait for more. I didn't push. I just said, "Night, Paige," and stepped out into the cool dark of the parking lot, hands jammed in my pockets with my heart doing backflips.

The sky was clear. The stars were lit up like sharp

points weaving through the trees in the distance. And I felt like I'd left something inside the bar I wasn't sure I'd get back.

Maybe it was just the pie plate I had yet to bring home, but maybe it was something more, and I should go back in and find out.

I took two steps across the gravel and came to a stop. I stood there in the dark, staring at the truck like it might tell me what the hell I was supposed to do next.

She'd said she used to love that pie. But the way she said it? It was like it meant something more. Like *I* meant something to her. Maybe she was ready to be more than friends, and maybe she was too scared to say the words out loud or make a move.

I scrubbed a hand over my face, wondering if I should've stayed. If I should've said more. Or if there was even any more to say at all.

The door creaked open behind me.

"Hunter," she said softly.

I turned. She stood in the doorway, arms crossed, like she'd come outside before she could change her mind.

Her expression was tight, unreadable, but her eyes looked like they were full of something she couldn't hold in much longer.

"Did you forget to tell me something?" I asked, voice low. Hope pounding through my veins like a fucking freight train.

She stared at me for a second. Then she stepped off the porch.

One step. Then another.

She walked right up to me, wrapped her fingers in the front of my hoodie, yanked me down to her level, and kissed me.

No warning. No hesitation.

Just kissed me like she'd run out of reasons not to.

It wasn't gentle. It wasn't slow.

It was months—years—of tension crashing into one moment. Her mouth was hot and soft, and she pulled me closer like she didn't want me to move. And I kissed her back like I'd been waiting my whole damn life to hold her like this. Because in this moment, I realized I had.

I gripped her waist, fingers sliding against that soft, pale sliver of skin I'd ached to touch only moments before.

Her breath stuttered against my lips, and I deepened the kiss just enough to let her know I wasn't going anywhere unless she made me.

And then, just as fast as it started, she broke the kiss and took a step back.

She was breathing hard. We both were.

Her eyes widened like she couldn't believe what she'd just done.

I didn't move.

Didn't speak.

Because this wasn't about me, it was about her and what she needed from me right now.

Her fingers hovered near her mouth. "Shit," she whispered.

Still, I waited. Silent.

And then, with her voice drifting away in the evening breeze. "That wasn't supposed to happen."

"Okay," I said, voice steady. "But it did."

She looked up at me, searching for something.

I didn't offer her an answer. Or ask her what she wanted from me. Because if I did, she'd run away. I knew it.

Instead, I just reached out, tucked a piece of hair behind

her ear, and said, "Do you want me to pretend it didn't happen?"

Her eyes flashed. "No," she said, voice shaking. "I don't. I don't want to pretend anymore. I meant that when I said it before."

My heart knocked once against my ribs. Hard.

She was still close. Still looking at me like she might bolt or break, like she wasn't sure which part of her would win.

I didn't touch her. I let the moment hang, soft and open, until she made the choice again—stepping closer, right into my space, pressing a hand to my chest like she needed to feel my heartbeat before she could believe any of this was real.

"Tell me I'm not losing my mind," she whispered.

"You're not," I said, my voice rough. "But if you are, I'll go with you."

"Tell me I won't ruin everything and drive you away," she pleaded. "I can't lose you."

"That would be impossible."

That was all it took. She surged up again, kissed me harder this time—hotter, hungrier, like the dam had broken and she didn't care about anything but getting her hands on me.

I groaned against her mouth and returned her kiss with everything I'd been holding back. My hand slid around her waist, pulling her in until her body hit mine and she gasped into the kiss, fingers tightening in my hoodie like she couldn't get close enough.

She was warm and soft and real in my arms, and the way she kissed me—like she was starving, like she'd waited just as long as I had—undid something in me. Unlocked a piece of my heart that had always belonged only to her.

"Paige," I murmured against her lips, letting my hand

slide up her back to drift into her hair. "You've got to tell me when to stop."

She shook her head, kissed me again. Then broke away, breathing hard.

"No," she said, her voice trembling. "I don't want to stop."

My hands stilled on her hips as her eyes searched mine —wide, wild, a little scared, but absolutely sure.

"But I do want to slow down," she said, softer now. "Because if I don't, I'm going to fall all the way into whatever this is. And I don't know if I'll survive it if it doesn't work."

I rested my forehead against hers, trying to steady the thudding in my chest.

"What if it doesn't fall apart? What if it all works out? What if I'm always here to catch you when or if you fall?"

"Maybe that's what scares me the most."

And I held her.

Right there in the gravel lot, under the flickering purple neon and the quiet hum of everything that was finally starting.

Neither of us said anything else.

Chapter 13
Paige

By the time I pulled into the driveway, my hands were still shaking.

I sat in the car for a solid five minutes, staring at the porch light and trying to decide if I'd just made the best decision of my life—or set a match to everything I'd worked so hard to keep safe.

I kissed Hunter Cassidy.

Twice.

And not soft little maybe-this-means-nothing kisses.

No, I kissed him like I meant it.

Because I did.

And that scared the absolute shit out of me.

But what scared me even more was how incredible it was - how completely, irreversibly right it felt. Like the kind of kiss that rearranges something in you. Like after that moment, nothing could go back to the way it was before.

And that scared the absolute shit out of me.

Inside, the house was still. The living room was dim except for the glow of the lamp by the couch. I dropped my keys into the end table, kicked off my boots, and padded into the kitchen like someone might stop me and demand an explanation for my actions.

The house was quiet as I grabbed a glass and turned on the tap for some water. My throat tightened as I tried to swallow.

Hunter was everything I never let myself want. Kind. Loyal. Safe. And worse, he'd never once used any of that against me. Never manipulated me by making me think he'd be there for me, then disappear.

I braced my hands on the counter and stared at the tile floor, trying to make sense of what had just happened.

His lips. The way he'd kissed me like he couldn't help himself. The way he'd *waited*—calm, silent, letting me be the one to choose.

And I had. I *chose* him. I kissed him. It was all me.

I let out a breath and opened the fridge, looking for nothing, really. Just movement. Something to do with my hands while my head tried to unscramble itself.

You're not falling in love with him.

You're just overwhelmed. You're tired. You're touch-starved. You're emotionally fried and probably a little bit feral.

That's what this was. It wasn't love. It couldn't be. Not yet. Except it felt like falling in love. Even better, it felt like coming home.

I pressed a hand to my mouth, remembering the way he'd said, *I'll catch you if you fall,* like it wasn't even a question. Like the idea of *not* catching me had never crossed his mind.

Who says things like that?

Who *means* things like that?

Along with Noah and my grandpa, Hunter was one of the best men I'd ever known. He meant every word he'd ever said to me. I had no doubts when it came to him. No, all the doubts were about me.

My chest squeezed, and I turned off the kitchen light before I could think about it too much more. I went to the bathroom to wash my face, then climbed into bed in my leggings and hoodie, and curled up around one of the throw pillows like it could keep me from unraveling.

I stared at the ceiling. At the shadows. At the old water stain in the corner that looked a little bit like a sea turtle. And whispered, "Shit."

Because I wasn't spiraling anymore, I was falling. And I didn't know if I could stop. I didn't know if I even wanted to.

I woke up to the smell of burnt toast and the sound of teenage bickering echoing down the hallway.

So, basically, normal.

I squinted against the morning light slanting through the curtains and reached for my phone out of habit. One new text. From him.

Hunter: Morning. Hope you slept okay. You don't have to say anything. I was just thinking about you.

Me: I've been thinking about you, too. But the kids are up. I'll talk to you later.

I didn't even realize I was smiling until Briar yelled from the kitchen, "Lark, stop leaving your weird science experiments in the fridge! I swear it blinked at me."

I threw back the covers and rolled out of bed. My body ached in that deep, exhausted way that wasn't physical—just the kind of fatigue that comes from feeling too much, from knowing something big was coming.

In the kitchen, Lark was drinking out of a mason jar with a sprig of mint and what looked suspiciously like a cucumber floating in it. She gave me a sleepy smile.

"Morning, Mom," she greeted me with a smile. "I started the coffee for you."

"Thank you, sweetheart. You put vegetables in your water now?"

"It's self-care."

Briar rolled her eyes. "It's annoying."

"Everything's annoying when you're thirteen," Lark snapped back. "Grow up."

I raised both hands before the bickering could escalate. "No fighting before coffee. House rule." I muttered as I made my way to the coffee maker.

Noah, home again for the night, padded in behind me, rubbing his eyes and reaching immediately for the mug I handed him. "Thanks," he mumbled, already drinking.

I loved these kids so much it hurt. Even on mornings like this. *Especially* on mornings like this. When you were free to be yourself, warts and all, that's when you knew you were truly at home.

We fell into our routine without speaking much—toast, cereal, coffee, repeat. Lark left early for a study group, Noah was packing up to go back to Portland, and Briar stomped back to her room to find her other ballet shoe for dance.

I poured myself another cup of coffee and sank into a kitchen chair just as a knock rattled the front door.

I cracked it open to find Piper standing on my porch with a bag of muffins and a raised eyebrow.

"You look like you've seen some things," she said, brushing past me to head into the kitchen. "Good things. Suspiciously good things."

I closed the door behind her. "Do you have some kind of sixth sense for romantic chaos?"

"No," she said sweetly. "I have *Eliza*. She said you were weird at the Coffee Cabin drive-thru on Hunter's birthday. I had no idea about the weirdness. Why didn't you tell me? I figured I'd check in. Again. And there's more. You were seen."

I groaned and flopped back down in my chair at the table, trying to avoid her eyes. Someone saw us? How? "Seen?" I wanted to play it off just in case no one actually saw me kiss Hunter. "What do you mean, seen?"

She studied my face. "Parking lot. Last night. Jasper forgot his hat. He went back to grab it, but turned around when he saw you and Hunter—"

"Shhh!"

"Kissing," she whispered. "Don't worry, I won't say anything."

"Twice," I whispered into the table. "Last night in the parking lot. And it was amazing and terrifying, and I'm probably going to ruin everything."

"Twice? Huh?" She patted my back. "You're not. Unless you start overthinking it. Which you are. Because that's what you do."

I shot her a look. And snagged a muffin from the bag.

"Not judging you. I do it too, don't feel bad. It's a

Darlington Sister trait. As long as we call each other out on it, everything will be okay."

I lifted my head and narrowed my eyes. "How are you so smug this early?"

"I slept. And I didn't emotionally implode in a parking lot last night after kissing my best friend." She shrugged lightly. "Yet. There's always time to implode, I just need a reason."

I gave her the abbreviated version of what had been going on between me and Hunter. The pie. The repair work. The kiss. Then the part where I said I didn't want to pretend it didn't happen, and then ran inside like I was about to burst into flame.

She nodded sagely. "Okay. So now what?"

"I don't know. I told him I didn't want to stop, but I needed to slow down, and he said he'd catch me if I fell."

"Oh my god." Her hand hit the table as a smile lit up her face.

"I know."

"That's the most romantic thing I've ever heard. Are we sure he's not fictional? I mean, I've known him forever, and I had no idea he was capable of that. I love this. You deserve this."

I pressed the heels of my hands to my eyes. "Piper, I kissed my best friend. My *safe place*. What if I screw it up and lose him?"

She pulled my hand away from my face and held it. "Then you get brave, and you fight for him. Because if this is real, and we both know it is, then you owe it to yourself to try."

Before I could spiral any further, my phone buzzed again.

Ren: Heads up. Eli's lawyer reached out.
They're not backing down. You might
consider telling the kids.

My stomach dropped.

I read the message twice, then slid the phone across the table like it burned.

Piper saw my face and went still. "What is it?"

"Eli," I said. "He's still trying to take the kids. He'd shut up for a while. How stupid of me to hope for the best."

Piper stood up so fast her chair squeaked. "Over my dead body."

I stared at the muffin in front of me, suddenly nauseous. "He's escalating. I never thought he would do something like this."

"Well, you never thought he'd cheat on you either."

"Yeah, well, messing with the kids is something else entirely. I can let some things go to keep the peace when it's just me, but I will not let this slide. He's in for a surprise. I'm lucky I had Ren to fight for me, to encourage me to go after what's fair and not let too much go during the divorce."

"And we're going to shut it down. I promise I'm here for you. And you already know Ren will take care of you."

"He's going to use *everything*, Piper. Me running the bar alone, the late nights. He'll probably try to blame Briar sneaking out on me somehow. And maybe even the fact that Hunter was here all night that night. Shit! And the kiss in the parking lot, damn it. If word of that gets around—"

Piper waved a hand. "Please. You think Honeybrook

Hollow won't find out about you and Hunter? And your suspiciously glowing skin?"

"Huh?" I blinked. "Excuse me?"

"You looked *happy* when I walked in, Paige. You're glowing. The whole town will figure it out by lunch. Once they see how radiant you are, it'll be on." She shrugged. "But look, it's Hunter. He's beloved in Honeybrook Hollow. Between him and his family, they keep every car, truck, and motorcycle running from Sweetbriar to Honeybrook Hollow and all the way up to Willowmist Falls. So hello? Any Hunter and Paige gossip that pops up will only help you. You have nothing to worry about."

I groaned. "I can't deal with gossip on top of custody threats and whatever else pops into his little pea brain."

"You can. And you will. Because you're strong, and smart, not to mention as mean as a honey badger, but most of all, you're not alone."

I bit my lip and tried not to burst into tears.

"You have your family. You have Ren. And you have *Hunter freaking Cassidy*, who would take a wrench to the face for you. Or hit someone in the face with a wrench for you. Either way, go you! Finally. You have a man worth your time in your life."

I swallowed hard, not answering as I tried to hold back the wave of emotion that rose in my throat.

She pulled me in for a hug, squeezing tight. "You've got this. And we've got you."

I closed my eyes; she was right. But I was still scared. Because when someone tries to take your peace, your kids, your life—you either stand up and fight for it or you lose everything. And I was so damn tired of fighting for everything I had.

Piper didn't let go right away. When she finally pulled

back, her eyes softened, the fierce sister-warrior in her giving way to something warmer.

"Okay," she said, "I can't fix Eli today, but I *can* start working on your face."

I blinked. "My face?"

"Your mood-face," she clarified. "It's tragic now. You've gone from glowing to Eeyore if he were going through peri-menopause."

I groaned. "I'm sorry. I feel like I have whiplash. Did you come over to insult me or—"

"—to save you," she interrupted. "From yourself. And from this vortex of gloom Eli keeps pulling you into."

"I'm okay. I don't need saving from anything—" I started.

She held up a finger. "Don't. Shh. I already have a plan."

"Well, that's terrifying."

"It's wonderful," she said, grabbing her coffee and taking a sip before continuing. "Your birthday is coming up."

I gave her a look. "Don't. Nope. Uh-uh."

"Oh, I will. Yep. Uh-huh. Forty, Paige. The big 4-0. You can't just let it pass by while you hide in your bar yelling at whatever appliance is acting up."

"I don't hide in my bar," I protested. "I—"

"Shhh," she said, taking a bite of muffin like she'd won the argument. "I'm thinking cocktails, twinkle lights, maybe that band from the summer festival, and cake. Obviously cake. Hello, I am the best baker in town. Multiple cakes. Like a cake buffet."

"Piper—"

"You can wear something sparkly. I'll wear something sparkly, and the girls will too. Do you think Noah will wear a sparkly tie? Or a vest?" I shook my head no because there was no way he would agree to that. "Well, shopping in Portland is imminent; we'll take him to lunch and see what he thinks. Oh! And we'll make Grandma wear sequins so she blinds people when she dances."

Despite myself, a laugh slipped out. "She'd do it."

"She'd *own* it," Piper said. "And you? You're going to let people celebrate you for once in your life. Twilight Tavern, your birthday, your divorce, and your burgeoning relationship with hottie Hunter. It will be amazing."

I shook my head, though my throat felt tight. "I don't know if I'm in the mood to celebrate anything right now."

"That's exactly why we're doing it," she said, softer now. "Because life doesn't stop being hard. But you deserve a night where you don't have to fight, where you can just be happy. Even if it's only for a few hours."

I stared at her, torn between wanting to protest and wanting to believe her.

"I don't need a party," I muttered.

"Maybe not," she said. "But you need a reminder that you're loved. And I am *really* good at reminding people of that."

For a second, I had to look away. Because if I didn't, she might see that she was getting to me.

She reached across the table and tapped the table in front of me. "Think about it. In the meantime, I'll just quietly plan it behind your back. I have what? Like a month-ish? By that time, you'll be so happy with Hunter you'll be begging for a party to show off. Trust me."

"Quietly plan? That's not how 'quietly' works," I muttered as I tried to muster a glare, but my lips betrayed me. "You're impossible," I said, failing to keep the affection from my voice.

She only shrugged, her smile gentle. "Only when it comes to the people I love."

"I love you, too."

A silence stretched between us, companionable and full of things unsaid. My fingers traced circles on the rim of my mug, and I let myself imagine—just for a moment—what it would be like to say yes to the party. To let go, even briefly.

Piper's phone chimed, and she glanced at it before shoving it away like nothing could distract her from this mission. "No pressure," she added. "Let yourself have hope, okay?"

I let out a breath. "Okay. I'll try."

She brightened. "That's all I wanted to hear. You'll show up and it'll be the best night of your life. I promise."

I rolled my eyes, but there was a little warmth in my chest now. A spark I hadn't felt in weeks.

Piper was going on about cake flavors when my phone buzzed again.

I pulled it closer, half-expecting another message from Ren about legal nightmares. The muscles in my shoulders eased when I saw the name.

> Hunter: Eat breakfast. Real breakfast. Not coffee and stress. If you say you don't have time, I'm bringing you bacon and eggs, and you know I'll do it.

A smile tugged at my mouth before I could stop it. I took a long sip of coffee, hoping the mug would hide the way my cheeks went warm.

Piper was watching me over the rim of her own mug,

her eyes narrowing like a cat stalking something shiny. "Is that him?"

"No," I lied, my voice coming out too fast and too high.

Her mouth curled into a slow, knowing grin. She leaned forward, elbows on the table, her napkin crinkling in her fingers. "Uh-huh. Let me guess—something sweet, slightly bossy, and guaranteed to make you blush?"

I shoved my phone into the front pocket of my pants and busied myself with tidying up the table. "Stop."

She made a satisfied *mm-hmm* sound, brushing a stray crumb off the table like she'd just wrapped up a successful interrogation. "This is going to be so fun. I'm putting him on the guest list and sitting you two at the same table. Maybe under mistletoe."

"It's not even Christmas," I said, shaking my head.

"Details," she said, waving me off. "It doesn't have to be Christmas for mistletoe to be effective at a party. Just saying."

"I'd rather you help me plan my grand reopening party for the bar. I don't need a birthday party."

"I've already decided to combine the two. How fun will that be?"

Before I could throw my napkin at her, my phone buzzed again. The vibration rattled against the table, and this time, I didn't grab it right away.

Piper's brows shot up. "Is it him again? Already? That's a good sign."

"I don't think so," I said slowly, pulling the phone out, "I'm afraid it's Ren with more bad news. My text notifications should come with a warning alarm."

It wasn't Ren with bad news. But I almost wished it was.

Eliza: Were you and Hunter making out in front of the tavern last night, or was that just the world's most romantic Heimlich maneuver? Asking for the entire town, because they're driving through asking me about it when they order coffee. I'd promise not to say anything, but it's already out there.

My stomach dropped like a stone into cold water.

Piper caught the shift instantly. Her chair scraped against the hardwood as she sat up straighter. "Oh my god. It's already *all* the way out there now, isn't it? I didn't think Jasper was the gossiping type."

"He isn't. Someone else had to have seen us." My voice wobbled. "And now half of Honeybrook Hollow knows we were having a parking lot make-out session under the neon lights."

"That was faster than I thought," her laugh was short and disbelieving. She leaned back, crossing one leg over the other.

I slouched back in my chair, rubbing at my temples. "Piper, if Eli hears about this—"

Her teasing expression shifted into something calmer and more deliberate. "He will hear about it, that's a given. But it doesn't matter. Don't forget that he's the delusional, dirtbag cheater who left his wife and three kids for another woman and tried to make his baby girl quit her dance class, the rotten bastard. That's not on you. You're allowed to have a life, and he's allowed to suck a bag of di—lemons."

I stared at the swirl of coffee in my mug.

I sighed, feeling the weight settle heavily. "Yeah, but logic doesn't really win against humiliation, does it? I just wish I could rewind and keep our business private for once." The ache in my chest tangled with embarrassment; I hated being the center of whispers, even when I'd done nothing wrong. "I just hope people move on to something else soon and let this drop."

"They will. Try not to worry. Eli is the problem. Not you."

"You know he doesn't see it that way. I mean, I don't care what he thinks about me; I'm over that. But the kids don't need to be involved in town gossip, and I'm beginning to think he will trash me as much as he can if he thinks it will get him what he wants."

"I know," she cut in gently, reaching across the table to nudge my hand until I looked up at her. "But you've got people in your corner. More than you think."

Her fingers wrapped around mine, warm and certain. "You're not alone in this. And I think you're about to find out just how *not-alone* you are. No one in their right mind will take his side. Please believe that."

"I wish I could stay home tonight and hide from this. But Jasper is off, and I have to be behind the bar, damn it."

"Want me to stop by?"

"No, it's okay. I'll have to deal with this sooner or later anyway. Might as well be sooner."

"Okay. You got this. You know that, right?"

I forced a smile and squeezed her hand. "Yeah. I always do. Thanks, Piper. Really. I mean it." She grinned, eyes crinkling with warmth, and stood to gather her things. I watched her sling her bag over her shoulder, lingering for a moment by the door.

"Get some rest before work if you can, okay?" Piper said, pausing as she reached for the handle. "Text me if you need anything, or if you want me to kick someone's ass."

I laughed softly, feeling lighter. "I will. Later."

"Later." She hugged me, then slipped out, leaving the kitchen a little quieter.

The rest of the night passed without incident. I kept my head down at work, pouring drinks and laughing with the regulars. The whispers faded into the usual background noise of the bar, and by closing time, I almost forgot there was anything to worry about at all. Then Hunter showed up, and all my worries faded away.

When my night ended, I drove home beneath a quiet sky, the crisp air clearing away the last of my nerves. I let myself in, shed my jacket, and settled onto the couch, a gentle relief blooming in my chest. For once, everything felt manageable—maybe not perfect, but enough. I was okay. Tomorrow would come, and I'd be ready.

Chapter 14
Hunter

The next few days drifted by, slow as molasses. The nights blurred together for me—a mosaic of clinking glasses, laughter, and the low throb of music from the jukebox as I waited to help Paige shut down the bar. We talked and laughed, back to our usual banter and jokes. But neither of us mentioned that night, or the half-life of a kiss that seemed to hover between us, unresolved and undeniable, yet heavy with the knowledge that it would absolutely happen again.

Why were we taking it slow?

Work kept me busy, but not enough to drown out the tension curled tight in my chest. I'd memorized every knot in the wood grain behind the bar, waiting for the time to pass until closing. Some nights Paige would catch my eye from across the room, her lips quirking in a secret smile, and I'd feel the world tilt a little closer to right, even if just for a heartbeat.

Being caught was a worry. Gossip had spread, and it made her uneasy. A storm was coming, the kind you could sense before it broke. News traveled fast in this town, faster than any of us liked, and I knew it was only a matter of time before Eli found a way to push himself back into her orbit. I knew she was worried, so I didn't push.

The day dawned with a cold, steely sky. I left early, needing air and time to think. I ducked into the town's diner for a quick bite before work.

The Pennywhistle Pantry always smelled like grilled cheese, fresh pie, and coffee that had been brewing since before sunrise. The red vinyl booths gleamed under the soft hum of neon signs, and the checkerboard floor was worn smooth by decades of locals sliding in and out for their lunch specials. It was the kind of place where you knew everyone, right down to the waitresses who called you "hon" and topped off your coffee without asking.

I'd gotten lost in thought as I stood in the doorway trying to find a table. Then I saw Paige standing at the counter near the register, a takeout bag in one hand, her jacket unzipped to show a soft, fitted T-shirt underneath, probably with a bar pun stretching across her chest as usual. Snug jeans hugged her hips, and the worn leather of her boots caught the light as she shifted her weight. Her shiny blond hair fell loose around her shoulders, and she was smiling politely at whatever the cashier had just said. My heart thudded to a stop as I fought the urge to claim her, take her in my arms, and kiss her right where she stood.

I knew exactly why she was here: to grab lunch before heading into the tavern. I could picture her eating a quick sandwich in the back, jotting notes on orders while she scarfed half her meal standing up. Maybe we could eat here together instead. I was already moving toward her, working up something easy to say, when the bathroom door swung open behind her and Eli stepped out.

His eyes locked on her immediately, and my steps slowed. I almost wanted him to confront her so I could step in and give him what he deserved. He got to her first, striding up like he owned the room. I held back, knowing she would be angry if I interfered and didn't let her take care of herself. I stopped near the end of the counter, every muscle in me going tight.

Paige saw him coming. Her posture changed instantly—shoulders back, chin up, but that flicker in her eyes said she'd been expecting a confrontation sooner or later.

"Not now, Eli," she said, her voice cool.

"Then when?" he shot back, too loud for the space. "You've been dodging my calls."

"I blocked your number. I'll only unblock it when the girls are with you." Her tone didn't change. "Remember? From now on, we will only be talking through our lawyers. If you have something to say to me, talk to Ren."

"That's ridiculous. We're both adults. We can settle this ourselves."

"You mean the way you tried to 'settle' it at my bar? Blindsiding someone is not how you settle things," she said, raising one brow. "No, thanks. This is what lawyers are for, right? Since your new one is determined to help you screw me over."

"I'm not the enemy here—"

"You are when you try to take my house from me. And my bar, and my children."

That one landed. His jaw tightened, but he forced a smirk. "You're overreacting. I'm just trying to do what's best—"

"What's best for who?" she cut in sharply. "God, I thought I married a man. Turns out you're just a spoiled little boy. I should have known better. Don't you even care what the kids will think? Or does that not matter to you anymore? Noah barely speaks to you as it is."

That was my cue. I closed the distance in a few long strides, the tension in the air snapping as I stepped between them.

"Walk away," I said, my voice low enough to make him look twice.

Eli turned his glare on me. "This isn't your business."

"It became my business the second you decided to corner her in public," I said, my voice rising just enough for the people at the counter to hear. "Here's what's going to happen—you're going to leave, right now, before I forget we're in a diner and put you through the front window."

The room had gone quiet, forks hovering in midair.

Eli scoffed. "What, you think you can—"

I took one step forward, close enough that he had to tip his chin to keep eye contact. "I don't think, Eli. I know. And if you give me a reason, I will. You want to play games? Do it somewhere else. You don't get to harass her in the middle of town."

Paige's hand came to rest lightly on my forearm—not pulling me back, just there.

Eli's eyes darted around at the people watching, and his fake charm slipped. He muttered something under his breath and turned, shoving out through the door hard enough to make the bell over it jangle wildly.

The quiet faded, replaced by the clatter of dishes and the low murmur of conversation resuming.

"You okay?" I asked, looking down at her. She was full of false bravado and defiance. He'd shaken her, and she was trying to hide it.

Her fingers lingered on my arm for a heartbeat longer

before she stepped back, still holding my sleeve. "Yeah. Thanks."

I didn't buy the "yeah," not with the way her grip on the takeout bag tightened, her knuckles pale, not with the way she clutched my sleeve in a death grip.

"Come on," I said. "I'll walk you out."

Outside, the crisp air hit us, the low autumn sun glinting off the diner's chrome trim. The gravel in the parking lot crunched under our boots as we made our way to her car.

"You didn't have to do that," she said after a moment.

"You know I did," I grumbled, wishing I *had* put him through the window. That motherfucker deserved it.

She glanced at me, the corner of her mouth twitching like she didn't know whether to smile or argue. We reached her car, and I opened the door for her.

"You do realize the entire diner probably thinks we're about to get married now," she said, sliding her takeout bag onto the passenger seat and making jokes to cover her tension. "Listen, I'm not scared of him, Hunter. Not really. He just makes me so mad, and I'm not supposed to say anything to him. Also, I've been sticking to the bar and my house. Being here today—" She ran a hand through her hair and paused. "Apparently, people know about us. Everyone seems to know we kissed in my parking lot."

"Good," I said, straight-faced.

That startled a laugh out of her. "Good? Really?"

"Yeah. Saves me the trouble of explaining that I protect what is mine." I held my hands up. "Don't get mad. I know how that sounded, and it's not what I meant, you're not property. I don't know how to say what I—"

"It's okay. I get it." She bit her lip, trying not to laugh at my stammering. "I liked how you stood up for me. I mean it. Thank you."

"You're welcome." I leaned one arm against the open door, lowering my voice. "Forget him. Soon enough, he'll fade back into the background again. It's almost your birthday. Heard from Piper that there's going to be a party."

Her mouth opened, then closed again. "You're seriously bringing that up now? When I'm torn between throwing a fit over Eli's bullshit and throwing myself at you in the middle of town? We can't let the gossip get out of control, you know."

"I'm just saying," I said with a shrug, "town gossip has a way of making things happen faster. If everyone thinks we're a thing, then we won't have to explain anything when I escort you to your birthday party."

She snorted. "You're unbelievable."

"And yet," I said, grinning now, "you still haven't said no."

Her lips pressed together like she was fighting a smile. "Get out of here before I change my mind about thanking you."

"Too late. I'm taking that as a yes."

She rolled her eyes in answer, but there was a softness there she didn't quite hide.

As she shifted into the driver's seat, I stayed leaning against the doorframe. "By the way," I added casually, "I'll see you early tonight."

Her brows lifted. "Early?"

"Gossip is out there. Eli is an asshole. You won't be alone. I have a few things to do at the shop, then I'm coming over."

She tilted her head. "Are you going to start charging me for this bodyguard service?"

"Nope," I said. "Consider it part of the pact."

She let out a little huff of laughter and shook her head. "You're ridiculous."

"And you'll see me tonight. Early." I said, stepping back so she could close the door.

"Maybe," she said, but the corner of her mouth curved like she knew she didn't mean it. "I'm fine. Seriously. Eli pissed me off, but I'm not really worried. He won't get anywhere with these games he's trying to play. Ren is the best; he never loses." She grinned and held up a finger. "However, I'm not arguing about you coming early. That part is my silver lining for the day."

I gave her a crooked smile. "Silver lining, huh? I like that. Try not to miss me too much until tonight."

She rolled her eyes again, but this time her laugh was genuine, bright as sunlight through storm clouds. "Don't flatter yourself," she teased, but I caught the way her gaze lingered a moment longer before she finally shut the door behind her.

I stood there until she pulled out of the lot, watching her taillights disappear down Sycamore Street—not because I didn't trust her to handle herself, but because no part of me could watch her go without making sure she got there safe.

I should have gone back to the shop. I told myself that three times on the way to the truck, and twice more while driving across town. But instead of turning left toward Cassidy's Automotive, my hands kept the wheel steady toward the tavern, following the route I'd taken a hundred times before.

The truth was, I didn't like the idea of her behind that bar *at all*, with gossip running wild and Eli making threats. And sure, Paige could hold her own—she'd done it for years—but knowing that didn't loosen the tight knot in my chest.

By the time the tavern's neon glow came into view, the parking lot had only a scattering of cars, all probably belonging to the usual weeknight regulars. The purple light washed across her windows, and I could see her behind the bar, head down as she wiped the counter, ponytail falling over her shoulder.

I slipped inside, the familiar creak of the door swallowed by the hum of conversation and low music from the jukebox. A couple of guys at the far end glanced my way, giving me a chin lift in greeting, but went back to their beers. I knew them. They weren't the gossiping type.

Paige looked up, and for a second her face softened in a way that hit me square in the chest. Not surprised, not annoyed—just like she was glad I was there.

"What are you doing here?" she asked, coming closer. "You're even earlier than you said you'd be."

I leaned against the bar, keeping my voice low. "Checking in. You okay?"

"I'm fine," she said, but her hand lingered on the bar near mine, close enough that I could feel the warmth radiating off her skin. "You don't have to babysit me."

"Maybe I don't have to," I said, "but I kind of need to."

Her eyes held mine for a beat longer than necessary before she reached for a glass and started filling it with ice. "You want a drink?"

"Sure. Coke?"

She slid it over, then drifted toward the other end of the bar to refill someone's beer. I stayed where I was, watching her move—confident, quick, at ease in her space. And still, every so often, she'd glance back at me as if she wanted to make sure I was still here.

The night wound down faster than I expected. The last of the regulars shuffled out with murmured goodnights, and Paige locked the door behind them after saying goodnight to her crew, telling them she'd see them tomorrow. The tavern went still, quiet except for the jukebox.

"You could have gone home," she said, stacking glasses. "Get some rest. Relax..."

"Could have," I agreed, "but I didn't want to."

Her hands stilled for a second before she set the last glass down. "Why not? You can see that I'm okay. It was a quiet night; there's not much left to do in here."

I stepped closer, slow enough to give her time to stop me. She didn't. "Because I need to be near you. Is that okay?"

"Yes," she whispered.

"It's quiet in here. The door is locked. Just us."

Her breath caught, just barely, and she leaned back against the bar as I closed the distance.

"You've been on my mind since that night. The night I kissed you." I said quietly. "Hell, longer than that. I need you, Paige. I want more."

She swallowed, her eyes flicking to my mouth before darting away. "Hunter..."

I rested one hand on the bar beside her hip, close enough now that the heat of her body warmed the space between us. "Tell me to stop, and I will."

She didn't tell me to stop.

Instead, she reached up, fingers brushing the side of my neck before sliding into my hair, pulling me down until our mouths met.

The kiss started soft—testing, tasting—but it didn't stay that way. Her other hand gripped the front of my shirt, pulling me flush against her, and I let my arm curve around her waist, anchoring her to me.

When her back arched slightly, pressing her chest against mine, a low sound escaped my throat before I could stop it. She tasted faintly of lemon water and something sweeter, something entirely her.

I deepened the kiss, tilting my head to fit her better, my hand tracing the curve of her spine. She made a soft, involuntary sound that went straight to my chest and lower, and I felt her shiver under my touch.

"Paige," I murmured against her mouth, "we should—"

"I know," she whispered, pulling back just enough to look at me. "But I don't want to stop this time."

The air between us thickened, charged.

I took her hand and, without breaking eye contact, led her toward the back hall. The jukebox kept playing, but the rest of the world faded, leaving only the soft thud of our steps, the faint hum of the cooler, and the pounding of my heartbeat.

Chapter 15
Paige

The pool table sat in the center under a low green lamp, casting soft light over worn felt and a couple of abandoned cue balls. The jukebox in the bar still hummed faintly through the wall, but in here it was just us. No windows. No curious eyes to see us from outside.

My butt hit the edge of the pool table as Hunter stopped in front of me, his presence filling the room in a way that made it suddenly feel smaller. Warmer.

"Is this okay?" he asked, his voice low, his hand hovering near my waist like he wasn't going to touch me until I said yes.

I nodded before I found my voice. "Yes. More than okay."

Something eased in his shoulders, and then he stepped closer, his palm sliding along my hip. The heat of his touch bled right through my jeans, steady and sure.

I leaned into him; my hands braced on his chest. "But I need to say this before anything else happens. I'm not ready for complicated conversations about what this means. Not tonight."

"Then we won't have them tonight," he said, without a single ounce of hesitation.

Relief loosened something tight in my chest, and I let myself pull him down into a kiss.

It started like the one in the parking lot—familiar and warm—but quickly deepened, hunger curling between us. My fingers slid into his hair, tugging gently, and he groaned against my mouth like he'd been waiting years to feel this.

When his hands slipped under the hem of my shirt, his palms warm against my skin, I broke the kiss just enough to whisper, "Condom?"

He smiled, quick and a little breathless. "I have one." He stepped back long enough to tug his wallet from his back pocket, the foil packet catching the low light. "Still okay?"

"Yes," I said, with more certainty than I'd expected to hear in my own voice. "I love how you check in with me. I'm okay, I promise."

His lips found mine again, slower this time, like he was savoring the moment. Each touch was deliberate—his hands mapping my waist, my ribs, the curve of my back—as if he was trying to learn me all over again but this time beneath my clothes, skin on skin.

When he pulled my shirt over my head, his gaze lingered on me like he was memorizing every inch. "You're beautiful," he said, not in the offhand way men sometimes did, but like it was a fact he'd been holding onto for years.

Heat spread through me, and I pulled him closer, wanting to feel his solid strength pressed against me. My legs bumped the side of the pool table, and he guided me back until I was sitting on the edge, his hips between my knees.

The kiss turned hotter, more urgent. He traced his lips in a line along my jaw, down my throat, and my breath caught when his stubble brushed my skin. My hands slid under his hoodie, finding warm, hard muscle, and I felt him shiver when my nails scraped lightly along his spine.

He murmured my name against my skin like it was both a prayer and a warning, and I knew—down to the very center of me—that this was going to change everything.

And I wanted it to. It was time.

He framed my face with his palms, his thumbs brushing lightly over my cheekbones like he was making sure this was real before moving any further.

"Tell me to stop anytime," he said, and the weight behind those words wrapped around me just as much as his body did.

"I won't," I whispered. "I don't want to."

That earned me the kind of kiss that stripped the rest of the world away. His mouth was warm and demanding, but not rushed, each movement deliberate—like he wanted to memorize the way I tasted, to study the way I breathed when he kissed me just right so he could do it again.

He eased me back on the pool table, his hands sliding under me to hold me steady. The felt was cool against my skin where my shirt had been, the edge pressing into the backs of my thighs. He broke away just long enough to pull his hoodie and T-shirt over his head, and I couldn't stop my gaze from roaming over him—over his broad shoulders, down the cut of muscle down his stomach, the trail of hair disappearing under his waistband. He was beautiful.

"Lift up," he ordered, spreading his hoodie out beneath me as I did. "You're staring," he said, a half-smile tugging at his mouth.

"Uh-huh, I am," I murmured, unapologetic. "I've earned it."

That made him laugh, low and rough, and then he

leaned back in, kissing me hard enough to make my toes curl. His hands slid down my sides, gripping my hips as he tugged me closer. The heat between us sparked sharp and insistent, and I didn't bother pretending I didn't want him. The thought of slow fled recklessly out of my mind.

He unbuttoned my jeans, his fingers brushing along my hipbone as he tugged the denim down. I helped, kicking them off to land with a soft thud on the floor. My heart hammered, not from nerves, but from the pure headrush of being this close to him, this bare, wanting more and knowing I was about to get it.

He kissed his way down my neck, over my collarbone, his breath warm against my skin. When his hands slid over the backs of my thighs, urging them apart, I gasped—half from the shock of it, half from how right it felt. He dipped his head, kissing the inside of one thigh, then the other.

"Hunter, please," I gasped right before he tasted me, gripping my thighs and spreading me wide to lick me from my opening to my clit. Never had I felt this way, ever.

I ran my hands into his hair to pull him closer. He knew what he was doing; he gripped my ass tight, fingers digging into my flesh as he licked into me and swirled his fingers in slow, deliberate circles. I cried out, falling apart embarrassingly fast.

"Fuck, the way you taste. The way you feel. So soft. So perfect. I can't wait to get inside you..."

"Hunter." My head spun from his words, his hands on my body, but mostly because of the way he looked at me. Like he was desperate for me, maybe even loved me a little bit. I had to stop thinking and get back out of my head. This was too much. "I'm saying yes. I want you. Please. Now."

I sat, tugging at his jeans, my fingers fumbling at the button until he helped, shedding them along with his boots.

And then there was nothing between us but the air, charged and thick.

"Still okay?" he asked again, his voice quieter now, a little hoarse.

"Yes," I said, without hesitation. "Hunter, I want this. I need you."

The way he looked at me then—like he'd been waiting years to hear me say that—sent a shiver straight through my entire body. He reached for the condom, tore the foil open with his teeth, and rolled it on without breaking eye contact.

When he lowered himself over me, his forehead pressed to mine, I could feel his heart racing against my chest. "If this changes anything for you tomorrow, tell me. I'll handle it."

"It's not going to change how I feel about you," I whispered. "If anything, I'm afraid it's going to make it stronger."

"Same for me. I've never wanted anything more."

"Hunter..." His name was a confession on my lips, hope and fear tangled together.

He kissed me softly, and in that quiet, I realized there was no turning back. Every part of me was open, vulnerable, and it wasn't just my body he was holding—it was all of me, laid bare and trusting him to cherish it.

"I can't believe this is happening," he murmured, and then he kissed me as he eased into me, slow and steady, giving me time to adjust to his size.

The first movement stole my breath. The second had me gripping his shoulders, my nails digging into warm muscle as he found a rhythm that felt like we'd been made for it. Every shift, every thrust was measured, intentional— not just chasing release, but building something that felt a lot like trust, like love and history, and what had always been meant to be finally being allowed to happen.

I gasped his name when he shifted slightly, hitting a spot that made my back arch off the table. His hand slid up my side, fingers splaying over my ribs, holding me there while his mouth found mine again and his thumb traced over my nipple.

Somewhere between his low, rough murmurs in my ear and the way his hips moved with that deliberate, devastating precision, I stopped thinking entirely. I let myself feel every inch of him, every shiver, every sigh he breathed against me.

When the wave finally broke over me, I clung to him, my whole body trembling. He followed moments later, his forehead dropping to my shoulder, his breath coming in hard, uneven bursts.

For a long moment, neither of us moved. The only sound was the faint hum of the jukebox and the slowing beat of our hearts against each other.

He brushed a kiss along my jaw, then my temple, before pulling back just enough to look at me. "You okay?"

His question broke through the haze, grounding me gently. I managed a shaky laugh, nodding as I brushed a stray lock of hair from his forehead. "Yeah. More than okay." My voice was softer than I meant it to be, full of all the things I wasn't quite ready to say out loud yet, but I saw the understanding in his eyes. He wrapped his arms around me, holding me close as our breaths slowly evened out together, the quiet between us comfortable and safe.

His smile was small but certain, and he pressed one more kiss to my lips—gentle this time, almost reverent—before helping me sit up and reach for my clothes.

As I pulled my shirt back on, I caught sight of our reflection in the dusty mirror on the far wall. My hair was a mess, my lips swollen and red, and Hunter was watching me like he'd just discovered his favorite view in the world.

And that was the moment I knew—whatever came next, however complicated it got—I would never regret this.

He met my gaze in the mirror, his expression softening into something impossibly gentle. Neither of us spoke, but the silence was full—heavy with promise, with meaning I didn't need to put into words. I reached for his hand, fingers threading through his, and for a moment, it was just the two of us suspended in the quiet aftermath, the world outside forgotten. It felt like the beginning of something new, even as we stood in the familiar shadows of the bar.

Hunter found my jeans and undies on the floor before I did, holding them out with a half-smile that was a little smug and a lot tender. "These are yours, I think."

I rolled my eyes, tugging them back on while trying not to smile too much. "You're lucky I'm too blissed out to sass you properly."

His low laugh rumbled through the room, warm and easy. "Guess I'll take advantage of that while I can."

We didn't rush. Not in that awkward, fumbling way you sometimes did after something like this. He tossed the used condom in the trash in the corner, slipped into his jeans, then leaned back against the pool table, watching me smooth my shirt down. There wasn't any distance in his gaze, no regret—just that steady Hunter way of looking at me like I'd hung the moon.

I grabbed my hair tie from where it had fallen to twist my hair back up, but his hand caught my wrist halfway.

"Leave it," he said softly. "I like it down. It's beautiful."

For reasons I couldn't quite explain, that made my chest ache in the best way. I let the tie fall to the table.

We finished getting dressed, then moved around the

space together without talking—me stacking the last few clean glasses, him grabbing his jacket from the hook by the door, switching off lights as he went. It was easy. Comfortable in a way that didn't make sense for what had just happened, but maybe that was the point.

In the main bar, the jukebox had shifted to a slow song, the kind that made the room feel warmer even in the dim light. He shut it down, and I flicked the back room light off. The faint scent of chalk dust lingered behind us as we crossed the floor to the door.

When I turned the deadbolt on the front door, he was already waiting with my coat. He held it open, and when I slid my arms in, his hands skimmed down my sleeves before settling at my waist.

"You sure you're okay?" he asked, voice low enough to make the air between us feel heavier.

"Yeah," I said, meeting his eyes. "I'm sure."

He studied me for a beat, like he was checking for cracks in my answer, then nodded. "Good. Then let's get you home."

He bent to press a soft kiss to my forehead before letting me go, a silent reassurance that lingered even after he stepped back. There was a comfort in those little gestures, a gentleness that never asked for more than I was willing to give. For a moment, I let myself lean into it, let myself believe this could be easy, that being wanted didn't always have to come with strings or shadows.

The night air wrapped around us as we stepped outside, the cool crispness of it a shock after the warmth of the tavern. The neon sign buzzed softly above, casting us both in violet light.

Hunter locked up behind me, his keys jingling as he pocketed them. He didn't move toward his truck right away, but he fell into step beside me as we crossed the gravel lot to my car.

"You're going to let me follow you home," he stated.

I gave him a look. "You think I can't make it a mile and a half without you behind me?"

"I think," he said, leaning one arm on my open door, "that I'll sleep better if I know you made it there without Eli lurking around or your radiator exploding."

My lips curved despite myself. "Fine. But only because you said, 'sleep better' and not 'keep you safe.' I can take care of myself. I only want you for *you*, not your protection."

His grin was quick and a little wicked. "I'll keep that in mind."

I slid into the driver's seat, my heart doing that strange, dangerous thing again. The thing that felt like hope. And as I pulled out, his headlights came on right behind me, steady in my rearview all the way down Sycamore Street.

Chapter 16
Hunter

I didn't sleep much.

Not because I was restless in a bad way—hell no. I'd been replaying last night on a loop until the sky outside my window started going pale.

Paige.

On the pool table.

In my arms.

Looking at me like she'd finally decided to stop running from whatever this was.

I'd gone home after following her back, making sure her porch light came on and that she made it inside. She'd glanced over her shoulder before shutting the door—one last look—like she was trying to say something without saying it.

I'd wanted to knock again. To ask her to let me in, not just into the house, but into the rest of her night, her morning, her body, her life. But I'd told myself to give her space.

She'd been through enough people crowding her, needing something from her. She didn't need me doing it, too.

But the truth was, I wasn't sure what "ready" even meant anymore. My chest was still tight with everything unspoken, everything hanging in the air after last night. I'd spent so long keeping my distance, telling myself I was protecting her. Now, the line between what I wanted and what I thought was best was blurring fast, and it scared the hell out of me.

I'd woken up with the smell of her shampoo in my head and the imagined feel of her hands clutching my shoulders like she was afraid I'd disappear.

I pulled on a T-shirt and jeans, made coffee, and tried to focus on something practical. But the thing about mornings in Honeybrook Hollow was, you couldn't avoid someone wanting to tell you the news of the day—especially when the news was about you.

By the time I stopped at the Pennywhistle Pantry for a breakfast sandwich, two different people had given me that grin—the one people use when they know something they shouldn't. And by the time I paid my tab, Nancy behind the counter was smirking like she was ready to start selling tickets to our next parking lot kiss.

I took my food to go.

The worst part wasn't the gossip—it was knowing that when it reached Eli, he'd find a way to twist it into ammo for the custody fight. He'd use anything. And even though Paige had the truth and a good lawyer on her side, that didn't mean the fight wouldn't gut her and the kids.

Back at the shop, Dad was leaning on the counter, flipping through a parts catalog. He didn't look up when he said, "Heard you were at the tavern late last night."

I froze mid-step. "From who?"

He gave me a slow, knowing look over the top of his glasses. "Hunter, this is Honeybrook Hollow. From everyone. These people monitor comings and goings like they're getting paid to do it."

I groaned, dropping the sandwich bag on the counter. "That didn't take long."

"Nothing does around here." His eyes softened. "You ready for what comes with that?"

"I've been ready for twenty years," I said without thinking.

And there it was. The truth, out loud.

I picked up the sandwich and headed for the bay doors before he could press me on it.

Because I already knew that whatever came next, I would never let her face it alone.

By the time the day wound down, I'd swapped out brake pads on two Fords, wrestled with a busted alternator, and still hadn't shaken the itch to see her.

Not just because of last night. Not just because of the gossip. Because I knew her, and I knew the way she carried things. She'd tuck the worry behind her smile until it got too heavy to hide.

The sun was dipping low, painting the streets in that burnished autumn light that made Honeybrook Hollow look like a postcard. I could see the purple glow of the Twilight Tavern's neon from half a block away.

Her car was parked out front, but the lot was empty otherwise. I didn't like that.

I pushed the door open, and the warm, familiar scent of beer, fried food, and citrus cleaner rolled over me. Music played low from the jukebox. She was behind the bar, sleeves shoved up, hair twisted into a messy knot. She was stuffing napkins into holders as if they had personally offended her.

"Hey," I said.

She looked up, startled for half a second before her face softened. "Hey, yourself. You're early. I open in an hour. I'm just setting up."

"I know. Figured I'd help you get ready."

Her brows lifted, but there was a tiny smile tugging at her mouth. "That's what you call it? Sure you're not here to check up on me?"

"Yeah," I said, stepping behind the bar like I belonged there. "Wiping things down. Taste-testing the beer. Making sure the jukebox doesn't get stuck on one of those sad eighties country songs."

She shook her head, but I saw it—the way her shoulders eased just a fraction.

"Everything okay?" I asked. I wanted to hold her. I wanted her to run to me instead of trying to play it cool as if she didn't need me when I knew she did.

"I heard from Piper. And then..." She trailed off, flicking the rag over a stubborn spot on the bar. "Let's just say the town is talking."

I leaned a hip against the counter. "About us."

She blew out a breath. "About the neon parking lot spectacle, you being here every night, among other things, yeah. Eliza texted me, too. The Coffee Cabin is like Honeybrook Hollow's gossip hub or something. Everyone who stopped by told her something different about us. It's freaking ridiculous, and half of it isn't even true."

"Let them talk," I said. "It's not their business."

"It's Eli's business if he decides to make it part of his case."

That steel-edged tone in her voice had me wanting to go find him right now. But instead, I slid her bottle of water in front of her and popped the cap. "Drink. Hydrate. You're running on caffeine and probably rage."

She smirked. "Bossy."

"Caring," I corrected.

For a moment, we just stood there—me on one side of the bar, her on the other—long enough for the quiet to settle around us like something solid.

"You don't have to be here this early," she said, softer now.

"I do."

Something flickered in her eyes. Not quite fear, not quite relief. "Careful," she said. "You keep this up and people will start thinking we're serious."

I didn't flinch. "I am serious."

The jukebox shifted to a slower song, low and bluesy, and neither of us moved for a beat. Then her mouth curved in a way that told me she was fighting herself again.

"Hunter—"

"I know," I said quietly. "You don't have to say anything. I'm just... here. Please let me be."

And I would be here. Tonight. Tomorrow. However long it took.

She stared at me for a long second, then glanced toward the front windows like she was checking for paparazzi. "Come with me," she said quietly.

I followed her through the narrow hall past the jukebox hum, into the back room with the pool table. Back here, the streetlights couldn't reach us, and neither could any wandering eyes.

She set the rag aside on the rail and leaned her hip against the table, crossing her arms. "I just didn't want to have this conversation in front of the windows."

I stayed a few feet away, giving her room. "What conversation?"

Her gaze flicked up to mine, cautious but clear. "That last night wasn't a mistake."

The words were simple, but they landed hard in my chest. "I didn't think it was."

"I just…" She exhaled, uncrossing her arms like she was letting herself unclench. "I need you to understand that I'm not quite ready for this to be public. I'm barely ready for it to be *real*. And I can't have Eli twisting it into something ugly in front of the kids. I want this to be good. I want this to be joyful and dreamy and romantic, and I'm afraid he'll try to ruin it with his bullshit. I don't want people commenting on my love life like I'm doing something scandalous. This is not sordid. This isn't some cheap fling. It's *you*, Hunter. You mean something to me, and I don't want town gossip cheapening what we have."

I nodded once. "Then we keep it between us. For now. On your terms."

That earned me the smallest, most grateful smile. "Even if we deny everything, or at least don't confirm it, I don't want to stop, though."

"Good," I said, stepping closer until I could rest my hands lightly on the edge of the table beside her. "Because I don't, either."

Her fingers brushed mine, tentative but warm. "Last night was exactly what I needed. But it's not just about needing *it*, you know, sex. It's *you* that I need. I want you. Only you and I don't want anyone else, okay?"

"I know," I said, my voice low. "I feel the same way. You're it for me, Paige. I'm in this."

She hesitated, her thumb still moving over my knuckles. "But, promise me, if you ever get tired of being with me—if you want out—I need you to tell me. Tell me before anyone else finds out, okay?" Her voice was steady, but the fear in it was unmistakable.

I caught the flicker of pain in her eyes, and suddenly it made sense. Eli had left scars—he'd cheated, lied, and made her feel small, and I could see now just how deep that damage ran. She shook her head, looking down. "I don't want to ruin this with doubts. I'm sorry. I know I'm scared, but I have to be honest with you."

"I'm not going anywhere," I told her. "Not if things get messy. Not if Eli's shadow hangs over us. Not if the whole damn town tries to make a show out of it. I'm here." I slid my hand over hers, letting my thumb rest over the gentle pulse at her wrist. "Paige," I murmured, my voice steady and soft, "I'm not going anywhere. I promise you, no rumor or sideways glance could ever change how I feel about you." The ache that lingered in her eyes began to soften, and I wanted nothing more than to guard this fragile hope between us. "You're safe with me—always. I want to be the person you can trust, no matter what."

She looked up at me, and for a moment, the uncertainty faded, replaced by something tender and genuine. I drew her closer, pressing a gentle kiss to her forehead. "Let's make this ours. Just you and me, as it should be—no distractions, no one else's opinions. I want to be with only you, I swear."

Her throat bobbed like she was swallowing words she didn't quite trust herself to say. Then she reached for my hand—no hesitation this time—and laced our fingers together. "I want you too. Scared or not, I'm in this."

I let her hold on as long as she needed.

Her hand stayed in mine, thumb brushing over the back of my knuckles like she was memorizing the shape of me.

I shifted closer, close enough that our knees bumped again. "You sure you want me this close right now?"

Her mouth tipped up at one corner. "If I didn't, you'd already know."

I gave her a slow smile, then set my free hand on her hip —just enough weight for her to feel it, to give her time to pull back if she wanted. She didn't. Instead, she tilted toward me, her breath warm when it hit my throat.

"Last night," she said softly, "I wanted to invite you home with me, but I was afraid if I didn't stop, I'd fall too hard. End up moving too fast. I don't know."

I slid my hand up her side, fingers resting just under the curve of her ribcage. "And now?"

Her answer was a whisper against my lips. "Now I think it's too late. I already did."

That broke something in me. I kissed her—slow at first, just enough pressure to feel the shape of her mouth against mine. She sighed into it, her body leaning into mine like she'd been waiting all day for this.

When I deepened the kiss, her arms looped around my neck, drawing me closer. The warmth of her pressed into my chest, the faint taste of her lip balm on my tongue—it was too much and not enough all at once.

"Hunter," she breathed, and I felt it all the way through me.

"Tell me if you want me to stop."

"I won't," she said, voice low but sure. "This is all I want."

My hand skimmed her waist, her lower back, memorizing curves I'd only let myself imagine for years. Her fingers tangled in my hair, and she kissed me like she'd decided there was nothing else worth thinking about.

I broke just enough distance to meet her eyes. "Do you want—"

"Yes." The word left her so fast it made my pulse kick harder. "Condom?" she asked. Her lips curved, flushed, and a little breathless.

"Yeah, I put another one in my wallet last night. Wishful thinking..." I kissed her again—harder this time— before forcing myself to pull back just enough to move us toward the little side office. She went ahead of me, tugging my hand, her laugh low and nervous but certain.

The door clicked shut behind us, muting the jukebox and the hum of the empty bar. In here, it felt like the whole world had shrunk down to her and me, the heat between us sharp and alive.

I reached for her again, backing her up against the desk, and when she pulled me down for another kiss, it was all instinct and years of wanting finally colliding in one perfect, dangerous moment.

Chapter 17
Paige

Hunter watched me like I was the only thing worth noticing, his hand still wrapped around mine. There was nothing impatient in the way he looked at me—just steady heat, a promise that I could take as much time as I needed. But we had to be fast; the bar was about to open, and the door was unlocked.

"I'm sure," I told him before he could even ask again. "I want this. I want *you*."

Something in his shoulders loosened, and the smile that ghosted across his face made my stomach flip. He stepped in closer, hands settling at my waist like they'd been made to fit there, his thumbs brushing against my hips.

The kiss that followed wasn't tentative. It was the kind of kiss you give when you've been waiting half your life to have someone's mouth on yours. His lips were warm, firm, coaxing me deeper until I had to brace myself against the desk.

"You're sure?" he asked one more time, his voice rough.

"Hunter," I said, smiling against his jaw, "if I weren't

sure, you wouldn't be standing this close. We have like twenty minutes until opening. Hurry."

That earned me a low, satisfied sound that I felt right down my spine.

He kissed me again, slower this time, like he wanted to memorize the shape of my mouth before he let himself rush. His hands skimmed up my sides, over my ribs, then back down again, lingering at the waistband of my jeans until I nodded. He made quick work of the button, the zipper, and then his hands were warm on my bare skin.

I tugged at his shirt until he pulled it over his head, my fingers immediately finding the soft hair at the back of his neck. He was solid heat and muscle under my touch, and when my palms slid down over his chest, he caught my wrists gently, holding them there for a moment.

"I've wanted you like this for so long," he murmured as he took the condom out of his wallet.

"Maybe I've known that all along," I whispered back.

The rest of our clothes fell to the floor in a slow, tangled trail. He rolled the condom on, his eyes never leaving mine. And when he stepped in, pressing me back against the desk again, I wrapped my legs around him without thinking.

The first push of him inside me stole my breath. I held onto him, nails curling against his shoulders, my head tipping back as he groaned into my neck.

"Paige," he said, like my name was the only word he knew.

"Don't stop," I whispered, my voice shaking.

He didn't. He moved with me like we'd been doing this for years, finding a rhythm that was as much about closeness as it was about heat. His thumb made circles over my clit, while he brushed his lips over my cheek, my jaw, catching my lips between each kiss, and his hands gripped me like I was something precious.

Every sound, every shift of him inside me, pulled me closer to the edge. And when I came, it was with his forehead pressed to mine, his breath mingling with mine, and my name falling from his lips like it belonged there.

He followed soon after, holding me close, his hands gripping my hips like I might break if he let go too fast.

For a long moment, neither of us moved. My legs were still wrapped around him, my arms looped around his neck, and the world beyond the office door could have been a thousand miles away for all I cared.

When he finally eased back, his lips brushed over mine in something softer, almost reverent. "Are you all right? Was that too hard? Too much?"

I smiled—small, tired, and maybe a little shaky. "It was amazing. You are amazing. It was perfect."

We were quiet together for a long moment. My legs were still hooked around his hips, my fingers resting at the back of his neck where his hair was just starting to curl.

His breathing evened out, the warmth of him still wrapped around me like I could keep it forever if I didn't move. And I didn't want to move.

He kissed me again—soft, unhurried—and I felt my body melt all over again. This was dangerous. The kind of dangerous where you want more before you've even let yourself process what you already had.

Reality seeped in, uninvited, like cold air under a door. The office wasn't soundproof. My crew could start arriving at any minute. And the pool room wasn't exactly a fortress against nosy eyes if anyone wandered back here.

"I think we should..." I trailed off, glancing at the pile of our clothes like they were evidence.

"Get dressed?" His mouth curved, but he didn't make a move to let me go yet.

"Yes. Before someone comes back here and finds us like this, I'm not ready to have Eliza reporting back *this* level of material from the coffee shop gossip circuit."

Hunter chuckled, low and warm, then kissed me once more before stepping back. The moment his heat left my body, I felt the air rush in, cool against my skin. I pulled my clothes back on, trying to do it in some kind of dignified order while he made zero effort to hide the fact that he was watching me.

"You're staring," I muttered, tugging my shirt down.

"I've waited years for you to let me," he said simply, pulling his shirt over his head.

Well. That shut me up.

Once we were both decent again, he stepped close, catching my hand before I could open the office door. "Paige," he said, and his voice was so steady, so sure, I felt it settle deep in my chest. "This doesn't have to be complicated unless we make it complicated. We'll figure it out."

I swallowed hard, searching his eyes for a second too long. "Okay."

He gave my fingers a squeeze, then released me.

When I pushed the door open, the bar looked exactly the same as when we'd left it—the soft glow of the neon beer signs, the low hum of the jukebox. No one behind the bar. No one at the nearest tables. I let out a breath and allowed myself to relax into this moment.

"See?" Hunter murmured behind me. "Flawless exit."

"Mm-hmm," I said, grabbing a rag off the counter to give my hands something to do. "Let's hope we're that lucky next time."

He stilled at my words, and when I glanced up, the look

in his eyes told me exactly how much he liked the idea of a next time.

Which, if I were being honest with myself, I did too.

Hunter lingered while I continued setting up, his big frame leaning against the end like he was perfectly at home here. He didn't offer to help—probably because he knew I'd tell him to go sit down if he did—but he stayed. Just close enough that I could feel the weight of him in the room.

The first of my crew trickled in not long after, along with the first of the evening customers. Routine settled quickly, the familiar rhythm of orders called and glasses clinking, a dozen small stories weaving themselves across the gleaming surfaces of the bar. For a few hours, it felt almost easy—us together, moving in sync, the outside world held at bay as I ran through the evening by rote.

As the clock pushed closer to midnight, the crowd thinned. Last call faded into the scrape of chairs and happy goodbyes. One by one, the crew peeled off. Soon it was just me, Hunter, and the echoing quiet of a bar that always seemed a little larger when empty.

When the last glass was dried and the till locked, I tossed the rag into the laundry bin and turned to find him already holding my jacket.

"Thanks," I murmured, slipping my arms through the sleeves.

He followed me to the door, waiting while I locked up, the purple glow of the Twilight Tavern's sign painting the walkway in soft light.

The night was crisp, the kind of cool that hinted at rain without any actual clouds overhead. I tucked my hands into my pockets as we started toward my car.

His hand brushed mine—just barely, like he was testing

the water—and when I didn't pull away, he laced our fingers together.

We walked the last few feet in silence, and I could feel the warmth of him even through the space between our bodies.

At my car, I turned to face him. The neon caught in his eyes, making them look impossibly dark and bright all at once.

"Hunter…" I started, not entirely sure what I meant to say.

He stepped closer, one hand lifting to cup the side of my face. "I'm not going anywhere, Paige. Not tonight. Not tomorrow. Not unless you tell me to."

I felt something in my chest go soft and unsteady. "I'm not telling you to. I won't."

That earned me the smallest smile, and then his mouth was on mine—nothing rushed, nothing frantic. Just the kind of kiss that says *I see you. I'm here. I'm not going anywhere.*

When he pulled back, his thumb brushed my cheek, lingering there for a moment before he stepped away.

"Get home safe," he said quietly.

"You too."

I watched him walk to his truck, his shoulders broad and sure in the neon haze, and for the first time in months, I didn't dread tomorrow. Because whatever was coming, I wasn't facing it alone anymore.

Chapter 18
Paige

The first thing I felt when I woke up was sore muscles in places I hadn't used in a very long time. The second was the ridiculous smile tugging at my mouth.

I stayed still for a moment, cocooned in my blanket, letting my brain replay last night like a movie I didn't want to end—Hunter's hands, his voice in my ear, the way his eyes had looked when he'd told me he wasn't going anywhere.

A vibration on my nightstand yanked me out of the memory. I reached for my phone, blinking against the light of the screen.

Hunter: Morning. Drink water. Eat real food.
And yes, that's an order.

I snorted under my breath. Bossy was apparently his love language, right after kissing me until my legs didn't work properly.

> Me: Good morning. I'm about to make coffee and maybe some toast. That counts as something real, right?

His reply came faster than I expected.

> Hunter: Toast is not a real breakfast. I could come over with something real for you.

A thrill of heat and something dangerously close to giddy shot through me.

Before I could overthink it, my bedroom door cracked open and Lark's head appeared, her hair in a messy bun, eyes narrowed. "Why are you smiling like that?"

"I'm not smiling," I lied. Poorly.

"Uh-huh," she said, then disappeared again, her voice drifting down the hall. "Briar! Mom's being weird!"

Perfect. Precisely the kind of subtlety my girls were known for.

By the time I arrived in the kitchen, Briar was rummaging through the fridge, and Lark was stirring Nutella into a bowl of oatmeal.

"Morning," I said, grabbing a mug.

Briar straightened, holding up a container. "Can I take the leftover mac and cheese for lunch?"

"Yes. Just don't—"

She was already halfway down the hall before I could finish reminding her to bring a fork.

Briar eyed me over her spoon. "You going to the bar early today?"

"Not too early," I said. "Why?"

She shrugged. "You just seem less stressed. Which is suspicious." She smirked at my look of confusion. "Translation: the stupid town gossips are working overtime. We've heard some things."

My hand froze on the coffee pot. "What do you mean?"

She lifted her phone. "Maddie told me people saw you and Hunter leaving the tavern together. And before that? Dad and Hunter almost had a fight at Pennywhistle Pantry. Her mom asked her about it. So yeah, Mom, everyone's talking. And we want to know what is going on with Dad. Please."

I set the coffee pot down carefully, like maybe if I moved too fast, the whole morning would shatter.

"Great," I muttered, pouring coffee into my mug. "Exactly what I needed this week. I'll tell you everything when Briar comes back in here. I'm not trying to keep secrets, just everything is happening fast, okay?"

Before I could take a sip, my phone buzzed on the counter.

Ren: Call me when you can. It's important.

That did nothing good for my stomach. I held up a finger to Lark, then stepped into the laundry room, shutting the door behind me before dialing him.

"Tell me it's not what I think it is," I said as soon as he answered.

"I'd love to, but Eli's lawyer just sent over new demands," Ren said. "He's doubling down—more claims about your 'unstable' work schedule, but now he's hinting about inappropriate overnight guests."

My grip tightened on the phone. "That's disgusting. And hello? Isn't that the pot calling the kettle black? Did he forget why we got divorced?"

"It's also easy to knock down if it comes to it," Ren said, his tone calm but edged. "He's got nothing but speculation. But I wanted you to know so you're not blindsided."

I pinched the bridge of my nose. "Thanks. I'll handle it."

"No, you won't. Paige, I have it under control," he said. "Remember that. You do nothing, okay? All I'm doing is keeping you informed."

I hung up before my voice could shake, leaning back against the dryer. My phone buzzed again immediately, but this time the contact's name made my breath catch.

Hunter: Don't panic, but I heard Eli's running his mouth again. I'm coming by early again.

Me: You don't have to. I got this.

. . .

Hunter: That's cute.

Despite everything, a laugh escaped me. The man could boss his way through my bad moods better than anyone I'd ever met.

I slid my phone into my pocket and rejoined the chaos of the kitchen. Briar was rinsing her bowl, and Lark had her backpack over her shoulder, ready to go.

They both gave me that look—the one that said they knew something was up and were waiting for me to explain.

"Okay," I said, setting my coffee on the counter. "I need to tell you both something before you hear it from someone else."

Briar froze. Lark shifted her weight, crossing her arms.

"Your dad's lawyer filed more paperwork," I said, keeping my voice calm. "Along with wanting to pay less child support, he's trying to change our custody agreement. He's saying my work hours aren't good for you, and that I have people staying over who shouldn't be here. I am not embellishing or making this more than what it is. I promise to only tell you the facts. I think you're old enough to handle it and observant enough to figure it out on your own."

Briar's mouth dropped open. "That's such crap. Grandpa is here every night that Noah isn't. What's the problem with that? We could even stay alone if we had to; we're old enough. You have to work, we know that. Like, it's his fault you're working. He left us."

"Yeah," I said automatically, but my throat tightened at

the fierce look in her eyes. "He was also talking about Hunter."

"Are you dating him?" Briar asked. "I'm okay with it if you are, just saying."

"Yeah, we won't say a word." Lark interrupted. "Forget about that. I don't have a problem with you dating Hunter either. The real problem is Dad is lying about you," she said flatly. "Hunter only stayed here that night because we were all traumatized, and you were both on the couch. Nothing happened, and who cares if it did anyway? Dad lives with Danielle, hello? Why would he lie like this?"

"I don't know," I said, avoiding answering their question about Hunter. "But Ren is going to fight this for us, and I need you to know that no matter what your dad says, none of this is your fault. You aren't to blame for his money troubles, or whatever is going on with them. You're safe here. This is your home, and it always will be."

Briar sat at the table, her movements jerky with fear, and probably a little bit of anger, too. "What if he makes us live with him?"

"That's not going to happen," I said, stepping closer. "You're both old enough that the court will listen to what you have to say. You might not get what you want, but you will be heard. And Ren has all the evidence he needs to show you're better off here if this is where you want to be. But if you hear anything at school, or if your dad says something to you, I need you to tell me right away. Promise?"

They both nodded. Lark's eyes were shiny, but her jaw was set like she was ready to take on a war. Briar stood to hug me without another word.

I kissed the tops of their heads. "We've got this. I promise."

"I don't want to go over there anymore," Briar whispered.

"I'm so sorry, sweetheart. We have an agreement I can't break. But I'll call Ren and see what he can do about that. Okay?"

She nodded. But Lark had already picked up her phone. I watched her fingers fly furiously as tears filled her eyes.

"Lark? It's going to be okay—" I started.

"Yeah, it will be." She looked at Briar. "I just texted and told him we aren't coming this weekend, that we're going to Grandma and Grandpa's instead." She looked at me. "I don't want him to come over here and try to pick us up or mess with you. No way he'll try to see us at Grandpa's house." She turned to Briar. "I won't let him do this to us anymore. I'm sorry I didn't say anything before, and I'm sorry I told you to ignore it."

Tears filled Briar's eyes as she hugged her sister. "It's not your fault. We're not the same. And it's okay if we handle things differently—"

I wrapped them both in my arms, thinking of the way my sisters and I were always there for each other like this. "I love you both so much, and I'm so proud of you."

"We love you too," Lark answered for both of them.

"Are you okay to go to school today?"

"Yeah," Briar mumbled. "I'm okay."

"Me too," Lark confirmed.

"All right. Let's get ready to go, then. It's time." As the morning light filtered in through the windows, we shifted back into the gentle rhythm of getting ready for the day.

Lark slung her backpack over one shoulder, double-checking the front pocket for her notebook, while Briar carefully slipped the container of mac and cheese into her lunch bag. I kept a close eye on them as they moved with quiet determination, handing each of them a water bottle and offering a reassuring smile.

They had just left, their voices carrying down the walkway as they headed for the bus stop. I shut the door, then flopped onto the couch to think, or nap, or perhaps lose my mind a little bit. I'd barely settled into my internal worry-fest when I heard the low rumble of a truck engine idling in my driveway. I glanced at the clock, frowning, just as the sound cut off and footsteps crunched up the walk. A firm, friendly knock echoed through the house. For a moment, I hesitated, then crossed to the door and pulled it open.

When I opened it, Hunter stood there with a paper sack in one hand and two coffee cups in the other. He looked annoyingly good for someone who'd probably been up since before sunrise, hair a little mussed, eyes warm in the soft morning light.

"Breakfast delivery," he said.

I arched a brow. "I didn't order anything."

"Yeah, you did," he said with that slow grin that always made my stomach trip. "Every time you skip breakfast, you're ordering me to show up like this."

I stepped aside to let him in, the smell of biscuits, bacon, and coffee curling around us like a hug I hadn't asked for but desperately needed.

We ended up in the kitchen. He placed the coffee on the table while I unpacked the bag. "You okay?" he asked, leaning against the counter like he had all day.

I stared at the biscuits for a moment before answering. "I don't know. I'm worried about the girls. Lark texted Eli this morning and told him they won't be coming to his place this weekend. And I can't..." My throat tightened. "I can't fix anything for them this time. I can't control whatever is going to happen, and I hate it."

He set his coffee down and closed the space between us, his hands finding my hips like it was the most natural thing in the world. "You're already fixing it. You're showing them you'll fight for them. That's more than most kids ever get."

"I don't want them to think this is their fault. I hate that Eli is hurting them like this."

"They have you. Which means, they'll be okay," he said, steady as bedrock.

"They asked if we're seeing each other," I said softly, trying for a smile. I was desperate to change the subject. I was so sick of Eli taking over my life again. "I didn't give them an answer. But they are okay with it if we are."

His lips twitched, the barest hint of relief flickering in his eyes. "Good. I think they're as amazing as you are. And I'll be here for them too. And Noah." He brushed a stray hair behind my ear, thumb tracing the line of my jaw.

"I hate that I'm dragging you into this. I have no idea what crap Eli will try to pull next, and I—"

He placed a fingertip against my lips. "Shh, please. All I care about is being with you. Eli can go to hell."

"Okay. But let me deal with him. This is my problem, not yours."

A quiet fell over the kitchen—not awkward, just the soft quiet that settles after a storm. I let myself lean into him, borrowing warmth, letting the tension of the morning ease away. It was a small, defiant act to let myself breathe and feel how rooted I was in this moment with him.

His hand gave a reassuring squeeze at my hip. "We're in this together. All of it. The messy, the hard, and the good stuff, too. Please believe it."

I nodded, my throat loosening. "I'm trying. It just feels

like I never get to choose what parts of my life belong to me."

He smiled, gentle and knowing. "Then let's take this one. Right now. Just us."

I managed a shaky laugh, and somewhere inside, the leaden weight shifted, just a little. My hands moved to his shoulders, and then he bent and kissed me. It wasn't rushed. His mouth was warm and sure, the kind of kiss that lingered, that made the world tilt just enough to remind me I was still capable of wanting something good. His thumb brushed lightly at my waist, coaxing instead of taking.

When we finally broke apart, his forehead rested against mine. "Is there anything I can do to make this easier on you?"

"You're already doing it," I said, and meant it.

"You're going to make me late for work," he teased.

"That's on you, bossy," I murmured, stealing one more kiss, slower this time, with the faint taste of coffee between us, before letting him go. "I'm going in early, too. I have a delivery to sign for. Then I'll be back here until tonight."

"I'll see you later then," he whispered against my lips before breaking away and heading to the front door.

"Promise?" I felt a bit foolish for needing the reassurance, but after the morning I'd had, I needed it.

"Absolutely." He pulled me in for one more kiss before turning to leave.

I followed behind, thankful that at least one part of my life seemed to be falling into place. I watched him walk down the steps, my chest lighter and heavier all at once.

Chapter 19
Paige

The Twilight Tavern's parking lot was still half in shadow when I pulled in, the morning air crisp enough to see my breath. The neon sign was dark, and the only sound was the gravel crunching under my boots. I'd come in early to meet a supplier who promised to drop off a special order—a batch of local cider I wanted to feature this month.

I was halfway to the front door, keys in hand, when I heard her.

"Paige! Hey, wait up!"

Danielle's voice carried too easily across the empty lot. I turned to see her jogging across the asphalt in boots that probably cost more than my monthly power bill. She'd always been used to the finer things. The way Eli had been struggling for money lately must be driving her up the wall.

My stomach sank. "Danielle. Where did you come from?"

"I parked in the back. I was afraid you'd drive away if you saw me." She reached me at the door with a breathless smile, like we were girlfriends about to grab coffee. "I was hoping to catch you! Can we go inside and talk for a minute? Mom to mom?"

"I'm waiting for a delivery," I said flatly. "You'll have to make it quick." I should tell her to get lost and keep quiet like Ren said, but I knew the only way to get rid of her was to either hear her out or physically remove her from my presence. I figured listening for a few minutes was better than an assault charge.

She fell into step beside me as I unlocked the door and entered. The bar was quiet, the chairs were still upside down on the tables, and morning light slanted through the blinds, striping the polished wood. I set my bag down behind the bar, checking my phone for a message from the delivery driver. Nothing, damn it. I wanted out of here.

Danielle wandered toward the bar, letting her gaze sweep the place like she was measuring it for curtains. "It's so cozy in here during the day. I never noticed."

"You've never been here before opening," I said, moving behind the bar to grab a glass of water.

She smoothed her hair, that perfect fake smile still in place. "Speaking of mornings, do you know where Eli is?"

"I don't know," I answered flippantly. "Go back outside and lift up a rock."

Her smile faltered, just for a second, before she pasted it back on. "Funny."

"Not really," I said, grabbing a glass and adding lemon slices to it.

"I was actually coming to talk about Briar and Lark," she continued, lowering herself onto a barstool like she had all the time in the world. "They seem a little off lately. Maybe it's the adjustment, or maybe they just need more structure at our house—"

"Off? That's cute. As if you don't know exactly what

the problem is. They will be fine," I cut in, staring her down so she'd get to the point and tell me what she was after.

"I'm only saying this because I care," she said, leaning forward, voice dripping with phony concern. "Transitions are hard. And Eli's under so much stress right now with business at the sandwich shop being so slow and the laundromat needing repairs. Meanwhile, you've got this place running like a dream..."

And here it was. The pivot. She wanted something from me.

"Yeah, this scenario is exactly my dream come true," I bit out.

"It's such a shame Eli doesn't still have a stake in it," she added, ignoring my tone. "That income would really help all of us. The girls, too," she added. "I hated having to suggest Briar quit dance class. She's such a talented girl. Eli wants her to dance. He wants to provide for everyone. And the bar—"

"No." I looked her dead in the eye. "Never going to happen."

Her brows pinched. "Paige—"

"No. I built this bar up. I ran it while I was married to Eli, did you know that? I ran all three businesses. I kept the books straight, paid the bills, and did the work while he was chasing bad ideas and showing up when it was convenient for him. I make more now because I know what I'm doing. He doesn't. He's not my problem anymore. If he runs the other two businesses into the ground, I do not care. Deal with him yourself and keep me out of it."

The sweetness in her smile dropped away completely for a heartbeat before she forced it back. "We need the money, and I think it's only fair that—"

"You are out of your damn mind. No," I said, letting my

voice drop. "You want *my* money. You think my bar is your shortcut. It's not. And by the way? You've been treating my daughters like a burden, don't pretend that you're aiming for future stepmother of the year. They see how you act. And so do I."

The air between us went still. Outside, a delivery truck rumbled past without slowing down, not mine, of course.

Danielle pushed back from the bar, chin high. "I was only trying to be helpful. Can we be polite with each other, please?"

"This is me being polite. It's the best I can do when it comes to you. It's time for you to go," I said. "Oh, and if you still can't find Eli after you leave, think about where he used to be back when *I* couldn't find him. If he'll cheat *with* you, he'll cheat *on* you." I shrugged lightly. "Food for thought." I guess I wasn't being polite. Whatever.

She left without another word, the door swinging shut behind her. I ran over to lock it, trying not to lose my shit.

I grabbed the phone from behind the bar and called my supplier, pacing between the tables. The manager answered, his voice chipper until I asked about my cider.

"Oh, uh, yeah, that order was canceled," he said, confused.

"Canceled? By who?"

"Someone from your number called yesterday afternoon, saying you didn't need it anymore. I double-checked the order form, and it matched your account info."

My stomach dropped, a cold, creeping unease settling in. "It wasn't me."

There was an awkward pause. "Sorry, Paige. I can put in another order, but it'll be at least a week before we can get it to you."

"Thank you. Do it, please," I said tightly, hanging up

before my voice could crack with the mix of anger and suspicion bubbling up.

I stood there in the quiet, my pulse sharp in my veins. The cider wasn't just late; it was not coming. Someone was messing with me.

And Danielle just happened to show up this morning, all smiles and false concern, fishing for information and reminding me how much she thought this bar should belong to Eli.

Coincidence? Maybe. But I'd been around long enough to know that some smiles hid teeth.

I moved through the space, searching for anything out of place. Things where they shouldn't be. Forgotten receipts. Anything that held a clue. The bar felt suddenly unfamiliar, like I was walking through a stranger's dream.

Once inside my office, I reached for the ledger on my desk, flipping through recent orders and deliveries, tracing every signature and note and matching them up with the records I kept on my laptop. Nothing jumped out, but suspicion clung to each page. I should talk to Eli about this, but the thought made my jaw clench.

Was I being paranoid? Could this just be a simple mistake?

Forget Eli. I called Ren, who told me to send him copies of my records and keep him updated on anything out of the ordinary.

I needed to get out of here. I should go home and take a nap. I was exhausted. Maybe sleep would bring clarity.

I left my office, the ledger still open on my desk, and stepped into the dimly lit doorway that separated the cramped back from the main part of the bar. The world narrowed to the threshold, and then I saw Eli standing in the glow between shadow and light.

He didn't move, didn't speak. The way he stood, half turned as if caught mid-thought, made something inside me go taut. I felt the press of old history in his silence—a memory of when this place belonged to both of us, before the lines blurred and broke. I didn't hear him come in; the bar had been locked. My gaze dropped to his hand, where a battered key glinted between his fingers.

"You still have a key?" My voice was sharp enough to cut glass.

He glanced at it like he'd forgotten it was there. "Of course. I helped build this place."

"That was years ago. It's mine now. Give it to me."

"What?" His eyebrows shot up.

"You heard me." I walked through the room, holding out my hand. "Key. Now."

His jaw flexed, but he dropped it into my palm. The weight of it was heavier than it should have been.

"Since when do I need permission to come in?" he asked. "We were married. We have kids together. This place was mine."

"Since you stopped being my husband," I said flatly. "And since you showed up uninvited in a locked building that doesn't belong to you anymore. It's mine now, Eli, and you are no longer welcome here. Maybe I should call the police." I watched him carefully. Weird things were happening here, and sadly, I wouldn't be shocked if he were part of it.

He stuffed his hands in his pockets. "I came to apologize. For everything that's been going on lately. And to offer to take the girls this weekend. Give you a break."

"Generous," I said, my voice dripping with acid. "As if you didn't get Lark's text this morning. You are driving them away. They don't want to see you right now."

"I have things to make up for, okay? Can you talk to them for me?"

"No. They're teenagers, old enough to have minds of their own. It's not up to me. It's up to them, and I'll back up anything they want. If they want to see you, I won't ever stand in their way or discourage them. I promise."

"We have to talk this through. We can't live this way."

"None of this has anything to do with me. Can't you see that? You caused all of it. We're divorced. You're not my problem anymore."

He swallowed, his gaze dropping to the scarred wood floor. For a moment, the silence pressed between us, thick as a fog neither of us wanted to walk through. I could see the words lining up behind his lips, the urge to argue, to justify, all of it simmering just below the surface. But he held it in, jaw working.

"What do you want from me, Paige?" he finally said, voice quieter now. "I know I've screwed up. I know I can't change what happened. But I'm here, aren't I? I'm trying."

I shook my head, not trusting myself to speak. My hand closed tighter around the key, as if its weight might anchor me. "Showing up doesn't fix what you broke," I managed, voice rough. "You can't just waltz in and rewrite the past."

His eyes flickered with something—hurt, maybe, or just fatigue. "I'm not trying to rewrite anything. I just want a chance to do right by them. And by you, if I can."

"It's too late for us, I don't care anymore, and you no longer have the power to hurt me. And as for Noah and the girls? That's not up to me," I said. "You burned all the bridges, Eli. If you want to cross, you'll have to learn how to swim."

A muscle ticked in his cheek. "It's not that simple."

"It is," I said, and the finality in my voice surprised even me. "Danielle was here. Right before you showed up, she didn't know where you were. Sound familiar?"

"I'm sorry, Paige. Damn it."

"Haven't you learned by now that apologies mean shit without accountability? You do the same thing over and over. You never change, Eli."

"What do you want me to do?"

"Oh my god!" I let out a frustrated screech. "Get the fuck out of my bar. That's what I want."

"Not until we talk this through. Please."

"Fine. Talk. This wouldn't have anything to do with the fact that your businesses are tanking, would it?"

His jaw tightened. "I'm trying, Paige. You think it's easy keeping everything going?"

"I know exactly how hard it is. I did it for years while you were busy chasing bad ideas and fucking Danielle behind my back."

Color rose in his face. "That's not fair."

I shrugged. "It's accurate."

He exhaled sharply, the apology draining out of his voice. "You know what? Forget it. I was trying to make things better."

"This isn't about making things better. It's about control. And I'm not giving you any more of it."

His mouth flattened. Without another word, he turned and stalked out, the door slamming behind him hard enough to rattle the glasses on the back shelf.

The room felt smaller after he left, the weight of the morning pressing in—Danielle's fake sweetness, the canceled delivery, Eli's bullshit apology. It was too much, too fast.

I locked up, deciding the bar could survive without me for a few hours. I just needed to go home and take a breath.

I'd barely made it a mile down the road when the steering wheel jerked in my hands. The car listed to the right, a rhythmic thump-thump-thump filling the air.

Flat tire.

Of course.

I pulled over onto the gravel shoulder, gripping the wheel until my knuckles ached. This day wasn't just bad; it was starting to feel like someone was stacking the deck against me.

I sat in the driver's seat for a full minute, forehead resting on the steering wheel, trying to decide whether to scream or cry.

I slid my phone out of my pocket, grabbed my bag, and stepped out into the crisp air. The tire was flat, flat, the kind you couldn't limp along on even if you tried.

I sent a text to Hunter and climbed back inside the car. Locking the door, wondering if I should just say fuck it all and take a damn nap in the back seat.

Through the silence, I caught the distant rumble of an engine and glanced up. A bright red Cassidy Automotive truck slowed to a stop behind my car, gravel crunching beneath its tires. My shoulders sagged with relief. No matter how bad the day had gotten, things always felt a little more manageable whenever Hunter showed up. I opened my door and stood at the side of my car, waiting.

He hopped out, his work jacket unzipped over a T-shirt, toolbox in one hand. "You okay?"

"Flat tire," I said, gesturing toward the obvious.

"I got this. Fifteen minutes, okay."

I huffed out a laugh that felt more like relief than anything. "One day, I'll ride to your rescue. I swear. You're going to get a hero complex because of me."

He grinned, setting the toolbox down and crouching by

the tire. "Well, you really do have terrible luck lately. I gotta say. But this—" he trailed off. "The timing of it is—odd. I'm worried about you, Paige."

"Yeah," I hesitated to say anything. I didn't want him to think I was paranoid or to worry too much about me. "I'm starting to think it's not luck," I muttered, glancing toward the horizon where the late morning sun was breaking through thin clouds. "It's starting to feel like—something else."

Hunter's hands stilled for a second, his eyes lifting to mine. "Sabotage? I mean—the freezer was weird. Remember the wiring? Do you think someone is messing with you?"

"I didn't say that," I hedged. "But between the canceled delivery earlier, Danielle showing up, and Eli letting himself into my locked bar—"

"He what?" Hunter's voice rumbled from his chest, low and dangerous.

"He used his key. I made him hand it over."

"That bastard." His jaw worked, but he didn't say anything more, just bent and started loosening the lug nuts.

"You know," I added, "the girls told him they'd be at their grandparents' this weekend. They don't even want to see him right now."

Hunter's expression softened, but his voice stayed steady. "Good. They deserve to feel safe. And so do you. I'm taking this tire to the shop. I brought you a new one."

I didn't answer, not right away. I just watched him work, the easy competence in his movements, the way he filled my space like he was meant to be here.

When he straightened, wiping his hands on a rag, I found myself saying, "Thank you."

He stepped closer, his palm brushing lightly against my arm. "Anytime."

Something in me cracked just enough to lean into him for a second, my forehead resting against his chest. He smelled like soap, coffee, and the faint tang of motor oil, familiar and safe.

"You've had a morning," he murmured.

"That's one way to put it."

His lips brushed my temple, feather light. "Come on. I'll follow you home. Make sure you get there in one piece."

The drive back was short, but I caught sight of him in my rearview every time I glanced up. It was comforting, like a lighthouse following me home instead of waiting on the shore.

I pulled into the driveway, my porch light still on from the morning rush when the girls had left for school. Hunter parked at the curb and followed me to the door.

"Thanks again," I said as we stepped inside.

"You don't have to thank me," he said, hanging his jacket over the back of a chair. "You know this is the part of the pact where I just show up when you need me, right?"

I gave him a look. "Pretty sure that wasn't in the original agreement."

"Guess I'm rewriting the terms." His smile was small, soft, the kind that tugged at places in me I'd been guarding for years.

I dropped my bag onto the counter and leaned back against it. "You want coffee? I'm making coffee."

"Sure," he said, settling into one of the kitchen chairs like this was a perfectly normal mid-morning ritual for us.

While the machine gurgled to life, I let the quiet stretch. Outside, a car drove past, the sound fading quickly into the stillness. My heart was still racing from the day's chaos, but it was slowing, settling into something steadier just from having him here.

Two mugs in hand, I joined him at the table. His fingers brushed mine when he took his cup, lingering just long enough to make me forget what I'd been about to say.

"You look tired," he murmured.

I laughed once, softly. "That's because I am."

He leaned in, resting his forearms on the table. "Then you should let me take care of you for a while."

The way he said it—no bravado, no pity—made my throat tighten. I reached across, my fingers wrapping around his. "You already do. You have no idea how much better I feel because of you. It's everything to me."

For a beat, neither of us moved. Then he stood, tugging gently until I stood too. His arms slid around me, and I let myself sink into him, the warmth of his chest steady against my cheek.

"You've got a lot coming at you," he said quietly. "But you're not alone in any of it."

I tilted my head back to look at him, my hands resting against his ribs. "I know. And I don't take it for granted, Hunter."

His thumb brushed along my jaw, slow and careful, before he leaned down and kissed me. Soft at first, the kind of kiss that could have ended in a sigh, but deepened when my fingers curled into the fabric of his shirt.

When we finally parted, he rested his forehead against mine. "I should go and let you rest before the girls get home."

"I don't want you to," I admitted.

His smile was warm and a little sad. "I want to stay, too. But I've got a car waiting for me at the shop."

He squeezed my hand once, then lifted it to his lips,

pressing a soft kiss to my palm. Gently, he closed my fingers around it, like he was asking me to keep it safe until he could give me the next one. I looked down at my closed hand, heart thudding like he'd left a piece of himself there. Then he stepped back and grabbed his jacket. "Promise to text me if anything feels off. About the bar, Eli, any of it."

"I promise."

He left, his truck rumbling to life, and I stood in the doorway watching until he turned the corner out of sight.

Inside, the coffee sat cooling on the table, the house too quiet. But the echo of his presence was still here, threaded into the walls, into me.

Chapter 20
Hunter

I hadn't made it far before I turned the truck around. Deacon could work on the rebuild without me; he was more than capable. I called him to let him know I was taking the rest of the day off.

"You're heading back to her, aren't you?" he said, not even bothering to hide the laugh in his voice.

"Yeah."

"About damn time, Hunter."

I ended the call and kept driving, every mile feeling longer than it should. I couldn't stop picturing her in that kitchen—hair loose, holding herself together with sheer stubbornness, pretending she wasn't two seconds from breaking or falling asleep on her feet.

Her porch creaked under my boots when I knocked. For a moment, I thought she wouldn't answer. Then the lock clicked, and she opened the door, surprise flashing in her eyes before it softened into something I couldn't name.

"Did you forget something?" she asked.

"Yeah," I said. "This."

Her breath caught, and before she could think of a

reason to stop me, I stepped inside, cupped her face in both hands, and kissed her.

She made a soft, startled sound that went straight through me, then fisted her hands in my jacket and pulled me closer like she'd been waiting for this.

"Hunter," she whispered when we broke apart, her voice unsteady.

"Tell me to go, and I will," I said. "But if you want me to stay…"

"I want you to stay."

I laced my fingers through hers, warm and sure, and led her down the hallway. The house still smelled faintly of coffee. The floorboards groaned under our steps.

Her bedroom was dim, curtains pulled, soft light filtering in just enough to catch the edges of the rumpled quilt. I sat on the edge of the bed, drawing her closer until she stood between my knees. My palms slid up her thighs, over the worn denim of her jeans, before settling at her hips.

I kissed her again, slower this time, tasting her, feeling the little hitch in her breath when my hands moved under her T-shirt. Her cardigan slid from her shoulders, landing somewhere on the floor. My fingers brushed over warm skin, trailing up her sides until she shivered.

"You're so beautiful." I searched her face for doubt, smiling when I didn't see any.

"So are you," she breathed. "I need you."

I reached into my wallet, set the condom on the nightstand, and returned to her.

We undressed each other in pieces, like neither of us could bear to stop touching long enough to get the rest of the way there. Her fingers skimmed over my chest, my stomach, leaving trails of fire in their wake. I dragged her jeans down her legs, kissing every new inch of skin, until she was trembling and whispering my name.

When I lowered her onto the bed, the quilt bunched under her, and the faint scent of laundry soap rose. She looked at me—steady, open, trusting—and it hit me harder than I was ready for.

Her hair spilled across the pillow in a golden halo, her lips parted on a sharp inhale as I slid my hands up the warm, bare skin of her waist. She arched into me instinctively, her thighs tightening around my hips, pulling me closer.

I almost couldn't believe this was real. She made the sweetest little noises when I touched her. The thought that I should have been the only one to hear them pounded in my head along with my heartbeat. But along with that intrusive thought came the knowledge that *this*—what was happening between me and her—was better than anything I'd ever felt in my life, and I knew she felt it too. I was here now, and that was all that mattered.

I needed more.

Bending, I kissed along her jaw, down the column of her throat, tasting the soft pulse beating there. Her fingers tangled in my hair, tugging just enough to make me groan. Every brush of her nails against my scalp, every desperate press of her body against mine, stoked the fire already burning through me.

I dragged my palm down her side, over the curve of her hip, until I could grip her thigh and hitch it higher against me. The sound she made—half sigh, half moan—nearly undid me.

"Hunter..." she breathed, tilting her head back, offering me everything.

I kissed her deeper, tongue sliding against hers, and felt

her shiver beneath me. Her hands fumbled at the hem of my shirt, tugging it upward until I yanked it off, the cool air hitting my heated skin. She traced her fingertips down my chest, lingering lower, until my breath caught and my hips pressed harder into hers.

Even though it had been years, God, since I was a teenager, I knew I would soon come in my pants if I didn't get inside her.

"I need you naked," I growled against the soft skin of her neck.

We moved fast after that, hands pulling at fabric, mouths finding skin. She tugged my belt loose with shaking hands, and the brush of her palm over me had me groaning into her kiss and throbbing in her hands.

Every movement was hungry and reverent all at once, as if I could memorize her body by touch alone. The way she gasped when I kissed the hollow beneath her ear. The way her nails dug into my shoulders when I pressed closer, grinding against her until she was trembling.

Sliding into her was like coming home after years away, a rush of heat and relief. She gasped softly, nails biting into my shoulders as I pressed deeper.

"God, Paige," I groaned, forehead pressed to hers. "Why didn't we know it would be like this? We could have been doing this for years."

Her eyes fluttered open, dark and shining. "I think we were both too scared of losing each other," she whispered, her breath warm against my lips.

I slowed, filling her deep, hip to hip, before stopping to pull her close.

My voice dropped to a softer, raw tone, filled with emotion. It almost hurt to hear the sound of it. I'd never felt more vulnerable in my life. "Remember that night after prom? In the back of my truck. The night of the pact. I almost kissed you then. I wanted to." I remembered it—too well. The quiet night air, the way she'd leaned close like she wanted me to kiss her. I should have done it.

"I would have kissed you back." Her legs tightened around me, pulling me closer. "It was always like that. Always something in the way. Things only changed after the divorce. That's when I finally saw you. Really saw you, like this—with me. Just us."

The words wrecked me. I kissed her again, hard, tasting every ounce of truth in what she said.

We moved together in a rhythm that felt inevitable, like we'd been waiting half our lives for this moment. Every kiss was deeper, every touch hungrier, until she came undone beneath me, crying out my name like it had always belonged on her lips.

I followed her, my release tearing through me as I buried my face against her neck, groaning her name.

Afterward, I stayed inside her as I shifted to my side and let my weight rest into the mattress, keeping her close. The blankets were half-slid to the floor, the air cool against our overheated skin. I tucked her against my chest and pulled the quilt up around us.

For a long moment, we just breathed together, hearts pounding in the same wild cadence. The world outside faded to a hush, nothing left but the tangled sheets and the quiet, aching certainty between us. I stroked her cheek with the back of my hand, memorizing the flushed glow on her skin, the soft curve of her smile.

"I wish we could stay here forever," I murmured, brushing her damp hair back from her face. "Just like this."

She smiled, slow and sleepy, her fingers tracing idle

circles against my skin. "We can't, but I want to," she whispered, voice barely a breath.

I pressed a kiss to her temple, and for the first time in a long time, I didn't feel like I was missing anything. Not anymore.

We took turns in her bathroom to clean up, then got back in her bed.

Chapter 21
Hunter

I watched her as the light slipped in through the bedroom curtains, spilling pale gold across the rumpled quilt and catching in the loose strands of her hair. Outside, the maple tree in her front yard swayed just enough to make the light shift, dappling her skin in warm, uneven patterns.

She was curled against me, bare leg hooked over mine, her cheek resting on my chest like she'd been built to fit there. I traced the smooth length of her spine, slow as I memorized the way she felt under my palm, so soft.

Her hair tickled my chin when I breathed in—lavender shampoo, a hint of her lotion, the warmth of her skin. The quilt was tangled around our waists, soft from years of washing, and her hand was splayed across my ribs like she'd forgotten she'd put it there.

I should've been content. More than content. She was here, in my arms, letting me hold her like I'd always wanted. But a thought had been pressing at the edges of my mind since we'd started seeing each other, and I couldn't quiet it anymore.

I slid my hand up her back, fingertips tracing the curve of her shoulder blade. "Paige?"

"Mmm?" She shifted slightly, her knee sliding higher against my hip, eyes still half-closed.

"Where do we stand? You and me. Can we talk about it, just a little bit? I need to know—I need to know that it's okay to want more."

Her lashes lifted, and for a second, the light caught in her eyes—brown with a golden ring around the edges, sharp and soft all at once. She didn't pull away, but I felt the pause in her body.

She didn't answer.

I kept my voice low, steady. "I need to know what this is to you. I'm in your house, in bed with you. I've been inside your body. And you have to know you're in my heart."

She took a breath and let it out slowly, her gaze holding mine. "I'm with you, Hunter. I am." Her hand flexed lightly against my chest, like she was preparing herself to let me down. "I just don't want to go public. Not yet."

The words settled in my heart like a stone.

I nodded, keeping my expression easy even though something in me tightened. I understood why she wanted to hide what had happened between us, but it still hurt. "Okay."

Her brow furrowed, the line between her eyebrows deepening. "It's not about you. It's about the kids. And the gossip. And—" She looked away briefly, her hair sliding across my arm, "I can't take all of that on top of everything else right now."

"I get it," I said, and I meant it. But it didn't stop the ache in my chest.

Her eyes searched mine. "You're not mad, are you?"

"No," I murmured, brushing my thumb along her jaw,

feeling the faint flutter of her pulse there. "Not mad." I just wished I could tell the whole damn town she was mine and that everyone knew I was hers so I could protect her like I needed to.

She relaxed against me again, tilting her face up. I met her halfway, our mouths brushing first in a slow, testing kiss, then again deeper, her lips parting under mine as her fingers slid up to cup the back of my neck. The way she kissed me made it hard to remember that she wanted to keep this quiet.

When she pulled back, her forehead rested against mine. "I like this," she whispered. "Us. I just need to keep it ours for now. I need to keep it safe."

I pressed my lips to her temple, feeling the warmth of her skin and the faint, steady beat of her heart under my palm. "Ours," I repeated.

She smiled faintly and curled back into my side, her leg still tangled with mine, her hand warm over my heart. Outside, the light faded as the sun slid behind a cloud, leaving the room nothing but shadows and the soft, shifting shapes of us tangled together on the bed.

She didn't hear the part I didn't say—*it's not what I want, but I'll take it if it's all you can give me.*

She shifted against me, sighing in that way she did when she was finally letting herself rest. Her leg slid free, but she kept her hand over my heart, fingers curled loosely like she was holding onto something without realizing it.

"This is just a nap," she murmured, eyes already drifting closed. "I have to be at the bar later. Grandpa's coming over to be with the girls."

I smoothed a strand of hair back from her face, tucking it behind her ear. "I know. I'll make sure you get up."

Her lips curved faintly, like she didn't quite believe I'd

wake her when the time came. "Don't let me sleep too long. No more than twenty minutes."

"I'll try," I said, even though part of me wanted to keep her here until morning.

She let out another slow breath and settled in, the steady rhythm of it telling me she was already half under. I stayed still, memorizing the way she looked like this—quiet, unwound, the furrow between her brows finally gone. She was fucking beautiful.

Her grandfather would show up soon. He'd take care of the girls, and she'd head out to the Twilight Tavern, stepping into her role like she hadn't just been here in my arms, telling me she was mine in every way except the one I wanted most.

I wanted to believe her "for now" meant temporary, that she'd get to a place where she could walk into the bar with me at her side and not care who saw.

For now, I'd take this. Her warmth against me. Her trust.

She made a slight sound in her sleep, curling closer. I pulled the quilt up over her shoulder, my palm resting there, and stared out the window at the shifting light.

I'd do whatever it took to keep this safe.

To keep *her* safe.

Even if it meant lying here in the quiet, holding her, and waiting for the world outside that door to give us a reason to stop hiding.

She slept for almost forty minutes, long enough for the sun to slide to its afternoon angle, pouring pale gold through the curtains. I let her sleep longer, even though she'd told me not to. She needed it more than she realized.

When I finally brushed my hand over her arm and

murmured her name, she blinked awake slowly, confusion softening into recognition.

"What time is it?" she asked, her voice rough with sleep.

"Just after two."

Her eyes widened, and she pushed herself up on one elbow. "Crap. The girls will be home soon."

I sat up with her, the quilt falling to our waists, and watched as she swung her legs over the side of the bed. The light caught in her hair, making it shine, but there was still a heaviness in her movements—like every muscle was remembering the weight she carried.

"You're still tired," I said quietly.

"I'm fine." She reached for her jeans draped over the chair and found her shirt on the floor. "I just need to get myself together before they get home. I've got work tonight."

"Paige..." I started, but she gave me a small smile over her shoulder, more like an apology than reassurance.

"They'll be fine. Grandpa will be here soon to hang out with them while I'm at work."

"I know they'll be fine," I said, watching her pull her hair into a messy knot that was already spilling loose again. "It's you I'm worried about."

She paused, clothes gathered in her arms, one hand on her bathroom door. "I can't stop, Hunter. Not right now."

I nodded, but it didn't make it any easier to watch her keep putting herself last. "I get it. I'm just worried about you, is all."

Her voice softened. "I have to make sure you understand. I'm with you. You know that, right? But I just can't—" she gestured vaguely between us, "—I'm not ready for the whole town to have an opinion about my personal life. Not with Eli playing games."

"I know. I understand." Her repeated words landed harder than I expected, but I kept my face neutral. "I get it."

Her eyes searched mine, like she wanted to be sure I meant it. Then she leaned down, pressing a lingering kiss to my mouth. "Thank you for being here."

She slipped into the bathroom. I found my clothes and quickly dressed.

By the time she came back out and slipped her arms into her jacket and grabbed her bag, I was on my feet, following her into the hallway. Outside, I could hear the faint rumble of a school bus a few blocks away, and I knew the house was about to get loud.

I stood there, hands in my pockets, watching her get ready to greet her girls—still exhausted, still carrying more than anyone should, and still determined to handle it all herself.

And I knew, without question, that something had to give.

The rumble of the bus grew louder, brakes squealing faintly before the sound of voices spilled into the quiet street. She moved toward the front door, tucking her hair behind her ear like she didn't want the girls to guess she'd just woken up from a nap.

Lark was the first through the door, her backpack sliding off one shoulder. She paused, glancing between us. "Hey, Hunter." Her voice carried that sly, sixteen-year-old knowing.

"Hey, Lark. How was school?"

She shrugged and told me it was fine. Then she kicked off her shoes and disappeared toward her room.

Briar followed, her pink knit hat slipping down over one eye. "Hi," she said brightly to me before turning to her mom. "Can I go over to Mia's after dinner?"

"Maybe," Paige said. "But only if Grandpa feels like taking you and picking you up."

Briar grinned and headed down the hall, humming to herself just like Paige often did.

Paige turned to me, a quiet relief in her eyes. "Everything is going to be okay."

"Yeah," I said, and I meant it. Still, the image of her earlier—sleep-mussed and warm in my arms—flashed through my mind, and I wished I could just keep her there, safe, for a little while longer.

She walked me to the door, her hand brushing mine in a soft, secret touch the girls wouldn't see. "I'll see you tonight?" she asked.

"Do you need me?"

Paige didn't answer right away. Her gaze flickered to the hallway, where Briar's laughter mingled with the muffled thud of Lark's door. She squeezed my hand, the gesture fierce for a second, as if she was anchoring herself to me. "Always," she murmured, voice so low I could barely hear. "But I'm not closing alone anymore. I'm exhausted; I can't keep doing it alone." She smiled, and I caught a glimpse of everything she couldn't say—worry lined in the corners of her eyes, hope twisting beneath the surface.

For a moment, the hallway was a passage between worlds: the bright, ordinary life she'd built for her kids and the quiet, aching space where we existed in secret. I wanted to reach for her, to promise I'd never let go, but the sound of Briar calling for her mom snapped us both back. Paige released my hand, stepping away just as the kitchen light spilled across the hardwood.

I nodded, swallowing the urge to linger. "Tonight, then," I said, trying to fill my words with steadiness instead of longing.

She smiled, small and brave. "Tonight," she echoed, and the word seemed to mean more than just a time—it was a hope, a promise, a plea.

"Okay. Goodbye." I stepped outside, the cool air cutting through the lingering heat of her bedroom and glanced back once before heading for my truck. I couldn't shake the feeling that I'd just walked away from something I needed to hold onto tighter.

I drove away with her words echoing in my ears, the sound bittersweet as I reached the edge of her street.

The secret was starting to gnaw at me, leaving bruises no one could see. I told myself it was for her kids, for Paige, for the sake of the fragile peace she'd built. But every time I hid my feelings, it chipped away at something inside me because I craved more. I wanted it all.

I drove the long way home, letting the silence stretch, unsure if I could keep doing this—keeping my feelings a secret when I knew I wore them in every fiber of my being and anyone who saw me with her was bound to figure it out. Rumors were already flying as it was.

As I drove, the sky glowed with the last traces of sunset, painting the world in colors that felt almost too tender for how raw I felt inside. Every mile I put between us seemed to weigh heavier. I wanted to turn back, to say something honest and reckless, like *I love you*, but I kept going, letting routine remind me where I was supposed to belong.

And when I finally turned onto my own street, I still didn't know if I should go to her or ease off until she was settled.

I texted her that I had a migraine. And I went to bed alone. She wasn't closing by herself anymore; she'd be okay without me tonight.

Chapter 22
Paige

It had been a week. Seven whole days without Hunter showing up at closing time, without the creak of the back door announcing him, without that quiet, soothing presence that made the long nights feel special.

We'd texted, sure—short messages.

How was work?

Fine. You?

Busy.

Nothing that hinted at the way his mouth had felt on mine, or the way his arms felt when he had them wrapped around me. It was as if we'd hit pause, only he had the remote and I didn't know how to get it back.

Truth was, I missed him—missed him so much it ached in my chest, like something essential had been taken out and I couldn't breathe right anymore. I felt stuck, tangled up in all the things I couldn't say and all the worries that wouldn't leave me alone. More than anything, I wished I could make my troubles disappear and just be with him, safe and simple, with nothing between us but the way I felt. The idea that I might be hurting him, even without meaning to, made me hate myself a little. I wanted to protect him from all of this, from me, but I didn't know how. The worry ate at me, and every time I thought of him, the more I burned for him. I just wanted to promise him it would be okay, but I didn't know if it would.

I'd taken the day off—something I rarely did—because I couldn't face the thought of being at the bar and not having him show up again.

And now here I was, sitting in Piper's wedding cake bakery having lunch with her like I had nowhere else in the world to be. Something Sweet smelled like heaven—vanilla, buttercream, and the faint tang of espresso drifting from the little coffee counter she had tucked into the corner. The big front windows spilled soft light across the glass cases lined with towering layer cakes, delicate pastries, and the prettiest cupcakes I'd ever seen. A couple at the far table was sharing a slice of strawberry shortcake, and the bell over the door chimed every so often as customers came and went, their chatter mingling with the hum of the mixer in the kitchen.

Piper slid into the chair across from mine, smelling faintly of sugar and spice. She gave me the kind of look that said she was about to dissect my soul. "What's wrong?" she asked, in that deceptively casual tone she used when she was about to dig her heels in.

"Nothing," I said, picking up my coffee.

She arched a brow. "Paige. You look like someone stole your best friend, and by that, I mean Hunter. What's going on?"

I sighed, staring into my cup. "It's nothing. I've just been tired."

Her eyes narrowed. "Tired, huh? Or maybe you're avoiding telling me that he hasn't been around, and it's making you twitchy."

I froze for a second too long, and her grin went feral.

"I knew it," she said, leaning in like we were plotting a jewel heist. "Something happened, and you're going to tell me so I can fix it for you."

"Nothing happened," I lied badly. "We've both just been busy. That's all."

Piper waved a hand. "Busy my ass. The man practically lived at the bar since your divorce. Now he's not coming around, and you're acting like someone stole your emotional support mechanic."

I couldn't help the little huff of a laugh that escaped me. "You're ridiculous."

"I'm *right*," she corrected. Then her expression softened, her voice lowering just enough to feel like a hug. "You like him—a lot. You're probably in love with him. And now he's pulling back, and you don't know why. That's what's bothering you."

I looked down at the swirl of coffee in my mug. "Maybe. Also, how do you know everything?"

I bit my tongue, feeling the sting of truth in Piper's words. Of course, I knew why Hunter was pulling back, even if I'd never said it out loud. The secret I kept between us was a wall only I could see—one I kept fortifying with every excuse, every time I tried not to think about his absence, every time I changed the subject when anyone got too close. Keeping things between us quiet had seemed safer, easier, but when I watched the disappointment flicker in his eyes, it gnawed at me. I told myself I was protecting myself and the kids from Eli's bullshit. But in doing so, I was hurting him, and now I knew it.

"I don't know *everything*, but I can guess." Thankfully, she didn't push the subject. "But you'll tell me everything later because you know I'm here for you, and you also know

I'll do anything you need to help you through this. Right now, we have a birthday-slash-grand reopening to plan. Or rather, I'll let you approve or deny a few things I've already planned."

I blinked. "Wait—*what?*" Only Piper could jump from subject to subject like this.

Before she could answer, my phone buzzed on the table.

A text from Jasper. He should be at the bar getting ready to open for the night.

Jasper: The walk-in cooler must have gone out overnight. Almost everything inside is warm and spoiled. I'm so sorry, Paige.

The bottom dropped out of my stomach. I stared at the words, my throat tightening.

Me: I'll be right there.

So much for a day off.

My first instinct was to call Hunter and tell him what happened, ask if he could take a look, or at least hear his voice. But I didn't.

Because I wasn't sure if I could anymore.

All week, we'd kept in touch—little things, nothing real —but it wasn't the same. Not the easy rhythm that had slipped into my days when he was showing up every night.

Not the warm *I'll see you tonight* that had made me feel safe in ways I hadn't realized I needed.

A swirl of guilt tightened in my chest. Was he struggling with something right now, needing me, and I wasn't there to notice? What did I really mean to him? Was I making things harder by keeping my distance? The silent question pulsed beneath everything: should I let myself be with him, choosing what feels right for us, instead of worrying about Eli and what people might think?

But the answer felt tangled. I wanted to do the right thing, to protect everyone, but I wasn't sure whose happiness I was actually safeguarding. Maybe what mattered most was being honest with myself—and with Hunter— about what I wanted, and letting the rest fall into place.

Now there was space between us. A small space, but enough that I could feel the draft. What if I had pushed him away completely? What if my decision to keep us quiet had sounded more like rejection than self-preservation? What if I'd lost him for good? What if I'd ruined everything? I turned my phone face down on the table, like that could shut the whole thought out.

Piper caught the change in my expression instantly. "What is it?"

"The cooler at the bar died sometime overnight. The food is ruined." My voice came out thin. "I've been fixing things, piece by piece, and this will be a huge hit. It's like I need to babysit that place. Every time I take a day off, something goes wrong."

For a split second, a darker thought swirled through my mind: what if someone had messed with the cooler on purpose? Was it really just an electrical issue, or was there something else going on behind the scenes—something I wasn't seeing? The suspicion made my skin prickle, but after a moment, I shook it off. I was probably just being paranoid, letting stress get the best of me. I forced myself to take a deep breath and focus on what I could control, reminding myself that sometimes things really do just break.

Piper's gaze flicked down to the phone in my lap, then back to my face. There was the faintest twitch at the corner of her mouth—like she knew exactly who I wanted to call but wasn't going to say it out loud. Not yet.

Her hand slid across the table to squeeze mine. "We'll figure it out."

The hum of the bakery filled the pause between us—the whir of mixers in the kitchen, the soft clink of a cake stand being set in the front case. But under it all, there was the same restless pulse in my chest because I wasn't sure if the thing I needed to fix most was the cooler at the bar or the space between me and Hunter.

Piper squeezed my hand once before letting go, her gaze sharpening in that way it always did when she was about to start trouble for my own good.

"Alright," she said, sliding her coffee aside. "We're not letting Eli, a busted cooler, or whatever is going on with Hunter ruin a single thing that we've got planned."

"*We've* got planned?" I lifted a brow. "And how exactly are *we* doing that?"

Her grin was pure mischief. She leaned in, elbows on the table, lowering her voice like she was letting me in on a secret. "Like I said, we'll combine the grand reopening with your birthday. Two birds, one giant glittery stone."

"Oh, no," I said immediately. "I've also been thinking, and absolutely not. Especially now. No way."

"Oh, yes," she countered. "*Especially* now. It'll be perfect. The place will be fixed up—"

"Except for the cooler," I muttered.

"Which *will* be fixed in time for the party. Don't you worry." She steamrolled right over me. "But for tonight, we'll use this nosy town to our advantage. They'll be curious, they'll want to know what's going on, and most importantly, they'll spend their money in your bar so they can get the story firsthand." Her smile softened.

I looked down at my coffee, the steam curling in the air between us. "I don't know if I have the strength for any of this. But I will acknowledge that the gossip angle is legit."

"Totally legit, so we're on for the party. As for now, you need cooler repair money; you and Hunter are the latest news. Use it to your advantage. Start crying before you head out to your car. Trust me. Bawl your eyes out, and the bar will be full tonight."

"But I can't open the kitchen tonight, Piper. I don't even know what I have left to serve. I have to close."

"No, you don't have to close. We'll grab some chips and salsa, nuts, crackers, pretzels, a bunch of veggie trays—basically cheap-ass non-perishable finger food to set out. We'll call it a special. Nobody has to know the cooler broke. It will be okay. I'll call the sisters, and we'll head to the store. We got this."

I took a deep breath and, for just a second, I let myself picture it—the tavern lit up, cheap-ass finger food on the menu, music drifting from the jukebox, people laughing, but most of all, spending money as they watched me for signs of mental distress or a case of the extreme feels. But most of all, I wanted to see Hunter there. But I couldn't picture him now without that hollow space between us.

Piper was still watching me, like she knew exactly what I was thinking. "Let me handle the food for tonight, and I'll have Lucy see if Spencer or any of his brothers know anything about refrigeration," she said. "You just go to work like normal. Yes?"

"Yes." I blew out a slow breath. "Thank you."

Her answering smile was all the confirmation she needed.

By the time I left Something Sweet, the sugar and spice scent clinging to my sweater felt like a cruel joke because I knew my bar would be a full-on olfactory assault when I got there. My phone buzzed in my pocket as I crossed the street toward my car.

Jasper: It's completely dead. Most of the food is bad. Smells pretty gross in here.

I stopped halfway to the driver's side, staring down at the screen. The cold knot in my stomach tightened with every word. The bar was cursed, or maybe it was me. One step forward, ten steps back.

I wanted to text Hunter. My thumb even hovered over his name. But I couldn't bring myself to hit send. Not when things between us were already stretched thin and awkward. Not when I was the one who told him I didn't want to be public.

If he came now, I wouldn't know if it was because he wanted to be near me or because I'd asked for help. And I didn't want his presence to feel like a favor. So I slid my phone back into my pocket, jaw tight, and drove toward the tavern.

By the time I pulled into the gravel lot, I could already picture the mess inside. The heavy stench of spoiled food, the empty shelves. Another hit to the budget. Another reason for Eli to add to his list of reasons to mess with me if he found out. I shoved the thought down and got out of the car.

Inside the tavern, the air was thick with the smell of spoiled meat and dairy. Warm blue cheese reeked, and I always had a lot of it. I pressed the back of my hand to my mouth, breathing through my nose as I headed into the storage area and stepped toward the walk-in.

The door hung open. The cooler was silent. Too silent.

"Jasper?" I called.

He poked his head out from the back room, face grim. "I tried the breaker, nothing. This thing is done."

I stared at the racks—empty trays, a few containers sweating in the heat, things I'd bought with the last of my monthly budget. "Everything is ruined."

"Not everything. I hauled the worst to the dumpster, mostly chicken wings and wilted produce. The blue cheese smell was heinous when I walked in. The stuff that was defrosting in there was still mostly frozen, so I jammed it into the deep freeze. We just have to air the place out. It will be okay."

My throat felt tight. "Thanks."

But even as I said it, my phone buzzed again. I half expected Hunter's name, even though I hadn't messaged him. Instead, it was Piper.

Piper: You okay?

Paige: Nope.

Piper: I'll be there momentarily with
reinforcements!!!

Paige: Do me a favor and don't tell Hunter.
I'll tell you everything later. Please.

Piper: Anything you need.

I wanted to talk to Hunter without the broken cooler in the middle. I wanted him for more than his handyman/hero thing, and I didn't want to take advantage of his kindness anymore.

I watched the message thread blink out, then slumped against the counter. The hum of the deep freeze was the only sound left in the kitchen—a brittle, anxious noise that reminded me that it might also be on its last legs. Hunter had repaired it, but it was old; who knows how long it would last?

Outside, dusk pressed against the windows; the air was heavy with that lingering, sour smell, no matter how wide I opened the door. I thought about Piper and her promise of reinforcements, wondered who she'd bring, and worried a little about the parade of sympathy that might march into my cramped little world.

I wiped my hands on a towel and tried to push back the rising panic. The cooler was just an appliance, I told myself. But the stakes felt bigger: the inventory, the money wasted, the reputation I'd fought to build from nothing. It was all me now. I was no longer behind the scenes, as I had been when I was married.

I closed my eyes, drew in a shaky breath, and forced myself to remember everything I'd already survived—messier breakages, bigger disappointments, my freaking divorce. This was just a cooler, just a day. I could handle it.

"Come on, Paige. You can do this," I muttered, pressing the towel to my chest like it might soak up the panic knotting there.

I dragged out the old box fan from behind the mop sink, its cord knotted and its blades dusty from last summer. Setting it in the doorway, I cranked it up to high, letting the noisy gust scatter the heavy air toward the street. It wasn't much, but it made the space feel a little less stifling.

Jasper poked his head in from the back, sleeves rolled. "Need a hand up here?" he asked, the hint of a smile undercutting the worry in his eyes. Without waiting for my answer, he moved to open the side windows. Then together, we worked silently—him wiping down the bar and tables with heavily scented lemon cleaner and me going to work on the floor.

Little by little, the smell dissipated, and I felt better about tonight.

Chapter 23
Hunter

Spencer was elbow-deep in a box of tools when I walked into the shop. The familiar smell of grease and metal was grounding, but I knew by the look on his face that whatever came out of his mouth next wasn't going to sit right.

"The cooler at Paige's place is dead," he said, not even looking up. "Piper called Lucy, Lucy told me. It was a game of "Darlington Sister Telephone." Thought you should know. I'm going over there to take a look."

The wrench slipped in my hand. "She didn't call me."

"Nope." He cracked open a soda and leaned back on the workbench. "You've been keeping your distance, huh? I mean, that's what I heard."

I didn't answer. Not right away. I tried to ignore the way my chest tightened at Spencer's words. I didn't need reminders—every hour, every moment I spent alone, Paige's absence filled my life like static. I kept my head down, sorted my tools into a bag, and pretended the conversation was strictly about broken appliances.

Spencer shrugged, the kind of gesture that didn't need translation. "She'll reach out when she's ready."

I wanted to believe him. But it felt like there was a wall between me and Paige, built out of all the things unsaid and the space she'd asked for.

Still, when Spencer grabbed his keys and gave me that look—the one that said, *Don't be an idiot*—I found myself falling in behind him like always. The drive over was silent except for the clink of tools in the back seat, the unspoken worry about how Paige was holding up.

The tavern was quiet when we drove up, not yet open for business. I knew she was here. I saw her car in the lot when we drove around to the back to park. I hesitated, fighting the urge to go see her. Instead, I focused on the task —hopping out of Spencer's truck, gathering our tools, anything to keep my hands busy and my mind off the ache I carried in her absence.

Spencer gave me a long look. "You think staying away from her is going to make your feelings any less obvious?"

My jaw tightened. "I'm not staying away. I'm just giving her what she asked for. Privacy. Space. Every time I walk into that bar, I feel like everyone in there can read me. She doesn't want that right now, so I'm trying to respect it."

He shot me a look like he was calling bullshit. "Fine. But come with me anyway. We'll get the cooler running before she loses any more of her inventory."

I followed him. Because staying away was one thing— but knowing she was hurting and not doing anything about it was something I couldn't live with.

When we slipped in through the rear door, luckily, the smell was contained to the trash. Inside, there was nothing but the faint traces of cleaner and the familiar echo of quiet before opening.

I knelt in front of the busted cooler, the tools heavy in my hands as I surveyed the mess. Wires poked out from the back panel—some frayed, others pulled loose like someone had been searching for a quick fix without caring where each piece belonged. It didn't look accidental. More like frustration, or maybe someone trying to cover their tracks. This was like a bad sequel to the freezer repair. But this time I was sure it wasn't an accident.

"I keep thinking someone is fucking with her," I mumbled. "Or whoever tried to fix it is just plain stupid. This is almost the same as the freezer, but more obvious. The freezer is so old it could have been just worn out."

"Huh?" Spencer knelt to look over my shoulder. "Oh shit. Do you think Jasper tried to fix it? Or did he screw with it? What are you thinking?"

"No idea." I was tightening a connection when the door creaked. "He doesn't seem the type to fuck with her. But what do I know?"

"Spencer, did you—" Paige's voice cut off. Then, sharper: "Hunter?"

I straightened, caught in her stare. Her hair was pulled up in a messy knot, with a few curly tendrils hanging down. Her snug tank top said, "Beauty is in the eye of the beer holder."

She was the most beautiful woman I'd ever seen.

Fuck, I wanted her. Time seemed to slow as I met her startled gaze. Her name caught on my tongue—too intimate, too raw—so I just nodded instead. Spencer, never one for subtlety, sidestepped out of the way, but I could feel him watching as Paige lingered in the doorway, torn between leaving us in secret and risking something by stepping forward.

I set the wrench down and wiped my hands, searching

for words that didn't sound like apologies or confessions or begging. Paige's eyes flicked to the cooler, then back to me, uncertainty warring with something softer. She hung in the threshold, the weight of unspoken things hovering between us like humidity before a storm.

"I didn't expect to see you here," she managed, her voice a little rough around the edges. I started to answer, but she glanced at the tools, the tangled wires, then at Spencer, as if to remind herself she wasn't alone with me.

Spencer cleared his throat, trying to cut the tension. "It's not as bad as it looks, I promise. Well, unless you're the health inspector. The dumpster is pretty rank out there."

That got the faintest hint of a smile from Paige—a flicker, then gone. The air shifted, just enough for her to take a step in, boots scuffing along the battered linoleum.

Uncertainty flickered across her face. I straightened, wiping sweat from my brow, and tried to read her—tried to see past that armor she wore whenever she felt cornered. The silence pressed in, thick as the heat from the dead cooler.

Spencer stood up, dusted his hands on his jeans, and said nothing. He watched us. Concerned as he realized that whatever was broken in the tavern wasn't just wires and coolant lines, but the invisible current running between Paige and me.

Paige stepped closer, the floor creaking under her boots. She glanced at the mess, at me, and for a heartbeat, her resolve slipped. It was there in the way she tucked a strand of hair behind her ear, in the way her voice faltered.

"You didn't have to come," she said, softer now, almost vulnerable. "I didn't want to take advantage—"

I shook my head, cutting her off. "I couldn't stay away. Not when you needed help."

She hesitated, conflicted, then nodded toward the cooler. "Is it fixable?"

"Yeah, we got it," I said, voice low. "At least temporarily."

She lingered, arms crossed, as if she might say more. But instead, she just watched—the silence between us tighter than any wire I'd spliced. Spencer rattled through the toolbox, grumbling under his breath, but it only made the tension more pronounced.

Paige let out a small breath, like she was weighing what would happen if she let me back in. I wished I could promise her things would go back to normal, but some breaks didn't mend with pliers and patience. Still, I met her gaze—steady, open, waiting for whatever came next.

For a second, the only sound was Spencer muttering to himself as he dug through the parts. Paige stood a little straighter, her arms crossed, but I caught the guilt in her eyes before she masked it.

"I—can we talk for a minute?" She tilted her head toward the back door, and I followed her out.

We stood there in silence. Her mouth opened. Then closed. She hugged her arms around her middle and took a deep breath in.

It was miserable. I'd never felt awkward around her like this. Not ever. Not even when we started having feelings for each other. "I'm trying to do what you asked," I said finally. "Keep things quiet. Stay out of the way. But it's not easy, Paige. You have no idea how hard it is for me to act like nothing's changed between us."

Her throat worked, like she was swallowing words she didn't want to say. Or maybe couldn't say.

"I'm not asking you to pretend," she said softly. "I just need time. I'm not ready for everyone to see."

I nodded, even though the ache in my chest made it hard to breathe. "Then I'll keep giving you time. It's okay, I swear." It wasn't. But it was my problem, not hers. She'd been nothing but clear about what she needed.

From inside the back room, Spencer muttered a satisfied, "There we go." The hum of machinery filled the silence between us, low and steady.

I wiped my hands on my jeans and looked at her one more time. She was still watching me, her arms folded, like she was trying to hold herself together. I wanted to reach for her. To close the gap. Instead, I backed toward the door.

"I'll get out of your hair," I said, forcing my voice steady.

She didn't stop me. Just stood there, watching, her eyes saying everything she couldn't before she turned and went back inside the back room.

Her silence pressed heavily on my heart like I could feel it. She was hurting me without trying to, and she knew it. The fact that she knew what she was doing to me hurt. But I shoved it aside because it wasn't her fault. It was the situation. Still, I didn't know how much more I could take. I didn't wait for her to call out a goodbye. I couldn't. If I stood there another second, I'd go back in there and reach for her, and that wasn't what she wanted. Not now.

The back door opened, then creaked shut behind me, the cold air slapping harder than it should have.

"Hey," Spencer said. "Take my truck. I'll get a ride from Lucy." He gave me his keys.

"Thanks."

"I'll ask around about Jasper. I'll figure this out. Go home. I got this. I'll call you if I find anything out."

"I—thank you. I can't be here right now. Watch her, please. I want you to help me install some cameras. Something isn't right here, Spence. I'm worried—"

"I got this. I'll keep an eye on her, and I won't leave her alone. I'll text Brody about cameras, okay? We'll take care of it. You go home and get some rest."

"Yeah, thanks. Appreciate it." I made it to the truck without looking back, even though every part of me burned to. Driving home felt wrong. Like I'd left something vital behind, like I'd left *her* behind.

But I trusted Spencer. She would be okay.

My hands gripped the wheel tight enough to ache, the leather warm under my palms. The roads blurred into one long stretch of gray, the late afternoon light cutting sharp lines across the street as I drove.

By the time I pulled into my driveway, I was wound so tight my jaw ached. The house was dark. I went inside, dropped the keys on the counter, and paced the length of the kitchen. Then the living room. Back again. Every step felt like it should be taking me somewhere, back to her, back to what I'd left behind. But it didn't. It just circled me right back into my own frustration.

A soft, plaintive meow curled out of the silence, and I looked down to find Ozzy weaving around my ankles. His yellow eyes tracked me as I paced, his tail flicking with every turn. Every time I paused, he'd butt his head against my shin, insistent, like he could sense the storm rattling inside me.

"Hey, buddy," I muttered, reaching down to scratch behind his ears. He purred, loud and hopeful, but when I moved away, he trailed after me, meowing again—a little accusing, a little worried.

I tried sitting on the couch, elbows braced on my knees, staring at the floor. It lasted two minutes before I was up again, restless energy buzzing in my veins. My hands itched, wanting to fix something, to put myself to work, but all I could picture was her face when she caught me in that cooler. That flicker of guilt in her eyes. The way she let me go without reaching for me.

I wanted to be angry. It would've been easier than this slow, gnawing ache. But there was no anger in me. Just the truth: I couldn't be near her without my feelings spilling out, written all over my face. And she wasn't ready to see them.

I had to be okay with waiting for her to feel the way I did. Or lose her.

So waiting was what I would do.

Ozzy, undeterred by my wandering, leaped onto the back of the couch with fluid feline certainty. He settled above me, his small body crouched like a sentry, yellow eyes fixed and unblinking. Every time I shifted, he pivoted too, tail draped and twitching, a silent question mark in the dim room. I slumped against the cushions, feeling the weight of his gaze—a gentle pressure, a quiet urging not to run from the moment.

I'd never felt this kind of pain before—wanting what I couldn't have when I knew it was everything right in the world.

The hours dragged. I reheated leftovers I couldn't taste. I tried a beer but left it sweating on the table half-full. I even flipped on the TV, but the noise grated, and I shut it off again.

By midnight, I was stretched out on the couch, staring at the ceiling with sightless eyes. All I could see and feel were memories of her voice, her eyes, her touch. Recalling how it felt to kiss her for the first time burned hot in my chest, so vivid it kept me awake long after I finally closed my eyes.

Somewhere in between one restless thought and the next, Ozzy climbed down from his perch. He pressed his warm, solid weight against my chest, spinning in a tight circle before settling with his head tucked into the hollow of my neck. His purrs vibrated through my bones—steady, comforting. I curled an arm around him, holding him close, letting the rhythm of his breathing coax the frantic edge from my own. For a while, I just lay there, listening to the quiet buzz of his purr and the echo of the thoughts I couldn't quite get out of my head.

I'd waited years for her. I could wait longer. But tonight, I let myself feel it—the hollow ache of walking away from the only person who had ever felt like mine, like home. I knew sleep wasn't coming anytime soon.

The ceiling was just as blank at three a.m. as it had been at midnight. At five, I gave up pretending sleep was coming and dragged myself into the shower. The water beat down hard and hot, but it didn't wash anything away.

By the time I walked into the shop, the early light was spilling across the gravel, thin and gray, the kind of dawn that made everything look half-finished. Deacon was already in the bay, grease on his hands, head bent under the hood of an old Chevy. Spencer leaned against the workbench with a cup of coffee, watching me like I'd already given myself away.

"You look like hell," Spencer said, voice dry.

"Thanks," I muttered, dropping my jacket on the back hook.

Deacon glanced up and wiped his hands on a rag. "Couldn't sleep?"

"Didn't," I said. And that was all I gave them.

I could feel their eyes on me, but they didn't push. We'd been raised knowing when to pry and when to leave well enough alone. Still, Spencer's face softened into something quieter, something knowing, and Deacon's jaw tightened like he already had an idea where my head had been all night.

I threw myself into work—bolts, grease, the steady rhythm of tools in my hands. But the motions didn't quiet my thoughts. Every turn of the wrench, every scrape of metal just brought me back to her. The way she'd looked at me last night. Like she wanted to let me in but couldn't bring herself to do it. Like my feelings were too much for her right now, and she wasn't ready to carry them.

I tried to swallow the lump in my throat, but it stuck.

Deacon passed me a socket set, watching me carefully. "Hunter," he said finally, low. "You don't have to tell us, but don't burn yourself out trying to carry something alone."

I nodded, not trusting my voice.

By midmorning, the shop was loud—air compressors hissing, classic rock spilling from the radio, Deacon cursing at a stripped bolt—but underneath it all, I still heard her.

Chapter 24
Paige

It had been a few days. Long, restless, twisting-in-circles kind of days.

I missed Hunter. I missed the way he filled a room without even trying, the quiet steadiness of him, the way I felt less alone whenever I was with him. And now, with him keeping his distance, it felt like I was being pulled in too many different directions at once.

Eli's bullshit threats. My feelings for Hunter—loud, consuming, impossible to ignore, no matter how hard I tried. And then the kids, the center of everything, the ones I had to protect above all else. But most of all, I needed too much. I was unsettled, my life was in turmoil, and I had to stop taking advantage of him.

I knew I'd hurt him. I'd seen it in his eyes the night the cooler broke, even though he hadn't said the words out loud. And I was so angry with myself for it. I hated that I was too scared to give him what he deserved. The guilt sat heavy on my chest, pressing down with every quiet moment I had to myself.

When I headed to work that morning, I wasn't sure

what to expect. The bar had become such a minefield—problems with equipment, Eli's shadow hanging over me, and now Hunter's absence. For the first time in weeks, I didn't know if I even wanted to unlock the door.

But when I pulled into the gravel lot, the lights were already on.

Piper. The party. How could I have forgotten?

Inside, I froze just past the doorway.

Piper and Lucy were there, moving around like they owned the place, half-buried in decorations. Piper balanced on a chair, looping brand new twinkle lights across the beams above the bar, while Lucy fussed with a bouquet of balloons and muttered about proportions. The tavern smelled faintly of leather and lemon cleaner. It looked different. It looked almost new.

Brand new light fixtures glowed overhead, brighter and warmer than the old ones. From the back, appliances that were clearly not mine hummed steady and strong, no longer threatening to drain me dry with repair costs. And a new margarita machine, gleaming, shining, and *quiet*—not the banshee-voiced relic I'd been cursing for months—sat proudly in its place. Even the jukebox was new, flashing with playlists that weren't stuck somewhere back in 1987.

"Surprise," Piper called without turning around. "Don't freak out, just go with it."

I slipped out of my jacket and set it over a barstool, my eyes wide as I took it all in.

"Spencer and Deacon were here all night," Lucy explained, not even trying to hide her grin. "Brody and Tucker were here for a while, too. The cooler is fine. Spencer got new parts, and they'll last for a long time. But the freezer was crap, so now you have a new one—happy birthday from me! They installed the new light fixtures and even programmed the jukebox. Don't ask how they did it all so fast. Cassidy magic."

My throat tightened. Cassidy magic. No—*Piper* magic. God, I freaking loved my sister. She hopped down from the chair, dusting off her hands. "See? You thought I was just being bossy about this party, but it wasn't about cake and balloons. It was about *this*. You never ask for help, so I asked for you."

I stared at her, my eyes filling up with tears faster than I could blink them away. "What?"

She spread her arms like she was unveiling a masterpiece. "This was the plan all along. New lights, working appliances, a margarita machine that doesn't sound like it's clawing itself out of the grave, a jukebox with songs from this century. The party is just the excuse. You'd never let us do it otherwise. Happy birthday, grand opening, Paige-is-forty-extravaganza day!"

Lucy smirked at her. "I thought you were calling it emotional camouflage day."

I let out a shaky laugh, gripping the edge of the bar. Emotional camouflage. Of course, she'd come up with that.

Because it was true, I'd waved off offers, insisted I could handle everything by myself. But now, standing here, surrounded by things I hadn't dared to hope for, I couldn't deny how much lighter I felt.

And underneath it all, I could see Hunter. Not here, not looking at me with those gorgeous blue eyes, but in the quiet fixes, the mended places, the things repaired and replaced without me asking. My chest ached with guilt and longing.

Piper was talking about centerpieces and cake, but all I could think about was how badly I wanted to see him. How badly I wanted to tell him he mattered. That maybe I was finally ready to stop hiding how I really felt about him and let everyone know we were together.

I was still staring at the new lights and contemplating my life when the front door banged open and a whirlwind of voices came pouring in.

"Delivery for the birthday girl!"

My mother swept in first, holding a garment bag nearly as tall as she was. Grandma trailed right behind her, sequins already glittering on her cardigan like she'd taken Piper's assignment to sparkle to heart. Piper clapped her hands and squealed as if she hadn't orchestrated all of this from the beginning.

"Sparkles," my mother declared, laying the bag across a booth with all the gravity of someone setting down crown jewels. "Wait until you see it. It reminded me of your prom dress. Plus, it's not a party without sparkles, don't you think?"

"Or heels," Grandma added, placing a shoebox on top with a flourish. "We never got to go shopping together, so we brought shopping to you."

I blinked at them, throat tightening as they unzipped the bag and pulled out a purple sequined dress. It was low cut and sexy as hell. I hadn't worn something like this in ages.

"This is too much," I protested, pointing at the neckline. "I can't pull something like this off. I'm not that girl anymore."

"You sure as heck can. And you are that girl. You'll always be that girl, don't let anyone take it from you," Grandma countered. "You need to go try it on. I'll fight you if you don't."

"Okay," I whispered. I hesitated, fingers ghosting over

the dress's sequins as if they might spark some forgotten version of myself.

Piper tugged at my elbow, urging me toward the bathroom with a conspiratorial grin. "Come on, Paige. You need at least one dramatic entrance tonight."

Before I could gather my thoughts and go try it on, the door opened again.

"Coffee run," Eliza sang, sweeping in with a cardboard tray. She pressed a hot cup into my hand and kissed my cheek. "Extra cream, extra sugar, because it's a party day. Happy birthday, big sister."

Behind her came Cara, cheeks pink from the cold, holding a bouquet of fresh flowers—wild, bright, colorful. She set them on the bar with a smile. "For good luck."

I pressed my palm to the lid of the coffee cup, warmth seeping into my fingers, my throat thick. I'd spent so long holding everything together on my own that I'd forgotten what it felt like to be surrounded. To be carried instead of carrying.

Piper caught my eye, her smile softening. "Paige? Are you okay?"

I swallowed hard, blinking fast. "I'm just overwhelmed. In the best way."

Mom crossed over, looping an arm around my shoulders, while Grandma fussed with the hanger, muttering about necklines and how you're never too old to sparkle.

The whole bar buzzed with life, warm and bright, and for the first time in weeks, I felt something I hadn't let myself feel—hope. And love. So much love, it pressed against my ribs until I thought I might burst. They were here. All of them. For me.

But somewhere under all of that warmth, beneath the sparkle and laughter and happy chatter, was Hunter. Still missing. Still, the ache I couldn't quite ease. He should be here tonight.

Then my grandma, as casual as could be, said, "Your grandpa is on his way to pick up the girls from school. Noah texted—he's halfway here. Want me to call anyone for you? I'm sure he'd drop everything and come."

"Grandma," I whispered. "I don't know what to do."

"Yes, you do."

Chapter 25
Hunter

The shop was quiet for a Friday night, too quiet. Usually by now, Deacon would have music going in the back bay, or Spencer would be giving me grief about how long it took me to finish a job. Instead, it was just the tick of the clock on the wall. The others were off, getting ready for Paige's party.

Spencer leaned against the workbench, arms crossed, grease still smeared on his shirt. "Still nothing," he said. "Checked the recordings twice. Whoever's messing with the tavern hasn't shown their face yet."

I rubbed the back of my neck. The laptop sat open between us, a handful of recorded camera feeds glowing back at me—the kitchen, the storage room, the back hallway. Paige didn't know he had set them up last night, and it killed me to keep that from her. But until we caught someone in the act, telling her would only make her worry more.

"Could be Eli," I muttered. "Could be somebody he sent."

Spencer nodded. "That's what I think, too. We'll catch

him if it is, then this will all be over." He ran a hand through his hair with a sigh and looked at me sideways. "You gonna head over there? It's the party tonight."

I didn't answer right away. My hands were restless, wiping down a wrench that didn't need it.

"Hunter," Spencer pressed. "It's her birthday. Don't you think—"

"I can't." My voice came out rougher than I meant.

He frowned. "Can't? Or won't?"

I set the wrench down harder than I should've. "She doesn't want us public, Spence. Doesn't want the town talking. If I walk in there tonight, everyone will know how I feel. And that's not what she asked of me."

Spencer studied me for a long second. "So you're just going to sit here in this shop and mope while she blows out candles without you?"

My chest tightened. The picture of it rose up in my mind—Paige under those new lights, the jukebox humming, Piper probably shoving a fancy drink in her hand, her family around her, laughing, loving her.

And me? Not there. Not beside her where I wanted to be.

"She deserves to celebrate without me making things harder," I said finally, my throat tight. "She's going through enough."

Spencer's jaw worked, but he didn't argue. He just grabbed his jacket off the hook. "Suit yourself. I'll be there, keeping an eye on things. Deacon too. Tucker has the kids tonight. Brody and Dad are on their way. Are you sure you don't want to come with me?"

"I can't," I all but growled. "Look at me, I'm a damn mess over her." It was as close to honest as I'd been with him.

I hesitated, caught between the urge to go with him and the ache in my chest that kept me rooted to the spot. My eyes drifted to the birthday card tucked beneath a pile of invoices on the workbench—a card I'd bought weeks ago, intending to write something clever or sweet, but every time I tried, the words dried up in my throat.

I picked it up, flipping it between my fingers, tracing the embossed edges. This feeling was a living thing, coiling tighter with every second.

Some part of me wanted to believe I was doing the right thing—giving her the space she asked for, not making a scene, not forcing her to choose. But another part, stubborn and hopeful, kept whispering that maybe she wanted me there, even if she'd never say it out loud. Maybe I should make the choice for both of us and let my feelings show.

I let the card drop back down and scrubbed a hand over my hair, the familiar smells of oil and metal grounding me, even as everything else felt uncertain.

"Shit," he finally said. "I understand. I'm sorry."

I nodded, grateful and gutted all at once.

"I get it, I do," He said as he reached the door. "I understand why you're holding back. But don't wait too long. She might need you more than you think."

The door shut behind him, leaving me with nothing but the glow of the laptop in the dark. I sank onto the stool by the bench and dragged my hands over my face. I should be there. But all I could do was sit in this damn shop, watching the clock tick, listening to the empty silence, and wondering how much longer I could keep trying to pretend I didn't want more.

I shut the laptop with a decisive click before I grew tempted to switch to the live feed. I did not need to see her having fun without me. And watching her without her knowledge would be wrong and creepy. Not to mention pathetic and sad.

My mind wandered back, like it always did lately, to that night years ago—the night of the pact. We'd been young, reckless, full of cupcakes and prom-night promises. *If we're not married by forty. We'll marry each other.* I had laughed when she said it, but even then, I'd wanted her more than I ever let on. More than I had ever been willing to admit to myself.

When I brought it up again a few weeks ago, I hadn't meant it as a proposal. Not exactly. But I had meant it as a reminder. Of what we had back then, our friendship. Of what we could have if we tried for more. I wanted her to remember the way we used to be together—comfortable, steady, like the world made more sense when it was just the two of us. I wanted her to see that we'd always been good, and that maybe, we could be great now. I leaned back, staring at the ceiling, restlessness already pressing in on me like a storm I couldn't outrun.

I wanted her. Not just for tonight, not just for the quiet moments after closing the bar. I wanted all of it. Her kids. Her chaos. Her mornings and her bad moods and her stubborn streak that could level a man if he wasn't ready for it.

But she didn't want the town knowing. She didn't want *us* in the open.

And if that was what she needed, then I'd grit my teeth and give it to her. Even if it meant sitting here in this empty shop, wanting her so badly it hurt.

The clock ticked on. Spencer's truck had long since rumbled out of the lot, heading toward the tavern. The hum of the heater filled the silence.

I dragged a hand over my face, ready to stand up and

lock everything down for the night, when my phone buzzed in my pocket.

I pulled it out, not expecting much. Probably Deacon, checking in about tomorrow's schedule.

But it wasn't.

It was her.

Paige: You should come tonight. Please. I want you here. With me.

The words blurred for a second before I blinked them clear. My heart gave one hard, uneven thud.

Chapter 26
Paige

The tavern had never looked like this before. It was close to perfect. Exactly like I'd always envisioned it. Twinkle lights glowed from the rafters, softening every corner. The new light fixtures gleamed overhead, casting warm pools over the polished bar and the tables Piper had insisted on covering in purple runners and little vases of fresh flowers. The jukebox—brand new and loaded with updated music—hummed with a mix of old favorites and songs that made people laugh in delight when the first notes hit.

Lark and Briar were in the middle of the room, giggling and dancing with my grandma, their hair curled and shiny under the lights. Noah had made it home just in time. He was standing near the pool table with Grandpa, the two of them watching the chaos like it was better than TV.

And me? I was in the purple dress my mom had insisted on buying, sequins catching the light every time I moved. The heels were higher than I usually dared to wear, but somehow, they worked. Piper had teased me mercilessly while she zipped me into it, saying if this didn't make me look like a woman who was forty and fabulous and finally ready to live again, nothing would.

The place was full—friends, neighbors, my regular customers, the people who'd seen me at my lowest and still showed up anyway. Laughter, chatter, and the clinking of glasses filled the air. For the first time in months, it didn't sound like pressure. It sounded like joy.

And then the door opened.

The hum of conversation didn't exactly stop, but it shifted. Heads turned. A ripple of attention moved through the crowd as he walked in—broad shoulders, dark jacket, his hair a little messy like he'd run a hand through it one too many times.

I felt it too—the way the whole place seemed to tilt toward him. People loved him here. Admired him. Trusted him. But to me, it was more than that. It was the way my heart lurched like it had just recognized home. I didn't think. I couldn't. I just ran to him. Ran *home*.

Past the tables, past the bar where Piper was grinning like she already knew what I was about to do. Past the cluster of women near the jukebox who had started whispering behind their hands, eyes fixed on him.

He hadn't spotted me yet—he was scanning the room, taking it all in. But when his gaze landed on me, it softened, like the weight of the whole night had just eased off his shoulders.

That was all it took.

I ran straight up to him, heels clicking on the worn wood floor, the dress shimmering with every step. And before anyone could start speculating—or maybe because I knew they already were—I slid my hand up his chest, rose on my toes, and kissed him.

Not a quick, shy brush of lips. A real kiss. One that left

no room for doubt. Hunter Cassidy was mine, and it was time to claim him like he deserved.

The tavern erupted in cheers, laughter, and a couple of whistles. But all I felt was the warmth of him, steady and sure, kissing me back like we'd never paused, never doubted, never stopped wanting this.

When I finally pulled back, breathless and flushed, I didn't care who had seen. For once, I didn't care about the whispers, the gossip, the risks. All I cared about was him.

He looked at me then, and in his eyes I saw everything—love so deep it felt like an anchor, threaded through with longing as if he'd been waiting for this moment for ages. Relief flickered across his face, softening the tension in his jaw, settling in the curve of his lips as if just seeing me had put every piece back in place. It was all there, plain as day, and the world seemed to narrow down to the connection humming quietly between us, undeniable and whole.

And then he kissed me.

His lips were warm, familiar in a way that still managed to steal my breath. When I broke the kiss, I stayed close, my hand lingering on his chest, the rise and fall of it beneath my palm reminding me he was just as rattled as I was.

The room blurred around us—clinking glasses, laughter, someone starting up another round of "Happy Birthday" in the corner—but it all faded under the pulse in my ears.

I'd done it. I'd kissed him in front of everyone. My best friend. The man who had shown up for me again and again, who had fixed my bar and my freezer and maybe even pieces of my heart without asking for anything in return. And now everyone knew.

I should've been panicked. Terrified of what Eli could do, of what gossip would spin out of this. But as I looked up into Hunter's eyes—those warm, beautiful, blue eyes soft-ening in the glow of the tavern lights—all I felt was relief.

The cheer from the crowd rose again, pulling me back into the moment. Piper was outright beaming from behind the bar, raising her glass in a mock toast before mouthing, *finally*. My mom and grandma were standing near the cake with the girls, clapping like they'd just witnessed a wedding instead of a kiss. Even Noah, who was usually too cool to react to anything, was grinning at me from across the room.

I swallowed hard, blinking against the sting of tears. Gratitude, joy, fear—they all tangled together, hot and messy in my chest.

But when Hunter's hand slid over mine, his thumb brushing once against my knuckles, everything quieted inside me. For the first time in a long time, I let myself stand there and simply soak it in.

"I missed you. I'm sorry," I whispered.

Hunter leaned down, his breath brushing against my ear over the noise. "Come with me."

It wasn't a question. But it wasn't a demand either. Just that quiet, steady tone he always used when he knew I needed space. I nodded before I could think better of it.

The room buzzed with chatter and music as we threaded our way through. People smiled, clapped me on the back, raised their glasses in teasing acknowledgment, but I barely heard them. My hand was in Hunter's, warm and strong, guiding me past the jukebox and down the short hallway toward the back.

We slipped into my little office-slash-storage room, the door clicking shut on the hum of voices. It was quiet here, shadows stretching long over the desk stacked with invoices, the scent of birthday cake and spilled beer lingering faintly in the air.

My heart was still racing, half from the kiss, half from the fact that I'd done it in front of everyone. I pressed a hand to my stomach, trying to steady myself.

Hunter watched me with hot eyes, leaning against the desk, his shoulders broad in the low light. His expression was unreadable, but his eyes, god, his eyes gave him away. Soft, careful, and so full of something I didn't know how to name without cracking open.

"I can't believe I just did that," I murmured, shaking my head. "Was that okay?"

"Are you serious right now?" He chuckled darkly. "It was more than okay. It was everything I've ever wanted."

The corner of my mouth tugged, a shaky, almost-smile. "Half the town probably thinks we're engaged now," I teased to lighten the mood.

His mouth curved just a little. "Let 'em."

I laughed then, short and nervous, but it loosened something in my chest. I crossed my arms, then dropped them again because it felt too much like shielding myself.

"You okay?" he asked after a beat, his voice low, steady.

I met his gaze, and for once, I didn't look away. "I don't know. But I know I needed you here. Tonight. With me."

Something flickered in his eyes, and then he pushed away from the desk, closing the distance between us. He cupped my face, thumb brushing my cheekbone. "That's all I needed to hear."

And when he kissed me this time—slow, lingering, nothing rushed—it wasn't about the crowd or the gossip or even the birthday cake waiting outside.

It was just us.

Hunter's mouth lingered against mine, slow and unhurried, but it didn't stay that way. His hands slid down, one anchoring at my waist, the other slipping lower to press me closer. The heat between us sparked fast, familiar, and I melted into it, my fingers sliding up his chest to grip the back of his neck.

"Hunter…" I breathed against his lips, not sure if it was meant as a warning or a plea.

"Paige," he murmured, voice rough, like my name had been living in his chest too long.

His mouth slanted over mine again, hungrier this time. I gasped, the sound swallowed by the way he kissed me—deeper, harder—until my back hit the wall beside the filing cabinet. The cool plaster sent a shiver down my spine, one that had nothing to do with the temperature and everything to do with the way his thigh slid between mine.

I clutched at his shirt, pulling him closer, needing more of him, all of him, right here in the dim back room while the whole damn town was only a thin wall away.

"We shouldn't be doing this here," he whispered, breathless.

"I don't care," I whispered as his forehead rested against mine.

"They'll know what we're up to." His lips brushed against mine with every word. "God, I've gone too long without touching you, and it damn near killed me."

Something hot and dangerous unfurled in my chest. My hands slid under his shirt, palms against warm skin, feeling the solid lines of him, the way his muscles tightened under my touch.

He groaned low in his throat, his hips pressing into mine, the movement making me bite my lip to keep from crying out. His hand trailed up my side, thumb brushing over a nipple, and I arched into him without thinking.

"Paige," he rasped, pulling back just enough to search my face. "We have to stop."

"We don't," I whispered, tugging him down into another kiss. "Don't stop. At least not yet."

It was messy, desperate, the kind of kiss that said too much—everything we'd been holding back. His hand slid under my dress, fingers skimming the bare skin of my thigh, and I nearly came undone right there.

The muffled sound of laughter drifted from the bar, jolting me back just enough to press a hand to his chest. My breathing was ragged, my lips swollen. "I need you," I groaned. "So much."

"Fuck, Paige, we can't... not here. Not now." His jaw clenched, his thumb tracing my cheek as if he couldn't quite let go. His voice was gravelly when he spoke.

"Then tell me where or when. Because I can't keep pretending I don't need you." I swallowed hard, torn between the pull of the party outside and the gravity of him right here, holding me like he was afraid I'd vanish if he loosened his grip.

My pulse was wild; my answer caught somewhere between my ribs and my throat.

Hunter's lips brushed mine again, softer now, but no less urgent. His breath was ragged against my cheek as his hand lingered high on my thigh, the heat of it making my whole body hum.

"We can't," He whispered again, though it sounded more like he was trying to convince himself. He pulled back a fraction, his forehead pressed to mine, his chest rising and falling hard against me.

"I know."

"Step away, Paige." His voice was low, gravelly, wrecked. "I can't seem to stop."

My hands fisted in his shirt, not pulling him closer, not pushing him away—just holding on, like he was the only solid thing in the room. I could still taste him on my lips, feel the pulse of his heartbeat under my palms.

"Hunter..." I breathed, unable to move.

Outside, the music shifted on the jukebox, the muffled cheer of voices swelling with it. The reminder that we weren't alone slid in between us, sharp as glass.

He let out a shaky breath. "They'll notice if we're gone too long."

His jaw flexed, his eyes searching mine. "We have time. You're mine now, and I don't give a fuck what anyone thinks about it."

God, the way he said it. Fierce. Unapologetic. Like I was worth the risk of every whisper in this small town.

But my chest ached with the weight of all the things still unsettled—Eli, the kids, the bar. Us.

I smoothed my hands over his chest, trying to steady both of us. "You're right. We have all the time in the world..." I started, but I didn't finish. Because the way he was looking at me—like I was the only thing that had ever mattered—made the words dissolve on my tongue.

So I kissed him once more, quick but sure, before stepping back. The loss of his warmth hit me instantly, like stepping outside on the coldest morning.

He ran a hand over his face, exhaling slowly, as if he was trying to pack every frayed emotion back inside. Then he nodded once, a muscle ticking in his jaw. "Later."

And that word—later—lit something low in my stomach, a promise tucked into two syllables.

I smoothed my dress, forced my breathing to calm, and reached for the doorknob. When I glanced back at him, his eyes were still on me, dark and steady, like he could pin me in place with nothing more than a look.

It took everything I had to turn away.

I opened the door, the noise of the party rushing back in —music, laughter, the faint clatter of glasses behind the bar. The air out there felt cooler, thinner, like I'd left every bit of heat and danger behind in that little room.

But Hunter followed me, close enough that I could feel his presence even without touching. His hand brushed mine briefly—just a ghost of contact, but enough to send a shiver up my arm. I didn't dare look at him. Not yet.

Out in the main room, Piper spotted me, then lit the candles on the cake. Eliza herded people into place, and Cara corralled my kids into the front for the big moment. The energy was bright, buzzing, full of love—and I tried to let it wash over me, to pull me back into the version of myself who could smile without her pulse still racing.

"Paige!" someone called from near the bar, waving me over. I pasted on a smile, adjusted the strap of my purple dress, and stepped into the crowd.

I laughed at a joke, accepted a hug from one of the regulars, let Piper kiss my cheek with frosting still on her fingers —but underneath it all, my skin still burned where Hunter's hands had been.

And when the crowd started singing, when the candles flickered in the dimmed light, I closed my eyes to make a wish.

The only thing I could think of was him.

Hunter peeled off toward the back, quiet and steady as always, but I felt the weight of his gaze across the room. It was like a tether between us, invisible but unbreakable.

Chapter 27
Hunter

I should've been inside, standing next to her while everyone clapped after she blew out the candles. Instead, I slipped out the back door, the cool night air hitting me hard enough to clear my head.

The stars were sharp overhead, the kind you only saw in Honeybrook Hollow, far from city lights. I shoved my hands in my pockets and leaned against the wall, listening to the faint hum of voices and music spilling through the bricks.

I'd caught her kiss earlier like a man who'd been holding his breath too long. The whole room saw it—Paige making a statement, right there in front of half the town. For them, it probably looked simple. Sweet. Maybe even inevitable.

But for me? It shook me down to the studs.

Because I wanted more.

Always more with her.

I tipped my head back, eyes closing as I thought about the pact—the one we'd made so long ago, laughing at the idea that we'd ever be this old. Back then, she'd never meant it as a real proposal. It was just words. A safety net. A way of saying: if the world lets us down, at least we'll have each other.

But the older I got, the more those words dug in. Some-where along the way, I stopped thinking of it as a joke. I wanted her. Wanted this. And not just because of the pact, not because I owed something to the past. Because of who she was now. Who she'd always been.

I had wanted to start something real with her. And I hadn't been sure if she wanted the same—or if I was just the person holding her together while the rest of her life spun out of control. But now I knew, and I felt like my heart would soar out of my chest every time I let myself feel it.

The door creaked behind me, voices spilling out, then quiet again when it shut. My pulse kicked, wanting it to be her. But it wasn't. Just someone sneaking out for a smoke.

I turned away, staring at the gravel lot instead of the glow spilling from the windows. My chest ached, tight with the kind of longing that doesn't fade no matter how much you try to smother it. She kissed me in front of everyone. She wanted me close. Finally.

The crunch of gravel behind me was soft, but I knew it was her before I turned. Some part of me always knew when it was Paige.

"You hiding out here?" she asked, her voice carrying that teasing edge she used when she didn't want me to hear the worry underneath.

I turned, and there she was—purple dress catching the light, her hair loose around her shoulders, cheeks flushed from the warmth and noise inside. She looked radiant. Like the center of the whole damn universe had decided to set up shop in Honeybrook Hollow and wear sequins for the occasion.

"Just needed some air," I said. My voice came out rougher than I meant it to.

She stepped closer, arms wrapping around herself against the chill. "I thought maybe you were avoiding me."

God. If she only knew.

"I'm not avoiding you," I said, forcing the words past the knot in my throat. "Not when you're everything I've always wanted."

Her eyes searched mine, like she was looking for something I wasn't sure I could hide. "Then what are you doing out here?"

"Trying to remember how to breathe."

That startled a laugh out of her, soft and a little shaky. She shook her head, blond hair catching the light. "You and your lines."

"Not a line," I said, taking a step closer, my hands still jammed in my pockets so I wouldn't do what I really wanted—pull her against me, then take her home so I could have her all to myself.

Instead, I tilted my head toward the tavern. "This party's for you. You should be in there, soaking it up."

"Maybe I'd rather be out here with you."

She was so close now I could see the little flecks of gold in her gorgeous brown eyes, could feel the warmth of her in the cool night air. And I thought—if she asked me to, I'd stay with her forever.

But she didn't. She just looked at me like she was working up the courage to say something big, then she let out a breath and slipped her hand into mine.

"Come back inside with me," she said softly.

And just like that, the ache in my chest shifted—still there, still sharp, but threaded with hope. I let out a low breath and turned our hands over, lacing my fingers through hers. Her skin was soft against the rough calluses on my palms, and I couldn't help rubbing my thumb over the back of her hand like I was memorizing the shape of her.

"Paige..." My voice cracked a little, so I swallowed hard and tried again. "You look beautiful tonight."

She rolled her eyes, but her smile gave her away. "You're just saying that because I'm in sequins."

"No," I said firmly, tugging her a little closer. The light painted her skin in gold, the purple of her dress shimmering every time she shifted. "I'm saying it because it's true. Sequins don't matter. You'd still knock the breath out of me if you walked out here in flannel and boots. But tonight, you remind me of prom night. Back in my truck. Purple and sparkly and wearing your heart on your sleeve."

That got me a soft laugh, one that warmed the cold night air between us. She tilted her head up toward me. Her lips parted just a little, and then mine brushed hers—light, teasing. The slightest touch, but enough to have my heart kicking against my ribs. She made the faintest sound, and it undid me. I deepened the kiss, sliding my free hand around her waist, feeling the soft fabric of her dress under my palm.

Her hand tightened in mine, the other sliding up to rest against my chest like she needed to feel my heartbeat.

When we finally pulled apart, both of us breathing harder than we should've been, she stayed close—her forehead nearly resting against mine.

"Hunter," she whispered, like she didn't know what else to say.

I wanted to tell her everything then. I wanted to say that I was hers and that I'd been hers since before I even knew what love was. But the words stuck, because I knew she wasn't ready for that yet. And maybe I wasn't either, at least not here.

So instead, I pressed a kiss to her forehead, lingering there. "You don't have to go back in yet if you don't want to. We can stay here, just us, for a while."

She let out a shaky breath, her fingers curling tighter into mine. "Maybe just a minute."

And so we stayed—just a man in love and the woman who didn't know it yet, holding on to each other under the glow of the tavern's parking lot lights while the party rumbled on without us.

The night hummed softly, cicadas buzzing in the distance, the faint thrum of music spilling from the tavern door. For a long moment, neither of us moved. I didn't want to. Being out here with her felt like the first breath after holding it too long.

Eventually, she let out a tiny laugh, nervous and sweet. "If we stay out here any longer, someone's going to come looking for us. And Piper will make it weird."

"She already makes it weird," I said, smiling down at her. "That's her job."

Her eyes softened, and she squeezed my hand. Then, slowly, like she was still gathering courage, she stepped back and tugged me toward the door.

The warmth of the tavern wrapped around us as soon as we walked in—music from the jukebox, chatter from the crowd, the clink of glasses behind the bar. Lark and Briar were laughing with Piper near the cake table, and Noah was leaning up against the jukebox with Spencer and Deacon, all three pretending they weren't scoping out the crowd.

And then the heads turned. Not all at once, but enough that I noticed—the way people's gazes slid toward us as Paige led me inside, still holding my hand.

Her cheeks flushed, but she didn't let go. Not right

away. And the part of me that had been aching, the part that thought I'd lost her, settled just a little.

Spencer caught my eye from across the room, his grin bright and knowing. I smiled back. He could tell me '*I told you* so' a million times, and I wouldn't care.

Paige finally slipped her hand from mine, but not before brushing her thumb against my palm in a touch so quick no one else could have noticed.

"You hungry?" she asked, her voice light but her eyes saying something else entirely.

"For food?" I asked. "Or for you?"

Her lips parted, her breath catching before she rolled her eyes and swatted at my arm. "You're bad."

I grinned, leaning in close enough that only she could hear. "I'll behave. For now."

Her flush deepened, and she turned toward the bar, leaving me to follow in her wake. And damn if I didn't feel like the luckiest man alive just to do that.

Chapter 28
Paige

The tavern hummed around me—laughter, music, the clatter of glasses—but it all blurred to background noise the second Hunter leaned against the bar beside me.

He didn't need to say anything. Just being near him was enough to make my pulse do that uneven thing I pretended wasn't about to send me into a joy orbit. My shoulder brushed his arm as I turned slightly, catching the sharp line of his jaw in the glow of the string lights. He looked good. Too good. So good, I was tempted to take his hand and get the hell out of here so I could have my way with him.

I tilted my head, unable to stop the smile tugging at my mouth. "You clean up nice," I said, soft enough that the music swallowed it.

His lips curved, almost teasing, but there was heat behind them. "You look..." His gaze dipped to the sweep of purple fabric at my waist, then back up, his voice roughening. "Unreal."

I swallowed, my cheeks warming under the weight of it. "Can you believe my mother picked this out?"

"Remind me to thank her," he murmured, his fingers brushing the back of my hand on the bar. Barely there. Enough to make me ache for more. "Like I said, it's prom night all over again, except a million times sexier, and I get to touch you this time."

"Purple sparkles," I said softly, glancing down at the shimmer of my dress before meeting his eyes again. "Not this shade, but close. You told me I looked—what was it? Like the only star in the sky. I thought you were just trying to cheer me up. But now I know it was more. For both of us. Remember?"

His mouth quirked, but his eyes darkened with memory. "I remember every second of that night."

"Me too," I whispered, my throat tight. "It feels a little like that right now. Like the whole world's out there, but you're the only thing I can see."

For a beat, we just looked at each other, the jukebox humming in the background, the tavern bustling with life all around us. But the moment felt suspended, private, just ours.

He leaned closer, his voice low enough that only I could hear. "Happy birthday, Paige."

My breath caught, a nervous laugh slipping out. "Thank you."

"You're so fucking gorgeous. I can't keep a thought in my head." His eyes held mine, steady and unflinching.

I drew in a shaky breath, my heart thudding unevenly. "You can't just say things like that in the middle of my bar when it'll be hours before we can be alone together."

He gave me that slow, dangerous smile—the one that made it impossible to breathe properly. "No, this is the best time to say these things to you."

The words hit me low, true, leaving me unsteady. My

hand tightened over his, the only answer I could give him without unraveling completely. And before I could second-guess myself, before I could talk myself out of it, I leaned closer.

"Hunter?"

"Yeah?" His voice was rough; his attention was locked on me like there wasn't anyone else in the room.

"Maybe we should have dinner together. Just us. No crowd, no town, no gossip. Just me and you. Like you asked me on your birthday, we need to talk this all through. Make plans. Figure this out. I mean, we're both forty now. All grown up—allegedly."

His expression shifted—surprise, then something so fierce and warm it stole my breath. "I'd like that," he said quietly. "More than you know." Then his eyes went dark, his lips curving in a way that made my pulse skip. "But, Paige," he murmured, leaning closer so I could feel his breath against my cheek, "if you knew how long I've been waiting to hear that from you, you'd know dinner's not exactly the first thing on my mind."

Heat flushed my skin, traveling down my neck. My fingers tightened on his. "Dinner was the safe version," I admitted, smiling despite myself. "What I really want is—"

His brow arched, teasing, but his voice was husky. "Say it."

The party buzzed along, surrounding us, but suddenly it was nothing but background noise. All I could feel was the way his thumb stroked the back of my hand, his gaze steady, pulling me closer without moving an inch.

"I want to leave," I whispered, the words slipping out before I could stop them. "Right now. With you."

His jaw flexed, a quiet sound escaping him, like he was barely holding himself together. He leaned in, lips brushing just below my ear, sending a shiver down my spine. "Careful," he whispered. "You say things like that, and I'm not going to let you change your mind."

I tilted my head toward him, my pulse racing. "Who said I wanted to?"

His soft laugh was threaded with something darker, something that set every nerve in my body alight. "You're killing me, Paige," he said, pulling back just enough to meet my eyes. "Standing here in that dress, saying things like that, looking at me like you do—do you have any idea what you're doing to me?"

"Maybe," I teased, though my voice shook. "But I like it."

He exhaled slowly, his hand sliding from mine to rest on my hip, grounding me. "We can slip out the back door," he murmured, half-teasing, half-deadly serious. "Nobody would notice."

"Let's not fool ourselves. Everybody would notice." I bit my lip, laughing softly, though I wanted to say yes. I wanted to let him take me away from the noise, from the crowd, from everything but the heat simmering between us. "Don't tempt me."

"Too late," he said, his smile slow and devastating. "You already tempted me first."

For one breathless second, it was all I could do not to take his hand and drag him toward the door. His gaze lingered on my mouth, and I swore my knees went weak.

But then, just beyond his shoulder, I caught sight of Briar and Lark laughing with Eliza by the jukebox, Noah leaning against the bar with Grandpa and Deacon. My family. My whole world. And I knew I could be patient, because Hunter was part of my world now, more than ever.

Reality slipped back in, soft but firm. As much as I

wanted to sneak out with Hunter and disappear into the night, I couldn't—not with my kids here, not when tonight was as much about them seeing me happy as it was about the party.

I forced myself to lean back a little, though I kept my hand in his. "My kids are here," I whispered, more to myself than to him.

He nodded once, his thumb brushing against my skin in quiet understanding. No judgment. Just that steady patience that undid me every time.

My phone buzzed in my pocket—because my mother would never buy a dress without pockets—I pulled it free, heart still racing, and read the message lighting up the screen.

Piper: I can feel the heat from over here.
Woo Hoo! Slumber party at Auntie Piper's
place so you two can be alone? Bow
chicka wow wow...

A laugh bubbled up, shaky and full of nervous energy. I glanced at Hunter, holding up the phone so he could read it too. His eyes warmed, his lips tipped up slowly.

"She's not subtle," I murmured.

"Not even a little," he said, his voice low, rough with something I felt all the way down to my toes.

I typed back with trembling fingers.

Me: Maybe. I'll let you know.

. . .

My thumb hovered over send, then I looked up at him again. His expression said everything—he wanted me to hit send, to let the night belong to us, finally.

But for now, I slid my phone back into my clutch and said softly, "Let's just stay here for a little while longer."

The way his gaze lingered on me told me he understood exactly what I wasn't saying.

Chapter 29
Hunter

The gravel crunched under the tires as Paige's car rolled into my drive, headlights sweeping across the front of the house before flicking off. My chest ached just seeing her pull up—like something in me had been holding my breath for years, and it finally let go.

She climbed out, the purple dress clinging to her curves, porch light catching the shimmer in the fabric. Her hair tumbled loose around her shoulders; her lips parted like she wasn't sure if she should run toward me or keep up appearances and walk. I didn't give her the chance to decide. I met her halfway, caught her hand, and held on like I was drowning.

"Hunter—" she began, but my voice broke over hers.

"I need to say this before I lose my nerve. Paige..." I swallowed hard, the words raw and jagged in my throat. "I'm in love with you. I've been in love with you for years. Longer than I could ever admit to myself. And I don't care if this complicates everything—you deserve to hear it, and I need to say it. Out loud."

Her breath caught, eyes shining, and then she whispered back, fierce and trembling all at once: "I love you too. I think I always have. I just couldn't let myself say it or even feel it until now."

The sound I made was half a groan, half a prayer. Relief and want collided in me, and I kissed her—hard, desperate, years of need spilling out in one breathless rush. She opened for me instantly, clutching at my jacket, pulling me in like she'd been starving for this too.

We stumbled inside, barely making it past the door before I pressed her against it, kissing her until her soft moan vibrated against my mouth. Her hands slid under my shirt, hot against my skin, and I nearly lost it right there.

"Bedroom," she gasped.

I didn't need to be told twice.

I lifted her, her legs locking around my waist as I carried her down the hall. She laughed breathlessly against my throat, the sound wrecking me, sweet and wild. By the time I laid her back on my bed, we were both shaking.

Her dress whispered up over her thighs as I pushed it higher, kissing down her neck, across her collarbone, lower until she arched up beneath me. Her fingers tangled in my hair, tugging, urging me closer.

"God, Hunter," she breathed, her voice low and desperate with need.

I peeled her dress over her head, tossing it aside. She was flushed, gorgeous, laid out in lace and satin that made my head spin. I kissed down her stomach, slow, savoring, before coming back up to claim her mouth again.

"You're so damn beautiful," I whispered, meaning every word.

Her hands roamed over me—my chest, my back, down over my ass, and back up—pulling at my shirt until I stripped it off. Her touch was everywhere, hungry and sweet at once, and I couldn't get enough of her.

We shed the rest of our clothes in a clumsy rush, laughing between kisses until there was nothing left between us but heat and skin. I fumbled for the condom in my bedside drawer, ripped it open, and slid it on. She watched me the whole time, lips parted, eyes dark with want.

"Come here," she whispered. "Get inside me."

When I sank into her, she gasped, clinging to me like she'd never let go. The sensation was overwhelming—heat, tightness, the pure rightness of her body around mine.

"Jesus, Paige," I groaned against her mouth. "Nothing has ever felt more fucking right in my life."

Her eyes shone, soft and fierce at once. "We belong together. We always have."

I moved inside her, slow at first, then deeper as she arched beneath me, meeting me stroke for stroke. Every gasp, every moan, every time she whispered my name unraveled me more. She clung to me, nails digging into my shoulders, lips seeking mine like she couldn't bear a second of distance.

I cupped her face, kissed her through it, and felt her tighten around me as she shattered, trembling in my arms. The sound of her pleasure broke me open, and I followed, spilling into her with a ragged groan of her name.

After, I collapsed against her, still buried deep, her skin damp and warm against mine. She curled into me, breath hitching as she pressed her lips to my chest.

"I love you," she whispered again, soft but certain.

"I have always loved you. Always." I pulled the quilt over us, tucking her against me, my hand splayed across her back like I could anchor her there forever. "I'm never letting you go," I murmured.

And for the first time in years, I believed I'd end up happy, because she was here, in my arms, where she was always meant to be.

Sleep crept in slowly, heavy and sweet, and I let the world fade away. I traced lazy circles on her back, breathing her in, feeling her heartbeat settle into the rhythm of mine. The room felt cocooned, quiet except for our breath and the distant sounds of the night outside my window. I whispered promises into her hair, promises I meant to keep, and she answered with the kind of sigh that spoke of surrender, of trust built over years of longing and loss.

We drifted, unhurried and tangled, our limbs a gentle knot under the blue patchwork quilt. At some point, I felt her hand find mine, fingers weaving together, and I squeezed back, anchoring us in the warm dark. The night lingered, soft and timeless, and I wished it could last forever —just her, just me, nothing else.

We cleaned up and got ready for bed.

Eventually, sleep claimed us both, wrapped up in each other, heartbeats echoing the quiet certainty between us.

The first thing I noticed when I woke was her. She was curled against me, her cheek resting on my chest, one bare leg tangled over mine beneath the quilt. Her hair spilled across my arm in a messy halo, and the faint morning light spilling in through the curtains made her look like an angel in my arms.

I didn't move. Couldn't. I'd imagined this so many times —her in my bed, her body warm against mine, her breathing soft and even like she finally felt safe here—and now it was real.

I pressed a kiss to her forehead, tasting sleep and sweetness, and she stirred. Her lashes fluttered, and then those big brown eyes blinked up at me, still hazy with sleep.

"Morning," I murmured, brushing my thumb over her cheek.

"Morning," she whispered back, her voice low and rough in a way that made me want to drag her right back under the covers and never leave. She shifted closer, fingers tracing idle patterns across my chest. "I could get used to this."

My throat tightened. "So could I."

We lingered there, quiet, the house still around us. It felt like the kind of morning that should last forever—no worries, no kids, no bar, no custody battles. Just us.

But the world never stayed away for long.

My phone buzzed on the nightstand. I thought about ignoring it, but something in my gut said not to. I reached over, careful not to jostle her too much, and glanced at the screen.

Spencer: Caught him. Just checked the feed—Eli was in the tavern last night, messing with the freezer. We've got him on camera. Recorded. He's done.

Every muscle in me went tight.

Paige noticed instantly. "What is it?" she asked, propping herself up on one elbow, her hair tumbling over her shoulder.

I set the phone down, my jaw clenched. There was no way around this anymore. She deserved to know.

"Spencer and I set up cameras in the bar," I said carefully. "After everything that kept going wrong. I didn't want to tell you until we had proof. Last night, they caught Eli. He was in there, messing with the freezer."

Her breath hitched, eyes widening. "What?"

"Yeah." I reached for her hand, threading my fingers through hers. "It's him, Paige. You're not imagining things. You're not cursed. It's Eli. And we've got proof now."

For a second, she didn't move. Just stared at me, her lips parted, her hand trembling in mine. Then her shoulders sagged, relief and anger warring across her face.

"He must have made copies of the key," she whispered, more to herself than to me. "I haven't changed the locks yet. I'm so stupid. He's been sabotaging me. The father of my children. What the hell, Hunter?"

"It's over," I said firmly, cupping her face so she'd look at me. "He doesn't get to take another damn thing from you. We'll send the footage to Ren. He can't touch you, not with this."

Her eyes filled, and she pressed her forehead to mine. "Oh my god. I can't wrap my head around this."

I kissed her then, soft and certain, letting her feel everything I couldn't quite put into words yet. The relief of finally knowing, the rage at Eli, and most of all, the promise that she wasn't in this alone anymore and not ever again.

When we pulled back, her eyes shone with something fierce and fragile all at once. "I don't know what I'd do without you."

"You'll never have to find out," I said, pulling her against me again, holding her like I never wanted to let go.

Chapter 30
Paige

My hands were shaking so hard I nearly dropped the phone. Hunter's thumb pressed circles into my palm, steadying me, but my voice still trembled when I said, "I'm calling Ren."

He didn't argue, just stayed right there beside me, solid and unmovable, while I scrolled to Ren's name and hit call.

"Paige?" Ren's voice was rough, like I'd dragged him out of bed.

"It's Eli," I blurted, my throat tightening. "Hunter and Spencer set up cameras in the tavern. They caught him—on video. He was in there last night, messing with the freezer."

For a heartbeat, there was nothing but the sound of rustling on the other end. Then Ren's voice sharpened, all business. "You're sure?"

"I'm sure." I swallowed hard, fingers tightening around Hunter's. His steady warmth kept me from coming apart. "We have proof. Spencer will send it to you."

"Good," Ren said firmly. "This changes everything. He's not just harassing you anymore, Paige—this is criminal.

I'll call the police. We'll press charges. This will shut him down in court."

My breath hitched. The words should have felt like a release, like finally being freed from a weight I'd been dragging for months. But instead, hot tears slid down my cheeks.

Hunter pulled me closer, tucking me against his chest, his jaw pressed tight against the top of my head. His whole body thrummed with quiet fury, every muscle wound up like a spring.

"Did you hear me, Paige?" Ren asked. "It's going to be over now. We'll make sure of it."

I swiped at my tears with the back of my hand, nodding even though he couldn't see. "Yeah," I whispered. "I heard you."

"Is Hunter with you?" he asked, his voice softening just a fraction. "You shouldn't be alone right now."

"Yeah, he's right here."

"Good. I'll take it from here. Sit tight. Don't let Eli near you. I'll be in touch as soon as I've spoken with the police and his attorney."

"Okay," I said, my voice breaking. "Thank you, Ren."

When the call ended, I let the phone slip from my hand onto the quilt. My body shook, all the adrenaline I'd been running on finally catching up to me.

Hunter caught my chin gently, tilting my face up to his. His eyes burned with a heat I'd never seen there before—not just protectiveness, but fury, the kind that came from watching someone you loved be hurt time and time again.

"He's done," Hunter said, low and certain. "You hear me? He doesn't get to touch you, doesn't get to scare you, doesn't get to hurt what's yours ever again. Not while I'm here."

That was what undid me. Not Ren's certainty, not the

promise of the law stepping in—but Hunter, holding me like I was the most essential thing in the world, swearing he'd keep me safe no matter what.

I pressed my face into his chest, tears dampening his skin, and whispered, "I don't know how I'd do this without you."

"You won't have to," he said fiercely, kissing the top of my head. "Not ever."

Hunter didn't let go of me for a long time. His hand stayed pressed against my back, warm and sure, like he could hold all the broken pieces of me together with nothing more than his touch. And maybe he could.

When the tears slowed and my breath evened out, he pressed one last kiss to my hair and eased back. "Stay here," he murmured.

"Where are you going?" My voice came out small, and I hated how raw it sounded.

"Kitchen," he answered, brushing his thumb over my cheek. "You need something in your stomach."

Before I could argue, he was up, tugging on his jeans, bare feet silent against the old wood floor as he disappeared down the hall. The faint creak of cabinets, the soft scrape of a chair pulled across the kitchen floor—it all carried back to me, calming me like some kind of lullaby.

I sat there in his bed, quilt wrapped around me, watching the morning light spill across the floorboards. My chest still ached, but the weight wasn't crushing me quite as hard. Not with him here.

A few minutes later, Hunter came back in, balancing two mugs and a small plate. He set one mug on the nightstand beside me, the steam curling up in lazy ribbons. "Coffee," he said simply.

The smell hit me first—strong and dark, exactly how I

liked it. Then he set a tray in my lap: two pieces of toast, butter melting into the edges, and a little jar of jam.

"Toast?" I asked, the corner of my mouth twitching in disbelief at being served breakfast in bed. "Thank you."

"You didn't eat dinner last night," he reminded me gently, sliding onto the bed beside me. "Coffee and stress aren't going to cut it anymore, Paige. Not when I'm around. We'll get something more later."

I huffed a laugh, even though my throat was still tight. "Bossy."

"Damn right," he said, leaning back against the headboard, his own mug in hand. "Now eat."

The first bite nearly undid me all over again. Not because it was anything special—just warm bread, sweet jam—but because he'd thought of it. Because while I was falling apart, he'd gotten up and made sure I had something simple and comforting to hold onto.

I blinked fast, staring down at the plate in my lap. "You're going to spoil me if you keep this up."

He angled toward me, eyes warm but steady. "Good. Somebody should."

That was all it took for my eyes to sting again, but this time I smiled through it. He reached over, brushing the back of his fingers across my jaw, then let his hand fall, like he knew if he lingered too long, I'd start crying again.

We ate in silence, the kind of quiet that wasn't heavy anymore. Just soft and safe.

When my toast was gone and the last sip of coffee had gone lukewarm, I leaned against him, the quilt pooled around both of us. His arm came around me instantly, tucking me close like it was the most natural thing in the world.

Chapter 31
Hunter

The morning air was brisk, damp from the rain, the gravel drive gleaming wet in the sun. Paige was inside, warm in my bed, finally letting herself rest. I'd stepped out for a breath, trying to cool the storm that had been riding me since we found out about Eli in the tavern.

Then Eli pulled up to the curb in his truck. My whole body went tight as he slammed the door and came stomping up my drive. He looked like hell—rumpled shirt, bloodshot eyes, jaw working like he'd been chewing on bitterness all night.

"You think you're real slick, don't you?" he snapped. "Going after my wife? Sliding in on Paige, waiting for your chance."

"Ex-wife," I said, my voice low, steady. "You threw her away, remember? You need to turn around and leave. Get the fuck out of here before I make you."

He laughed, sharp and ugly. "Don't give me that. You've been circling her since high school, haven't you? Always hanging around, jealous as hell because she picked me instead of you. You wanted her back then, and now you're finally getting your shot."

I clenched my jaw, fighting the urge to break his nose right there. "What I wanted back then isn't the point. What matters is she's not yours. Not anymore."

His lip curled. "The bar was supposed to be mine. You think I don't know how much money it makes? My businesses are sinking, and she's over there building herself an empire that should have been mine."

The door creaked open behind me. Paige stepped out onto the porch, hair spilling over her shoulders, one of my sweatshirts hanging loose on her frame.

Eli's face twisted, and he aimed the venom at her. "Figures. You always thought you were better than me, Paige. Turns out you're just a slut. Spreading your legs for him while your kids are god knows where—"

That was it.

I stepped forward, fists clenched at my sides, the blood roaring in my ears. "Watch your mouth."

Eli swung first, and I let him. I wanted him to, so I could hit him back. He was wild and sloppy, but his fist cracked against my jaw hard enough to snap my head to the side. Pain flashed, sharp, but I barely staggered. He came at me again, but this time I caught his arm, shoving him back.

"You've wanted this for a long time, haven't you?" I growled. "Since you first saw me with Paige at the bar, right?"

He swung again, and I didn't hold back. I dodged it and took my own shot. My fist connected solidly with his jaw, sending him stumbling back a few steps, his boots skidding in the grass.

"I let you have one swing, Eli. Just one," I said, voice

low, dangerous. "Come at me again, I'll put you down and you won't get back up."

He spat blood onto the lawn, glaring past me at Paige. "You'll regret this—both of you. Don't think this is over. The kids, the bar—it's all mine."

Paige's voice shook, but it carried. "The kids don't want to see you, Eli. And the bar? You never lifted a finger to build it. It's mine and it always was. You don't get to take credit for something I bled for. You got two of our businesses out of the divorce. It's your own fault you're running them into the ground. Not mine."

For once, he had no comeback. Just a furious sneer as he yanked his truck door open, slammed it shut, and tore away, tires screaming against the street. The silence afterward was heavy, broken only by the pounding of my pulse.

I turned to Paige. She was trembling and pale, her eyes wide but steady. I climbed the steps and pulled her into me, cupping the back of her head. My jaw throbbed where his fist had landed, but the only thing I cared about was the way she trembled against me.

"He's done," I told her, voice rough. "He doesn't get to hurt you, doesn't get to touch what's yours. Not while I'm breathing."

She pressed her face into my chest, tears hot against my skin, and I held her tighter, swearing to myself I'd never let Eli lay another claim to her life.

My jaw ached where he'd landed that first wild swing, but I hardly noticed it. All I could think about was Paige—shaking in my arms, her breath uneven against my chest.

"Come on," I murmured, brushing a hand over her hair. "Let's go inside."

She nodded, and we slipped back into the house, shutting the door on the silence outside. The living room felt warmer, safer, the sunlight pooling across the worn rug. She pulled her phone from her pocket with trembling fingers and typed fast.

"I need to tell Ren," she whispered. "He has to know before Eli tries something else."

I nodded. She hit "send," then set the phone face down on the table as if it had burned her.

For a moment, she stood there, arms wrapped tight around herself, staring at nothing. I stepped closer, resting my hands gently on her arms, grounding her.

"You okay?" I asked, even though I already knew the answer.

Her chin wobbled. "No. I mean, yes. I don't know."

She hesitated, then slipped away from my side, heading for the kitchen. I listened to the clink of ice cubes as she rummaged in the freezer, her movements determined but shaky. In a minute, she came back, pressing a folded dish towel with ice gently to my aching jaw.

"You shouldn't have had to do that," she said, her voice thick. "Thank you." She fussed over the swelling, worry etched across her face as she searched my eyes for pain. "Are you sure you're okay?"

I nodded, catching her hand and squeezing it. She hovered, unwilling to leave my side, her gratitude and concern radiating between us like warmth.

I guided her to the couch, pulling her down beside me. She folded in, curling toward me until her forehead pressed against my shoulder. My arm wrapped around her automatically, holding her close.

"I hate that he still has this power to shake me," she said, her voice muffled. "After everything he's done. After the lies and the cheating, after all this time. I should be stronger."

"You are strong," I said firmly. "But he was part of your

life for a long time. That doesn't just disappear overnight. He knows how to hit you where it hurts. Time will make that go away."

Her breath caught, and she tipped her face up, eyes glassy. "When he said you'd wanted me since high school—I couldn't stop thinking. Maybe if we'd tried back then, things would be different now. But I was a mess as a kid. I'd lost my dad. And you..."

"I had lost my mom," I finished quietly.

She nodded. "And we were best friends. How could we risk losing each other?"

"Yeah." I swallowed hard, running a hand down her arm. "After she died, I didn't let myself want anything too much. I never let myself get too close to anyone after that. Because if I did, it could be taken away, and the thought of losing you was unbearable."

Her fingers brushed over my jaw where Eli's fist had landed. Gentle. Shaking. "That's how I felt after my dad. Like if I wanted something—someone—it would just get ripped away. It was safer to choose someone who wasn't..."

"Me," I said, not bitter, just honest.

Her lips pressed together, and her eyes shimmered. "I was wrong."

I cupped her face in my hands, holding her steady, making sure she saw me. "Paige, I've been afraid, too. But I'd rather face every fear I've ever had than spend another year pretending I don't want you."

Tears spilled over, and she leaned into my hands, her breath warm against my palms. "I don't want to be afraid anymore," she whispered.

I kissed her softly then—the kind of kiss that felt like a promise.

When I pulled back, her phone buzzed against the

table. She reached for it, glanced at the screen, then read aloud in a shaky voice, "Ren says it's going to be okay. He'll call the police. He's taking care of everything. He says it'll all be over soon." Her hand shook as she set the phone back down. I tugged her against my chest again, pressing my lips to her hair.

"Then it's over," I said. "It's over, and you're safe. That's all that matters."

She melted into me, and for the first time all morning, I felt her body loosen—like she was finally letting go of the weight she'd been carrying.

Paige didn't move for a long while. She stayed tucked against me, her head beneath my chin, my hand stroking up and down her arm in slow, steady lines. I could feel the tightness in her slowly easing, like she was letting herself borrow my strength until her own came back.

The house was quiet except for the faint hum of the heater keeping us warm. A soft thump broke the stillness, followed by the sound of claws clicking on the hardwood. Ozzy padded in from the kitchen, tail flicking as he hopped up onto the couch like he owned it. He gave a single, judgmental meow before curling himself into Paige's lap, settling there with all the weight and authority of a creature who knew he was welcome anywhere and had found a new friend. He'd been asleep in his cat tree when we got here last night, and I'd closed the bedroom door behind us.

The smallest laugh broke out of her, muffled against my chest. She ran a shaky hand over Ozzy's back, her fingers smoothing his fur. "Hello there, cutie," she whispered.

"He knows quality company when he sees it," I said, brushing a strand of her hair back from her face.

Ozzy purred, and it was loud, like he was determined to drown out every rough edge left in the morning. Paige's shoulders eased more, and her hand lingered on his back as she tilted her face toward me.

"You always take care of everyone, don't you?" she said softly. "Your brothers. Me. Even him."

I met her gaze, the way her eyes shone, tender and raw. "I don't know any other way to be."

Her lips parted like she might say something, but instead she reached up, her palm warm against my jaw, her thumb brushing the spot Eli had hit. The touch was gentle, reverent even. "Does it hurt?"

"Not compared to the thought of losing you," I admitted, my voice low.

Her breath caught. Then she leaned in, kissing me with a softness that was nothing like the heated urgency we'd shared before. This was slower. Deeper. The kind of kiss that held weight, that carried everything we hadn't yet said out loud.

Ozzy stretched in her lap, his purr vibrating against us both, as if even he knew we'd crossed into something that would last forever.

When we finally broke apart, her forehead rested against mine, our breaths mingling. "I don't know how to do this," she whispered. "But I want to try. With you. I love you."

"I love you, too." My hand slid down her back, holding her close, sealing the moment. "That's all we need."

We stayed there, tangled together on the couch, the sunlight warming the room, Ozzy's purr thrumming steady between us, as if the world had finally slowed enough to let us just be.

Chapter 32
Paige

It had been a few weeks, and for the first time in what felt like forever, I was happy. The girls were okay. Therapy was helping. They went twice a week—together sometimes, separately when they needed it—and even though it broke my heart to see them walk into those offices with brave little faces, it gave me peace to know they had someone safe to talk to. Someone who wasn't as close to the situation as I was. Someone who could help them untangle the mess Eli had left in their lives.

Noah checked in constantly, calling from Portland between classes and sending me memes when he thought I sounded stressed. He was okay. He'd been taking the breakup in stride, and every time we spoke or texted, he seemed a little steadier, a little more sure of himself. It was reassuring to see him finding his own way back to happiness, slowly but surely.

Briar and Lark were finding their footing again, a little more secure every day. And me? I was trying to believe it was really over.

Ren secured a restraining order against Eli and said it

was airtight. He'd also found out that the truck that followed Briar when she snuck out was just a random kid from the area, drunk after hanging out at one of the bonfires. He swore he had no bad intentions toward Briar, but there was no way to know if he was telling the truth. Hunter had told me about the truck after things had settled down and how he and his brothers had been keeping an eye on me and the girls. Sometimes I could hardly believe how lucky I was to have him in our lives.

Even though Eli had dropped every legal filing against me, he still had his businesses and was actually working to get them up and running again. Danielle had filed for divorce and moved back in with her parents, putting some distance between herself and the mess he had left behind. The fallout was complicated, but everyone seemed to be finding their own way through it, piece by piece.

There were still whispers in town. People loved a good story, and this one had everything: heartbreak, betrayal, scandal, a parking-lot make-out session, and a bar that had nearly gone to ruin before coming back shinier than ever.

But none of that mattered, not really. Because every night, when I locked up the tavern, Hunter was waiting for me. Not out of obligation, not because something needed fixing, but because we wanted the same thing: for us to end our days together.

I leaned against the bar now, the soft thrum of the jukebox filling the background with something slow and sweet, and looked around at what I had. The Twilight Tavern finally looked like the place I'd dreamed of owning. But it wasn't the bar that had me smiling.

The door swung open, that familiar creak of the hinges, and in he came—broad-shouldered and smiling. His face told me more than words ever could—and I knew that the worst was behind us. For once, I didn't have to fight every battle alone.

Hunter slid onto a stool at the far end, where he always sat when the night was quiet, and I made my way over like muscle memory.

"You're early," I said, my voice softer than I meant it to be.

He shrugged, propping an elbow on the bar. "Deacon had the shop covered. Figured I'd rather be with you."

That little flutter in my chest turned into a full sweep. I busied myself wiping down the already-clean counter, because otherwise I'd probably climb over it just to get to him. "I love that you still come by to close with me." It had been a slow night, so everyone had gone home a few minutes ago.

"Yeah." His voice was steady, but there was something underneath it. Something that made me lift my head.

Our eyes met, and I saw it—the weight he carried for me, for my kids, for all of it.

I leaned on the bar across from him. "I don't know if I ever said thank you."

"You don't have to."

"I do," I insisted. My throat felt tight, but I pushed through it. "Hunter, I thought I was protecting everyone by keeping things quiet and handling everything on my own. But all I was doing was pushing you away. And you still showed up even when I didn't deserve it."

His jaw tightened, but his eyes softened. "Paige, I was never going to leave you in it alone. Not then, not now."

The jukebox shifted to an old love song—something twangy and slow, the kind of thing couples would dance to if the place were fuller. For a second, I let myself imagine swaying there with him in the empty bar, the lights low, his hand warm against the small of my back.

Instead, I said, "The girls are doing better. They trust you."

His gaze sharpened, that quiet intensity that always undid me. "Good. Because I meant what I said, Paige, I'll always show up for your kids. For you."

Emotion rose thick in my chest, and I swallowed it down, pressing a hand against the cool wood of the bar. "I don't know what's coming next. But I know I'm strong enough for all of it, and I want you with me while I figure it out."

He stood, slow and deliberate, and closed the distance between us. His hand came to rest over mine on the counter, warm, solid. "Then that's where I'll be."

The room went quiet in that way it sometimes does when the air is thick with something meaningful. I tilted my head up, caught in the look he was giving me—the one that made my knees weak and my heart pound—and whispered, "Dance with me?"

No crowd, just the two of us swaying behind the bar. His arms came around me, mine looped around his neck. His hand pressed firmly against the small of my back as we swayed in the empty bar. The lights overhead were soft, the jukebox playing soft and low, and I leaned into him, letting the warmth of his body sink into mine.

It was easy to forget everything when we were like this. Easy to let my guard down.

"Is this what prom would have felt like if I'd gone with you?" I whispered, my cheek against his chest.

His chest rumbled with a low laugh. "Yeah. Except I wasn't really into dancing back then."

I tipped my head back, caught by the wicked glint in his

eyes, and smiled. "And we won't have to go out to your truck afterward. Or maybe we should."

His gaze dropped to my mouth, and the air shifted. The lazy sway slowed, turning into something heavier and more charged. He bent his head, brushing his lips against mine in the softest tease of a kiss.

The first kiss was tender, but the second was fire. His hand slid from the small of my back down over my hip, pulling me closer, until I could feel the hard planes of his body pressed against mine. My fingers curled in his shirt, holding him there, needing him closer.

I gasped into his mouth, and he swallowed it with a growl low in his throat, kissing me harder. The bar disappeared. The world disappeared. There was only Hunter, his mouth on mine, his hand slipping under the hem of my shirt, his thumb grazing skin that burned under his touch.

I broke away only long enough to breathe. "I love how you make me feel."

"Maybe we should go out to my truck right now and find a dark place to park," he rasped, his forehead pressed to mine. "I'll show you how much I missed you today."

I nodded, dizzy from the way he was looking at me, like I was the only thing he'd ever wanted. "You have the best ideas."

His hand tightened on my waist, his mouth finding mine again, this time deeper, hungrier. Heat coiled low in my belly, and every nerve screamed for more. He didn't answer.

I pulled back with a shaky laugh, breathless. "Let's lock up and get out of here."

His jaw clenched, his eyes dark with restraint. He pressed one last kiss to my mouth, fierce and lingering, then drew in a deep breath. "Damn, Paige."

"Yeah," I whispered, still clinging to him. "I need you." We stood there, pressed together in the quiet glow of the tavern, the heat between us simmering.

He didn't hesitate. We slipped out into the cool night, laughter tumbling between us as we hurried past the neon-lit windows and across the parking lot. The world felt spun with possibility, electric in its quiet.

Hunter opened the passenger door, and I slid in, heart hammering, nerves and anticipation tangling beneath my skin. He rounded the hood and climbed behind the wheel, his silhouette dark and sure against the glow of the dashboard lights. For a moment, he just looked at me, his thumb tracing lazy circles atop my knuckles.

Neither of us said a word as he started the truck and pulled out onto the empty road. The town faded behind us, replaced by fields and forest, the windows down just enough to let the cool air brush over our skin.

Music spilled softly from the radio—a song we both knew but neither named. Hunter reached for my hand, threading our fingers together, anchoring me to the present. We drove on, each mile smoothing the static between us, turning the urgent heat of the bar into something slower, sweeter, and impossibly tender.

When he finally stopped, the only witnesses were the stars shining in the endless sky and our own breathless, unspoken hope.

Chapter 33
Paige

The bed of Hunter's old pickup had never been glamorous, but that night, under a sky littered with stars, it felt perfect.

He'd driven us out past the edge of Honeybrook Hollow, up the winding road where the trees opened wide and the air smelled like pine and wild grass. He spread a soft quilt over the truck bed and helped me up.

I leaned back on my elbows, staring at the night sky. "You know," I said, my voice carrying in the stillness, "seventeen-year-old me thought the back of your truck was the height of cool. I can't believe you still have it."

"It's a classic. My dad knows how to pick 'em." He chuckled, stretching out beside me, his arm sliding under my shoulders to pull me close. "And seventeen-year-old me thought the same thing. Still does."

The crickets filled the silence, their steady hum grounding me. My life had been chaos for so long, but here, in the truck bed with him, everything felt peaceful. Safe. Right.

When I turned to look at him, he was already watching

me. His expression was steady, serious, but soft in a way that made my breath catch.

"What?" I asked.

He shifted, reaching into his jacket pocket. My heart stuttered as he pulled out a small box and held it between us.

"Hunter—"

"I know we used to joke about that pact," he said, his voice low and certain. "But Paige, I wasn't joking when I brought it up again. Not really. When we were kids, I didn't know what we'd go through or how much we'd change along the way. But I knew—even back then—I always wanted you in my life. It just took us longer to get where we belong."

The box flipped open in his calloused hand, revealing a simple ring. Gold, with a single diamond that caught the starlight. Not flashy. Just round and brilliant, and beautiful in its simplicity. I pressed a hand to my mouth, breathless as it sparkled under the starlight.

"I've loved you a long time," he said, his gaze locked with mine. "And I don't ever want to spend another day pretending I can live without you. So, Paige Darlington, will you marry me?"

Tears blurred the stars above us. My laugh broke out, wet and shaky. "Yes. Yes, I will marry you, Hunter Cassidy."

The relief on his face hit me like a tidal wave, stealing what breath I had left. He pulled me into his arms, kissing me hard, deep, until the crickets faded, the night air vanished, and there was only us.

When we broke apart, I pressed my forehead to his. "So, is this what happens when you keep a pact?"

He grinned, slipping the ring onto my finger, his thumb brushing over it once it was in place. "No. This is what happens when you finally get everything you've ever wanted."

I curled into his chest, my hand fisted in his shirt, my heart so full it felt like it might burst. And under that blanket of stars, in the back of his old Chevy truck, I finally let myself believe we'd made it home.

Epilogue
Paige

The Honeybrook Inn's reception hall had never looked prettier. Twinkle lights draped from the rafters, flowers spilled over the tables in mason jars, and Piper's cake—three tiers of lavender buttercream perfection—stood proudly in the corner, already making my mouth water.

It wasn't a huge wedding. Just family, and a few close friends. But it was more than enough. It was everything I'd ever wanted, even if I'd never let myself admit it before.

My kids stood at my side, all three of them glowing in their own way.

Lark sniffled openly into a tissue Piper had shoved at her. "You look so pretty, Mom."

Briar rolled her eyes, but her mouth curved. "Obviously."

Noah grinned, adjusting the tie Hunter had insisted on buying him. "Took you guys long enough."

I laughed, blinking fast against the tears threatening to ruin my makeup. "Thanks. I love you all so much."

When the music started, I turned—and there he was.

Hunter Cassidy, standing at the end of the aisle in a suit that fit him like sin and salvation, his eyes locked on mine like no one else existed.

My heart tripped over itself as my kids walked me up the aisle, because this was the man who had waited for me, who had shown up when everything else was falling apart—the man who had kept every promise he'd ever made to me.

The vows were simple. Honest. We didn't need elaborate speeches—we already knew what we meant to each other.

When it was over, as he kissed me in front of everyone we loved, the room erupted in cheers.

But it was the kids who got me.

Briar's arms locked around my waist the second I stepped off the little platform. Lark squeezed Hunter's hand like she never planned to let go. And Noah leaned in, voice low but steady.

"I'm so happy for you, Mom. You look peaceful. Thank you, Hunter."

Hunter's arm slid around my back, pulling all of us in closer. "I love you guys," he said as we slid into a group hug.

The reception was loud and joyful—music blasted through the hall, people danced, Piper's cake was being devoured like it was the last one on earth. Then Hunter caught my hand under the table and tugged me to my feet, then toward the back door.

We slipped outside into the cool night air, the sound of laughter and music muffled behind us. Twinkle lights framed the porch, casting everything in a golden glow. He backed me against the railing, his forehead resting against mine, his breath warm and steady.

"Just needed a minute with my wife," he murmured, his voice low and rough in a way that made me shiver.

I smiled, my hands sliding up his chest to loop around his neck. "Your wife, huh? I love how that sounds."

"My wife," he repeated, and then his mouth was on mine—slow and sure, a kiss that tasted like forever.

The town could have disappeared, the lights gone out, the music faded to nothing, and it wouldn't have mattered.

Because right there, in the quiet glow of the night, I had everything I'd ever wanted.

Would you like to fall in love with another small town?

*Turn the page to read the first chapter of **In My Heart**, from my Sweetbriar Mountain Series!*

In My Heart - First Chapter

Luke

One more swing and the tree fell. The scent of dirt blasting into the air filled my lungs while the sunlight filtering through the pines cast the forest floor in spiky patterns of shadow and light. I let my senses fill, grounding myself against the regrets threatening to derail the progress I had made since returning home from Afghanistan.

I was a father.

I had a son. If I got a handle on myself, I might be able to meet him and see his mother again. My Lily was also back in Sweetbriar, our small Oregon hometown. The thought of seeing her again after everything I had done and how I had ended it all—

I cut Lily out of my life. I had thought she deserved so much more than what I could offer. After a certain point, the things I'd seen and done in the Army had blended together into a black cloud of hurt and pain and I could no longer process what was happening to me. My grandfather tried to help but you can't help someone who feels worthless, so I cut him out too and stayed away from Sweetbriar.

Frustrated, I wiped the back of my hand across my sweaty brow, then took swing after swing at the fallen tree, splitting it into manageable pieces. Some of it I would use for firewood; the rest I would carve into animals, or chess pieces, or paperweights, or whatever else crossed through my thoughts the next time I needed to disconnect from the world.

My muscles burned and my still-injured back ached as I straightened but pain wasn't enough to make me forget what I had done. Nothing ever was. I could never disconnect from Lily. She was branded on my soul. No matter how far apart we were or how many years went by, she was always there. Memories played on a loop in my mind like an old black and white movie—sometimes skipping, sometimes blurry, but never gone. Those memories pulled me through some of the worst moments of my life, even when I had wanted so badly to let go of everything and fade away.

When I found out she was coming home my life burst back into color. Everywhere I went in this town held a moment we shared. She was on my mind constantly and it was driving me to distraction. It hurt. The desperate yearning in my chest grew bigger every day, overwhelming all other facets of my world until all I could think of was how to convince her to let me back into her life again.

I wondered how she was now. My heart broke for her when I found out her husband died. Then I was sick at myself for being happy I might have a shot to get her back. And my son? I wanted him too. I wanted my life to be the way it should have been before I fucked it all up.

All these years, I had told myself I'd done the right

thing. But now that I was home and finally healing, I knew letting her go was the worst mistake of my life.

After my medical discharge from the Army, I was a disaster. My grandfather Jed, or Pops as I had always called him, a Vietnam vet, convinced me to get help. I was diagnosed with PTSD, which should have been obvious to me, but it hadn't been. Denial is a powerful tool when your only goal is to forget. Pops took me to his therapist, talked me through panic attacks, comforted me when I realized all that I had thrown away, then gave me Rocky, my sort-of emotional support dog. Rocky had failed out of Jed's ESD program, but I fell in love with the brown and white boxer when he refused to leave my side. He woke me from nightmares, nudged me whenever I got down on myself, and provided me with the kind of love only the best, most loyal dogs could. Rocky was currently dozing off under a tree.

Pops and his employees trained service dogs of all kinds on his ranch right outside of Sweetbriar. I stayed with him for about a month before moving back to the house where I grew up. And it must be said, there is something about being surrounded by puppies and wide-open spaces that could put anyone at ease. It was the perfect way to begin settling back into a normal life.

I inherited my childhood home after my father passed. He'd made quite a few changes to the house while I was in the Army, to the point it almost felt like a different place. But the land was the same—fifty acres that backed into the Cascade Mountains in Oregon. I had since readjusted to the quiet sounds that had been so familiar in my childhood: animals rustling through the brush, the rush of the river, wind blowing through the trees. After being surrounded by people and near constant activity it was difficult at first, but

I finally realized getting acclimated to peace and solitude was a blessing.

"Yo, McCabe!" My former sergeant, Liam, called to me from the trees. He was my brother, bonded irrevocably not by the blood that flowed through our veins but by the blood we had lost together over the last few years.

Rocky's ears pricked up, but he didn't budge; by now he knew Liam almost as well as he knew me.

"Hey." I took another swing and left the axe in the wood. "How was work?"

"Typical. Boring. Quiet." He grinned at me. "Small town life is exactly what I needed."

"I grew up here. It's not always boring and quiet, you know." Like any small town, Sweetbriar had its fair share of gossip and low-key intrigue.

His lips tipped up in a grin. "Duly noted. How was therapy?" I was glad to see him smile. I wasn't the only one who was a mess when we got here.

"The physical stuff is always easier. Talking about myself was never my thing." Liam and I served together, we were both medically discharged due to the same IED attack. I convinced him to come with me to Sweetbriar and help me run my late father's construction company.

"Swinging that axe can't be good for your back," he remarked.

I shrugged. "As long as I do it right, I'm fine."

He smirked. "You're full of shit."

"I needed to—" I ran a hand down my face, unsure of what I was trying to say. But Liam knew.

"You needed to get it out. The way you feel about her being here . . . it's real now. No more *if* or *when*. They're both in town and it's just a matter of time before you see them."

"I'm nervous as fuck," I admitted.

"I can't blame you for that. You've been building this up in your mind for a long time."

"It's everything, man. If I screw this up, what do I have?"

"Hey, look. For one, that's not going to happen. And two, both of us know by now it's not healthy to think that way. We have each other, and Jed, and my grandmother. Neither one of us is alone."

"Is that your therapist or mine talking?" I joked. The mood out here had gotten too serious for my liking.

"Hard to tell lately, but that doesn't make it not true." He passed me a bottled water before sitting by Rocky beneath the tree and scratching him behind his ears.

"You're right." I sighed.

"Let's go get coffee. That's what I came out here for." He chuckled.

"Good idea." Lily's sister, Violet, owned the only coffee shop worth going to in town. If I got lucky, maybe I'd run into Lily there. Last time I spoke to Violet, she had mentioned hiring Lily for the summer.

"Call Jed, have him meet us."

"The old man texts now. I taught him how to use his smart phone. The memes are endless."

He huffed a laugh. "Let's go."

I shot Pops a text, Liam woke Rocky, then we took off. Liam drove, just like he always had when we were deployed.

"Pops is busy. Just you and me this time."

He nodded his answer as he took us out of the mountains and down into town. I lowered the window in back for Rocky and cranked the air conditioner up high for me and

Liam. It was an unusually hot summer day in Sweetbriar and, since returning from Afghanistan, we were all about creature comforts. Air conditioning, warm blankets, endless hot showers, and sleeping in. Don't get me started on hot coffee and good food. Violet got my business more than once a day, and I'll leave it at that.

We also set our own hours at my father's—well, now *my* company, McCabe Construction. Dad had built it to unbelievable levels while I was gone. I'd inherited enough money that I never had to work again if I chose not to. But I couldn't sell the business and leave his employees jobless. Plus, I needed something to do, so I stayed and gave them all raises, just to spite my father's cheap ass ghost in case it was lurking around somewhere, still disapproving of my choices.

He pulled into Violet's parking lot and cut the engine.

"There's my guys!" Violet greeted us from her perch behind the counter. She was older than me by a few years and I'd known her my whole life. She'd always been like an older sister to me. "The usual?"

"Please," Liam affirmed with a huge smile while I hung back and nodded. It was after lunchtime, and her shop was always slower this time of day. We practically had the place to ourselves. She turned her back to prepare our orders and I contemplated how to get her to start talking about Lily without having to ask.

She slid our coffees and a plate of scones across the counter. "Lily won't be in town until tomorrow. She was up all night with Calla. The poor little thing is cutting a tooth." Calla was Lily's baby, about six months old.

"Thanks, Violet." Liam paid for our orders and headed to the sofa in the back corner of the shop. I let Rocky follow him.

I took my drink with a sheepish smile. "Uh, I was going—"

She reached out and patted my arm with a knowing grin on her face. "And now you don't have to ask me about her. You're welcome."

"Thank you, Vi. You've made this easy on me, and I appreciate it."

"Well, I'm glad you're finally home. You and Lily belong together. You always have."

"I didn't realize how much I missed her in my life until I got back and got my head on straight. She's essential—I can't be myself without her."

Her eyes melted as she gave me a smile. "I love the way you talk about her."

I pressed my lips together and studied my shoes, embarrassed. What if Lily wouldn't talk to me? I'd end up a lovesick idiot with his unrequited feelings on display for an entire town to ridicule.

"Hey, it's okay." Her smile grew sympathetic. "Your face shows your love, Luke. It's in your body language and the words you choose when you talk about her. You have always loved her, ever since you were little kids. Once she sees you and hears you out, that simple fact will sink in."

"I hope you're right. But I'm not going to rush anything. We started off as friends, and I have to be okay with it if that's all she wants."

"I know. But if ever any two people belonged together, it's the two of you."

"Well, I can't imagine not having her back in my life. She's been in my heart forever, Violet. I never let her go."

"None of us let you go either. You're part of the family, Luke."

Violet gave me a nod and turned around to tidy behind the counter. I joined Liam and kept trying to come up with a way to get close to Lily again.

Keep reading In My Heart

Scan the QR code to keep reading In My Heart!

About the Author

Nora Everly is a lifelong bookworm. She started reading the good stuff once she grew tall enough to sneak the romance novels off the top of her mother's bookshelf and it has been non-stop ever since.
Once upon a time she was a substitute teacher and an educational assistant. Now she's a writer and stay at home mom to two small humans and one fat cat.
Nora lives in the Pacific Northwest with her family and her overactive imagination.

Find her at noraeverly.com
Get all the Nora News!

Also by Nora Everly

The Sweetbriar Mountain Series:

In My Heart

Heart Words

From the Heart

Heart to Heart

Change of Heart

Cross Your Heart

Honeybrook Hollow:

Next to You

Make You Mine

By Your Side

Meant for You

Sweetbriar Holiday Stories:

Holiday Hearts

Conversation Hearts

The Cozy Creek Collection:

Fall at Once

From Smartypants Romance:

Oh Brother!

Crime and Periodicals

Carpentry and Cocktails

Hotshot and Hospitality

Architecture and Artistry

Teachers' Lounge

Passing Notes

Star Crossed Lovers:

(*As Piper Everly, co-written with Piper Sheldon*):

<u>Midnight Clear</u>

Get exclusive sneak peeks of upcoming releases through Nora's newsletter and Facebook group, The Everly Afters.

www.ingramcontent.com/pod-product-compliance
Lightning Source LLC
Chambersburg PA
CBHW010737310726
48971CB00010B/2868